Troubled Waters

R. Wesley Clement

Troubled Waters
Copyright © 2024 by R. Wesley Clement

ISBN
978-1-962868-97-6 (Paperback)
978-1-962868-98-3 (eBook)
978-1-962868-96-9 (Hardcover)

DEDICATION

Troubled Waters is a work of fiction taking place in the very real and vibrant city of Portland, Maine. The Old Port is a jewel for the city and the gifted artists and entrepreneurs who work and play there. The mighty Atlantic Ocean is indeed a lure for the thousands of tourists who visit the coast of Maine. The boat in the story, *The Last Tango,* is berthed at Chandler's Wharf and is owned by my brother Zane an able Seaman in his own right. All characters are imagined though some names may sound familiar.

A story much like a successful sailing venture requires support from the crew. Before this story set sail I received assistance from the following: Zane helped me immensely with all things nautical and geographic. My wife Carey provided unwavering faith that we can weather any storm. Love from my children who have charted their own successful course in life offering me the opportunity to find my way forward. Son Khristian, daughter Shellee and lifetime friend Lynda Quinn, thanks for reading the story and sharing your views and reviews.

Thank you Nina Padilla for the oil painting of the boat and setting for the cover. Nina is a young artist who is just embarking on her own voyage using her paints and palette to fuel her ambition. She can be contacted at ninanicolepadilla@gmail.com Finally this voyage is all about weathering the storms that surface in our own lives. When Elvis sings she offers us hope. Sean moves forward with his life offering resilience. Freddy offers creative vision. Jacob's background music sparks our memories. Stella is the support we all long for. Lieutenant O'Connor provides persistence and Mrs. Waslowski wisdom. One additional character you will meet represents all the storms we must weather to find a safe harbor. This story began as my son-in law received the news that he would be battling cancer. The voyage ended as he completed treatment. We pray he finds warm and sandy beaches.

TABLE OF CONTENTS

Dedication iii

Chapter 1   Morning madness 1

Chapter 2   Jacob's ladder 6

Chapter 3   November 2009 431.25 Gallons of Coffee Ago... 14

Chapter 4   Late Coffee And A Piano Solo 21

Chapter 5   1992 Thank you, thank you very much 32

Chapter 6   Blue Christmas 38

Chapter 7   1994 Resilience takes a different form 41

Chapter 8   2014 Stella 50

Chapter 9   1992 Coffee Clique 57

Chapter 10   1992 Bewitched and bewildered........................67

Chapter 11   2009 Meanwhile back at the coffee shop............73

Chapter 12   1993 A flea market future 77

Chapter 13   2003 A young cowboy named Billy 83

Chapter 14   North By Northeast...88

Chapter 15   2009 Dreams and nightmares............................96

Chapter 16   Sail on 105

Chapter 17   Smoke on the water..108

Chapter 18   A formal education 116

Chapter 19 2009 Heartbreak Hotel....................................123

Chapter 20 Elvis is in the building......................................134

Chapter 21 Jacob's ark..139

Chapter 22 X-ray vision...146

Chapter 23 Jacob and Elvis Just duet................................149

Chapter 24 Bringing balance to the boat...........................154

Chapter 25 Hammers and saws and lots of coffee.............159

Chapter 26 Squeaks an' squawks.......................................163

Chapter 27 Polly want a cracker.......................................167

Chapter 28 Captain Jack...175

Chapter 29 Casco Bay and beyond...................................180

Chapter 30 A month of tying knots..................................185

Chapter 31 If it walks like a duck.....................................190

Chapter 32 "'Tis an ill cook that cannot
lick his own fingers' — Romeo and Juliet........194

Chapter 33 One door closes as another opens....................199

Chapter 34 The wagons begin to circle..............................204

Chapter 35 More mystery and medicine.............................209

Chapter 36 All news is local..215

Chapter 37 Heading down the eastern seaboard.................221

Chapter 38 An uneasiness as the garment unravels.............225

Chapter 39 In an octopus's garden in the shade.................229

Chapter 40 Stockings are hung..234

Chapter 41 Snow covers all tracks.....................................238

Chapter 42 Language barrier..242

Chapter 43 Pins and needles..246

Chapter 44 Happy Holidays..253

Chapter 45 Winter of discontent 259

Chapter 46 No known cure...266

Chapter 47 A different kind of storm 272

Chapter 48 One if by land. Two if by sea 279

Epilogue...288

CHAPTER ONE

MORNING MADNESS

Gray snow, ice, naked trees and an emerging sun surround my wife Stella as she stands in red flannel pajamas, daring her to make the journey down our steep drive.

Taking the trash to the curb might not sound exciting. Hefting that recycling bin doesn't raise much emotion. Yet I yearn to do both. During the growing season, a trip around the lawn thirty minutes a week with a mower and ten minutes with rake and clippers justifies a cold beer on a warm day. You the MAN! I'll take a ball game with that beer, thank you very much.

Using the garbage can as a stabilizer, her flannels tucked into snow boots, Stella begins her descent. She used to watch me make this run and reward me for my derring-do. Those were the days my friend … I hum the old show tune as Stella slides from side to side, one arm waving as if riding a bull.

I don't want to watch, but I do anyway. Reaching the curb, Stella raises her arms to the crowd of one. Climbing back up the drive, she is forced to use the gray snow and ice at the edge of the lawn for purchase but slides backward a step for each one forward. Stella raises her eyes to look at me and suddenly squints, the rising sun hitting her between the eyes.

Her blindness passes and now she can see me through the glass. I point at the blue recycling bin, sitting outside just below the window and mouth "second run." Her glare could melt the snow. I raise my arms and shrug, *what you gonna do,* releasing the curtain. She must be making her second trip with the recycling bin, that bright blue rectangle that will keep humanity from burying itself in processed plastic, but this time I really can't watch.

Then there's barking and Stella's raised voice muffled by the window. I nod to myself, hearing the opening lines of our weekly little neighborly drama with an ending yet to be determined. I'm pretty sure how Stella would like to see it end.

After what seems like an eternity but is really only the time needed for Stella to literally chill out and compose herself, the door creaks. A rush of cold air hits me. I breathe it in. Bask in it. I miss it. Sitting at the table, I toast her with a steaming cup of Starbucks. "Your form looked fine, but if you're going to compete in the downhill, fitted tights might offer you more flexibility."

Stella, her cheeks reddened from more than the morning chill, fails to feel my humor. "Smart ass. That friggin' dog is at it again!"

"Heard that. Did the owner make an appearance?"

"You mean Squirrel Nuts? I heard his voice meekly begging Fido to 'stop that right now and get back here.' There are tipped cans and ripped bags up and down the street."

Picturing the mess awaiting the neighbors who deposited their garbage last night and will be reassembling this morning, Stella shakes her head and grunts, "That coffee smells good." She gives me an appraising glance. "How did you sleep?"

"Honey, you ask me that every morning. My answer remains the same. I don't sleep. I nap." Taking a sip of my hearty brew, I continue, "I can tell you with certainty the minute hand *does* pause for sixty seconds each and every minute throughout the night."

Stella joins me at the table with a coffee, her chair protesting the dragging effort as she sits with her arms draped over the chair back. A little color still flushes her cheeks.

"Actually, you dress up those flannels," I say looking her up and down. "You should start a Victoria's Secret line, maybe call it

Soft & Sexy and a little bit Fuzzy." She does in fact look especially sexy sitting there. "Can I have a little of that cream?"

Stella lends me her cheek, all the while checking her phone for messages, her slightly lighter brew waiting for a little attention.

"You came in late this morning. Lots of action last night?"

Stella sighs, takes a sip of a blend called *Morning Madness* and puts her phone down with a look of one who fights the good fight nightly.

"Hump day. They should call it lump day. All these kids, and those still acting like kids, think they can get through the next two days hung over, sleep deprived, bandaged and banged up. Wednesday night is worse than the weekend." She leans towards me. "Last night in the ER, debris from five injured in bar fights, four drug or alcohol overdoses, three car accidents, two boyfriend-girlfriend domestic incidents with injury. All we missed was the partridge falling out of the damn pear tree."

A long sip, a head shake and a glad-that's-over sigh brings this aptly named morning's blend to her lips. Looking down into her cup, Stella remarks, "Starbucks should have a blend named *Midnight Madness* if you ask me."

"Why don't you get a day job? With your nursing skills and experience and," I couldn't help adding, "your way with dogs, you could run a clinic or a doctor's office. At worst, a vet's practice."

Stella ignores my wit. "Honey you throw that at me every morning, and my answer is always the same. I don't want to find out if that big hand pauses or not. I want to stay so busy I don't have time to worry about that minute hand pausing." She brushes the hair out of her eyes. "I just want to stay busy and not have to think at all. Besides, except for Tuesday and Sunday, you work nights too." She gives me eye contact then. Serious eye contact.

"I love you," she says, "just the way you are, always and forever. No regrets. The sooner you can accept that you'll always get to watch me slide down the driveway in my pajamas, even catch me without them on occasion, the sooner we can make plans to live our new normal life."

Stella turns her chair and sits back. She doesn't sip this time but takes a long pull, all the while her eyes locked on mine. "So let's switch topics here. Anything exciting happen at your own critical care unit last night that I will maybe read about in the police log?"

"Well, we got the usual tour of Portland via Freddy, History 101. Billy Joel was in the house. Elton John too. In great form, I might add. Jacob is amazing." I close my eyes and reflect on the night before. "A guy did get hit with a wayward dart but refused medical attention. And the King himself, or in this case, herself appeared, rekindling the past. All in all, just another night in the Old Port. The numbers are up though. New patrons every night, repeats too."

I clear my throat. "As far as this new normal, I can accept what and who I am, but that doesn't mean I can't want the best version of myself available." I look down at my useless legs that still have life but no movement.

"If that damn insurance company would quit jerking me around and sending me to one company specialist after another, wasting time while trying to save themselves a few bucks, I could maybe find out what that new normal is going to look like and stand on my own two—"

My cup lands with a sharp report. With that, I push myself up while falling forward, then catch myself with the crutches and, repeating the effort, make my way to the couch—the home of my remote, my bedroom, my office, my dining area when Stella isn't home for the foreseeable future.

Stella shakes her head, watching me without comment, then gets up and moves to the kitchen.

"Your Aunt Loretta called and left a message, want to hear it? Why she doesn't call you directly is beyond me."

"Loretta knows half the time I don't answer my phone. I don't text. I don't call on my own. She knows you'll sit on my right shoulder like a good angel till I call her back." I look back at my empty cup. "Bring me another cup of *Morning Madness* will you? I'm feeling mad as hell this morning."

Stella empties the pot, adds a teaspoon of cream and re-enters my sanctuary. I sniff the aroma of my special blend, bring it to my lips, sip and swallow.

"Okay. Play the message."

My Aunt Loretta's voice always takes me back to the twice-yearly family reunions with my fourteen aunts and uncles and too many cousins to keep track of. Good people all, hard-working, ultra-competitive, fun-loving, humorous, always ready to sink a dagger at the first sign of weakness. From cribbage to volleyball to horseshoes or three-on-three basketball. All fueled with family casseroles and desserts.

"Sean, I've been doing research on the internet. Usually I'm asking you for something, this time I'm offering. Something to do with an experimental trial. I thought of your situation. Anyway, call me. Love yuh."

Stella sits down in my office—since the blankets and pillow are still balled up from the tug of war I had with myself overnight, maybe it's still my bedroom—on my right side, the good angel side and stares at me with those blue eyes until I say, "I promise to call my aunt." Her eyes continue to speak. "Today! I promise I'll call her today!"

The good angel moves back to the kitchen and I will soon have a breakfast bagel and one final cup of grog.

"By the way, when Jacob calls, tell him to pick me up an hour early. I have something to do."

Stella looks at me quizzically, cracks an egg and turns toward the coffee pot. And so it goes.

———

CHAPTER TWO

JACOB'S LADDER

The wind nips at the noses of those braving the sidewalks of the section of Portland called Old Port, cold as hell, grey slush beginning to harden as the late winter sun stares you in the eyes. Stiffly walking working stiffs lean into the wind; each step taken, an in-your-face challenge. Heads bend forward. Street signs quiver. Colorful scarves and watch caps offer disguise in the ocean wave of winter-gray coats and outerwear.

Street drains emit plumes of steam while the Atlantic Ocean offers a stark, if not asked for, opinion that there's cold, then there's coastal cold.

I study this perilously perched population from the passenger seat of Jacob's van, envying one and all in spite of the conditions. He picked me up at two thirty, two hours before we open the doors of our friendly neighborhood bar on Fore Street named *Troubled Waters*. A play on words in a hundred ways, which if nothing else brings a smile to the lips of both patron and passerby as they review their own current situation.

We traverse the slippery streets with the radio tuned to an easy listening station, and Jacob seems to know every song being played. Our bar is located in what had long been a neglected area of Portland recently revived by one man's dream, one man's realization that the mighty ocean just off our beaten path will always be a magnet for mankind.

R. Wesley Clement

Welcome to our *Troubled Waters*. Imagine yourself playing along the wharves and piers. Pause, ponder, raise a glass and return to the sea, if only in your mind.

Stopping at my lawyer's office, thankfully located on the first floor, Jacob opens the heavy wooden door with me riding his back like a derby jockey. The receptionist hardly looks up, though she smiles at Jacob. I have been here so often our odd entrance doesn't raise an eyebrow. There is no one in the waiting room, so we barely pause down the home stretch and enter my lawyer's office.

"They are this close to a meaningful offer, Sean," offers Braden, my lawyer, who also happens to be my cousin, holding two fingers an inch and a half apart. I study the distance.

"Braden if I had that inch and a half attached to my own lower limb, I could make a perch for one more parakeet and I'd have a trio chirping this happy news."

Braden belly laughs, his face reddening.

"Too much information, Sean. I prefer the image of the killer volleyball games we played at the summer reunions and you leaping up and spiking that ball into the faces of our uncles."

I have to smile … good times those. Braden leaves to get us a coffee, and Jacob follows. I'm left sitting across from Braden's desk.

The image of three parakeets holding a casual conversation on my lower limb—branch maybe, alright twig it is—has me chuckling to myself. The quiet suddenly engulfs me and I realize they've been gone longer than necessary. The door is open, I turn my head. They are standing at the coffee pot, discussing something privately, quietly—hey this is my dollar we're spending here, Jacob.

I can't help admire Jacob, though, as I study his broad back, so broad he's eliminating Braden from my view. For most people, carrying a 160-pound man on your back would appear a burden, but not for Jacob.

The two return and after small talk and razzing and glad handing all around, Jacob drains his brew, rises and bends over, I wrap my arms around his neck and hoist myself aboard. We make our way through the outer office as an arriving client holds the door, wide-eyed and speechless. A line from an old Alaskan series I saw on cable leaves my lips "On you Huskies!" as I pretend to whip Jacob. Everyone laughs, which was my intent. I hate sympathy.

* * *

Jacob and I are partners, and I guess it's obvious he does the heavy lifting. Pulling up outside the bar, Jacob puts on his flashers and in tandem we enter the bar.

Jacob sets me on the raised, round piano stool. My useless legs dangle just above rubber rollers added to allow me movement using shortened cross-country ski poles give me leverage. With my new ride, I can move along the back of the bar at a height that allows me to greet and serve my patrons eye to eye. Looking around, I'm proud of what we've accomplished. I'm not ready to give it up.

I hear Jacob grunt as he emerges from the cellar with a quarter keg hanging from each hand like bowling balls. He squeezes behind me, sets the kegs in their proper place, hooks them up and hits the tap, draining a quart of foam. He reaches under the counter to grab his specially designed 32-ounce pewter mug licking his lips before testing the delivery.

During working hours, Jacob keeps the mug attached to his belt. As he raises the mug to his lips, I'm reminded of last week when he used that same mug as a gentle prod to remove a malcontent. He just stuck it right in that asshole's face and kept it there, all the time guiding him to the exit. The whole bar raised their own mugs in tribute.

Jacob is huge, but for the most part he's the gentle giant we all had in school. He also plays a mean Billy Joel/Elton John songbook at the keyboard we have set up next to a booth we try to keep unoccupied for our own use as an office. He has a terrific singing voice. Things quiet down when Jacob's on mike.

The mug is really a prop, one that lets him toast the outrageousness of life and, when necessary, keep the peace without damaging his talented hands. He doesn't drink during working hours, just tastes any new keg he has to tap. Still, the mug always hangs from his belt. A patron showing poor taste but failing to respond to Jacob's humor gets a nudge from his mug, which usually does the trick. For everything else there's MasterCard, as the saying goes, or 911.

Taking stock, I count a dozen stools spanning a 20-foot bar. Five small tables each with four chairs makes up the seating capacity. We have a single booth that serves as our office when it's not claimed by a patron. Usually that patron is Freddy. A unisex toilet framed in white Christmas lights has made everyone more respectful regarding graffiti and controlling the direction of body functions.

If a bar could truly reflect a business model it would mirror the old joke, *two guys walk into a bar,* and those two guys would be Billy Joel and Elton John. My dad played their music almost exclusively on our trips throughout the country, once in a while throwing in a little Eagles and a smattering of country as long as it was a ballad you could cry to.

"There's got to be a history attached or it's not worth listening to," he'd say.

Finding Jacob was a godsend. For an hour and a half, five nights a week, Jacob plays Billy Joel songs that seem to mirror the regulars we hope to depend on for our livelihood. The seaman, the sailor, the homeless, the knave, the injured, the wounded, the veteran brave.

Elton John ballads get a fair amount of air time as well. My dad would have loved Jacob. We also get a lot of young professionals who work those seventy hour weeks, arriving hollow-eyed and eager to get lost in the moment for an hour or two before heading home to collapse and start all over at six in the morning.

We get a fair share of ladies too. Not the barely legal. We are not equipped with all the sweet renderings that ruin a perfectly good liquor. Our ladies tend to be women with a reason to stop for a drink that doesn't start with a need to be carded. A word of advice here from the lips of one of my uncles: "If you can't see through it, don't drink it." Word of mouth has been our best advertising, and our faithful continue to multiply.

Did I tell you we make a mean burger with fried onions and peppers served on bakery-fresh bread? A crock-pot of beer-based beef stew and a gotta-have fish chowder that Stella makes that's always simmering on the edge of the grill. A warm-blanket-on-a-cold-night kinda food. News of the quality of our food has served us well.

The bar opens at four thirty. We are reminded of that when a snow ball strikes the single small window above the door. Jacob lumbers to the door and, with a sweeping gesture, welcomes our first customer of the day. Freddy the fixture, smiles up at Jacob and moves to the bar. Jacob offers, "I bet you throw like a little girl." Freddy just smiles in response.

I get Freddy started with a Bud Light and chuckle to myself. Freddy is a fixture in a good way. He is our benefactor, or more aptly stated, he comes from old money. You might say he's fixed. Freddy's father made money the good old fashioned way back when revival of the Old Port section of Portland was just a dream.

Without going into a long history lesson here, let me just say this area was a blight for a long time. In the seventies, Freddy's father, an accountant, oversaw the writing off of a lot of foreclosures and business failures in this section of the city. Like a crow flying a cornfield, he saw opportunity.

He started buying up old warehouses with little or no capital, found tradesmen who wanted to moonlight and brought a little reality to his dream. Marketing these properties, he offered very generous lease agreements as long as the tenant had an action plan that made financial sense and agreed to pay any improvements needed to open for business.

 R. Wesley Clement

He revitalized one of the properties himself, making sure anyone entering his office had a view of the Atlantic Ocean. Everyone wants to see the ocean, right? Long story getting shorter, he took the city's seal of a phoenix rising from the ashes as his own. Recognizing the pull of the sea, he added a nautical twist. Now, even his letterhead and marketing strategies feature a wharf in the background, sailboats playing in the harbor, a seal, a lighthouse and islands on the horizon.

Freddy finishes his first beer. He'll nurse himself through three more till the evening crowd gathers, then he'll pontificate on the abbreviated history lesson I just offered and add an Irish twist on all things with the word Portland attached. He actually does know a lot, but after an hour or so it gets tiresome.

As his attentive audience dwindles, Freddy will fuel his story with Jameson Whiskey as the history of the area moves from the 1700s to the fires that burned the city to being named the state capital. By the time he adds an invasion by the confederates, he'll seem ready to go to war with himself. He'll get louder, more determined to end this war within himself and lose even the casual listener. By nine o'clock, he'll be ready for Jacob to play a ballad that lets him leave the battlefield, welcoming his numbness, music cradling his head.

"Live to fight another day, Freddy?" I ask nightly as I shut him off.

"Love yuh, Sean," mutters Freddy, his last words before he heads for the booth that Jacob and I claim as our own. Late in the night, we'll call a cab and send him to his berth at Chandlers Wharf. I might mention here that Freddy owns this property we occupy Using the same business model as his father, his lease-to-buy terms are generous to a fault. Thanks Freddy, sleep soundly.

* * *

Elvis joins us at seven thirty, four nights a week. She's our twenty-three-year-old waitress who isn't sure who she's supposed to be or where she belongs. From her earliest memories, she's been defined as Elvis. No last name, simply Elvis. Elvis-styled haircuts. Serenades by the man day and night. Even a handmade Elvis mobile. Who wouldn't be confused?

She used to work security at Chandlers Wharf. Freddy, who is forty-two-years-old, is hopelessly in love with Elvis. He even knows it's hopeless; Elvis told him so. But he loves her anyway. He actually got her the job here. His motives might not have been pure—he gets to be with her, kinda sorta, four nights a week. She has proven to be pure gold for our business.

Jacob opens every music session with *Piano Man.* As he lowers himself onto the stool, it gets quiet. It seems it's always *nine o'clock on a Saturday* every night in *Troubled Waters.* Jacob invites the patrons to join him and some semblance of the song emerges. Depending on the night, the song is sometimes played with altered lyrics, giving identity to our own lively cast of characters, and suddenly Jacob is playing to them personally.

Elvis moves through the crowd filling mugs and shot glasses with a pitcher and various bottles, never forgetting to add to a tab in the process. Like I said, pure gold.

After an hour or so, Elvis takes the stage. Jacob transitions seamlessly, providing the background music. Elvis does Elvis better than anyone I've ever heard except maybe the great man himself. Elvis even looks like a softer version of young Elvis, like when he first began—an innocent. Hair jet black, 5'6" and lean, blue eyes that mirror the ocean on your nicest day at the beach. A natural sneer emanates from her full lips with the whitest teeth ever to enter this bar or any other, I'm thinking.

Elvis attracts more than just a passing glance from what is mostly a male audience. She's quick of wit and nimble of foot and weaves her way around tables, avoiding reaching hands with a smile. *Troubled Waters is* the new game in town and it will take a while to establish our identity. It hasn't taken Elvis any time at all to set boundaries for all her admirers, however, and one patron who never leaves his bar stool has taken notice. I like to think I'm a pretty good observer of the human condition. Missed it with this guy, though. It might have helped if he had interacted with Elvis, but he never did. He simply watched with an odd look on his face. Then he stopped coming in altogether. Till much later, at least.

I'm not thinking about Elvis at the moment though. My lawyer cousin Braden has come in and wandered over to Jacob, whispered in his ear. That's the second time today they've had more than passing conversation and it has me guessing. As I study Jacob from the distance of seven bar stools, my old life wanders into my head and the trip to Seattle, Washington, where I first met Jacob fills my mind.

CHAPTER THREE

NOVEMBER 2009
431.25 GALLONS
OF COFFEE AGO

I read the pamphlet giving the background and history of Starbucks for the third time. Nap, dream shop Sky Mall magazine, swap small talk with my seat mate and finally hear the news I've been waiting for. Landing in Seattle in ten minutes; the weather is clear—a rarity I'm told. Looking down on the coastline, the long stretches of water and islands remind me of the rock-bound jagged edges of Portland, Maine. As we get closer, I see a vast body of land beyond those islands.

Along with reading the information packet, corporate Starbucks insinuated one might want to bone up on the geography and history of the state. Trivia contests, spot quizzes and a writing contest that tells our own Starbucks story would all end with valuable prizes awarded—no free coffee certificates, we were promised.

From my brief Wikipedia search, I know that the body of water I see is Puget Sound, which has managed to create a body of saline water, allowing Seattle to be an active port city. I'm also struck by another similarity to Portland, Maine. Portland is hilly; Seattle is very hilly.

I had come to know the streets and byways of Portland in a very personal way. I ran them. I thought I'd get in a run or two out here as well. Hopefully there was at least one other runner in the group. After high school, most of your athletic competition is over unless you're very good. That would not include me. I discovered, however, I possess excellent wind and endurance. I finish strong.

The Back Bay area of Portland provides an incredible scenic opportunity to stay fit. Workout stations dot the scenic route. It also provides an opportunity to greet like-minded health conscious people. At least, that's where I met my wife. She was paused at one of those numerous fitness stations with her leg draped atop a bar that stood, I swear, at least four-and-a-half feet in the air, with her head resting on her lifted leg.

I just had to stop. I'm always kidding that I met my wife for the first time at a bar. Then, I tell the real story. Sweating like a pig after navigating a hilly section of the city, I transitioned to the Back Bay area for a cool down on more level ground. Then I saw her. I managed to look past those gorgeous legs and made eye contact.

"How do you do that?" I asked. That simple query would lead me to a year-long series of asking that same question for a hundred different reasons as our relationship blossomed. A truly amazing woman.

You don't need a car to survive in Portland, and I didn't own one. I did own a bike, and it took me most everywhere I needed to go. It's helpful to know someone who owns a car however, if you plan on romancing someone. Stella had a vehicle. It was my lucky day.

My mind shifted gears and I found myself staring out over the city of Seattle. I went back to comparing the two. If you include the communities that make up greater Portland, its population was also over half a million. I should feel right at home.

A sudden dip and then the captain was on the intercom, assuring us we were about to land. It brought me out of my coma and I returned my tray table, stowed my reading, brought my seat forward and said a silent landing prayer.

Entering the terminal, a sea of cards bearing the Starbucks logo and names of attendees in coffee brown letters waves feverishly. A company representative from each state has been invited to an all-expense three-day conference at Starbucks headquarters. I represent the grand state of Maine. I'm sure there were other reps from the Northeast on my flight, but I had yet to meet them. The company, through consolidation and acquisition, was poised to be the first brand you'd think of when you thought *travel coffee.*

It would be our task, upon returning, to hold a conference in our home states with licensees and managers. Selling the five-year plan would be our homework assignment. There would be teambuilding activities, taste-testing, games and contests all within the smelling distance of coffee. Lots of coffee. On the third day, a presentation from the company CEO promised additional surprises.

The men's room filled as relief in several ways was realized. Leaving the terminal I entered one of a caravan of nine passenger vans and was whisked immediately to headquarters. Each van carried the iconic logo that was becoming a visual reminder for the weary traveler to stop before entering or leaving the highway. Couple that with a push to be the stimulant of choice in the work world and Starbuck, the first mate of *Moby Dick* fame, was poised to become a captain of industry.

After a ride that did in fact include a lot of hills and nearly as many complaints about being crowded like cattle, we arrived at corporate headquarters. It was cold but clear; a rare winter day during rainy season.

As the vans unloaded, the parking lot doubled as an overpopulated aerobics class as an unplanned group stretch began; most of us had been on a plane for hours. West Coast fair-weather clouds dotted the sky. If they stayed in the air long enough maybe, I'd catch up to them in a few days on my return to the mighty Atlantic.

This was my first view of the entire group and it quickly became apparent it was still (business wise at any rate) a man's world. Of the fifty or so gathered, I counted maybe five females. There were more ethnic groups represented than I expected, though the greater portion could have used a regular exercise program.

Headquarters was a beautiful building high on a hill, the sun bathing the glass and steel structure in light, an ever-watchful Starbucks logo standing sentinel above the entrance. We were directed along a corridor with an outside wall of glass offering a view of Seattle below, a postcard for the city and its harbor. Sailboats, some moored, others on the move, mirrored the clouds above, playfully pushing one another.

Ushered into a room with a raised platform as the centerpiece surrounded by pods of comfortable chairs, we were directed to move to a pod with the region we lived in posted on a message board. These four pods form an arc around three-fourths of the stage.

After we were seated and generally greeted and challenged by a boisterous vice-president, a facilitator in each pod began the first in a series of team-building exercises. My pod, the eastern region, had fourteen seats filled.

Our first challenge was laid out. We were handed a piece of paper with a map of the United States. Each state was identified. Challenge one: identify the state capital for as many states as you can. Five minutes. No sharing answers. Begin.

Various stages of school life entered my mind. I smelled chalk dust along with the over-powering scent of Miss Prince's perfume as she towered above us, her dainty glasses perched, every hair in place. Coloring a map in elementary school. Creating the major mountain ranges out of a thick paste. I could still taste it. Several state capitals emerged, overpowering the smells and taste. I jotted them down.

My mind filled with middle school social studies class quizzes and spelling contests with girls showing their braces, their attention to detail making us boys shrink in our efforts. We boys just wanted to make it to recess, climb the mountains of snow created when the parking lot was cleared and yes, eat dirty snow. We learned something apparently, because my pencil added several more capitals. Our great land was beginning to fill up with a dispersing population.

High school history lessons with pages and pages revealing the founding and settlement of each region and state capital emerged like roadside flowers on my trip down memory lane.

Having grown up in Maine, I had no difficulty remembering the capitals in the east. As I moved my eyes to the southern coastline capitals, I could almost smell the body odor from Chester, the boy who sat directly across from me in fifth grade. Juvenile farts moved my pencil along the Gulf of Mexico. Capitals shouted out their names in my middle school mind: Texas, New Mexico, Arizona, California! All sharing a border with Mexico.

My pencil hardly paused. I had formed a ring of state capitals that covered the north, south, east and west. It's when I moved to the inside that ring that I found myself in a little trouble.

My mind shifted gears to family vacations. We traveled through New Hampshire, Vermont, Massachusetts, Connecticut, New York, Pennsylvania, West Virginia and Kentucky on our way to Tennessee. One of my uncles had moved to Nashville to try to establish a career in country music. My Dad envied the heck out of his brother's voice, and we went to watch him in his one appearance at the Grand Old Opry. My father cried.

Third born and first to attend college, Dad became a history teacher. Every summer we traveled to a different region of this Vast Treasure as my father termed our country. Along the way, my two sisters and I were treated to our own personal summer-long history lesson.

We learned about the reasons and rationales for the way the highway system was numbered. We learned how to identify the different makes of automobile, along with the names of the industrial giants who started the brands.

My father lamented that foreign competitors were taking over the roads. Our own Chevrolet wagon seemed to take this invasion personally as well, for whenever we came upon a Toyota or Honda or a lesser known model, the engine would growl and we would pass in a rush, a smile plastered to my father's face.

See the USA in a Chevrolet he would sing at any given moment. My mother, who never said much of anything, could glare with the best of them. My father sang every Billy Joel song, threw in a little classic country, then repeated Billy's lyrics, on and on. Long sighs would emanate from the woman riding shotgun.

Whenever possible, we stopped in the shadow of the capitol of the state. We visited state museums, leaving with enough information to write a brief history. There are educated people and then there are walking historians. My father was one of those.

I remembered a summer trip to Park City, Utah, to visit a cousin—any excuse to travel would do for my father. I could still see him at the kitchen table with his maps. I was fourteen and didn't want to go since I was a starting player on my Babe Ruth baseball team.

"Cooperstown will wait," he chided. With my father, everything could wait except his next planned excursion.

My dad is no longer with us. Despite all he knew about most things, he still fell under the addictive attraction of smoking. He always had a window open during these trips as if he'd researched the perils of secondhand smoke—missed the part about firsthand smoke, I guess. I felt his absence every day. A whole generation fell victim to what was just supposed to be a nasty habit.

I found myself smiling at the sense of humor he always displayed about the meaning of life and family. Even during the nine months he suffered with stage four lung cancer, he stayed upbeat and positive.

"I hope to hell there are places to visit and things to see up there. No wingback porch rocker for me," he said.

The quiz was taking me to places I hadn't visited in a long time. I found my pencil moving to the rhythm of a Billy Joel ballad.

We were all brought to attention by the scent of coffee hitting our nostrils. Platters of pastries were placed on a table to the right of our pods. Pencils down. We were advised to take a break, our papers would be collected and scored. I looked down at my paper and every state had a seat of business. I could hear the voice of Miss Prince admonishing us to make sure we'd put our names on our work.

It was at the pastry table that I first met Jacob. He was not in my pod. He was from California. It said so on his name tag.

CHAPTER FOUR

LATE COFFEE AND A PIANO SOLO

Jacob Morrison came from money. New money. He considered himself a self-made man with a work resume to back it up.

A difficult child, once he was old enough to tie his own shoes, his independent streak raised havoc with family dynamics that weren't exactly normal to begin with. An alcoholic father killed in a single car crash when Jacob was six left him in a house with two younger brothers and his mother. Nobody told Jacob he needed to grow up immediately, but he sensed it and acted upon it.

His one friend for as long as he could recall was music. It was also the only memory of his father that he cared to remember. Before going on what would sometimes be a week-long bender his father would start the day with a song on his lips.

Lifting the headphones from Jacob's head, Michael Matthew Morrison would give his own rendition of an entertainer, right down to holding the invisible mike just below his lips. Jacob would laugh and sing along if he could remember the words. His father did a fair Eagles medley, loved Bob Seger and his war experiences seemed to draw him to the lyrics of Billy Joel.

Being a veteran and having taken part in controlled violence, in the national interest of course, it didn't keep his father from internalizing the fact that he'd killed people. Excuse for his problem drinking, probably not, but reason, most definitely. Did he love

Jacob and his two brothers? Absolutely. Did he try to get help for his problems? What problems? He held down a job, paid his bills and was loved by all and forgiven his lapses. What problems?

When he was killed, all the problems Michael Matthew Morrison had ignored came crashing down on his loving wife and children. Not before Michael Matthew Morrison was loved one last time, however. Full military honors for his service, a mournfully haunting bugle, bagpipes and an edited script of his life left Jacob confused about who was being laid to rest.

Strangers and grandparents he hadn't met more than twice in his life doted on Jacob and his little brothers while chowing down and quietly telling the boys what a great friend and son Michael Matthew Morrison had been.

It was quieter in the house the next day, then very quiet two days later when the grandparents left to continue their retirement. Three weeks of uncertainty was settled with finality as boxes were packed, a yard sale held and a dazed Jacob, carrying his pillow and blanket, found himself leading his two little brothers up three flights of stairs into a small apartment where he would share a room and a bed.

Mother Lacey, finally done with her crying, sat the boys down and told them she was going to need to find a job. With no extended family in the area to provide support and a teenage girl with an infant of her own from the first floor offering to take care of the boys, Jacob grew up real quick.

Music became a trusted ally for Jake's anguish, telling him stories in every genre possible, lulling him to sleep, quieting an inner anger. Truth be told Jacob could point to no obvious reason why he was always on the edge of exploding, but music kept him from breaking into a million pieces.

School offered no sanctuary. Jacob became the class clown. He never involved anyone else; he simply acted out. His schoolmates' laughter got everyone off task and the teachers would send Jacob to the principal's office. On the third visit, the principal, a savvy old guy with twenty-nine years of dealing with the best and worst of student behavior, asked Jacob one question.

"I understand you provide the gift of laughter for your classmates, even at your own peril. Tell me, Jacob, are you having as much fun as they are?"

Jacob couldn't answer. He was not yet capable of self-examination.

"I don't think you're having any fun at all, Jacob. I'm going to make space just outside my office and for the remainder of the year, you will take your lessons here. If you can make the walls laugh at your antics, have at it. When I have the time, I will sit with you and perhaps we can come to some agreement and maybe become friends as well. Mrs. Darvin will get you set up. You are dismissed."

Perhaps over time, Jacob and the principal could have solved Jacob's anger issues, but the turning point happened by accident.

The weather was good most of the year and Jacob started scouring the immediate neighborhood for opportunities to make money. Removing his ever-present music from his ears he'd wandered into yards asking to do odd jobs; the neighbors responded.

One of these neighbors played piano with the windows open. Jacob struck up a friendship and the neighbor offered to teach him the fundamentals of music. Jacob took to the piano like a man dying of thirst craving water—he couldn't get enough of it. With his earnings, he bought his first keyboard and the headphones gradually retired to his bedroom. Jacob learned to create his own music.

As he got older, he introduced his little brothers to the world of work, asking for a small share of their profits.

"It's only right, I found you this job. Don't want it? Just say so. Plenty of young men out there looking for an opportunity." His brothers made eye contact with each another, shrugged, sighed and paid up.

A tall boy for his age, when he was twelve, Jacob insisted on a paper route in a wealthy suburban neighborhood. He had plans to buy an even more expensive keyboard, someday a piano.

Getting up early, the sun still yawning, its pink tongue lighting the horizon before casting its eye on the world, Jacob would bask in the early morning solitude. Everything and everyone seemed unhurried and hushed. The coolness of the morning would wrap itself around Jacob as he pedaled the two miles to pick up a hundred papers at the gated entrance, placing the bundle in the canvas carrier on his back, folding on the fly, letting the news spread far and wide.

Jacob was running his own business. Birds and squirrels could testify to the nose-to-the-grindstone way Jacob did his work. Pickup and delivery was his mantra. His approach to school took on a businesslike approach, and when he rejoined his classmates, the principal took full credit for the change in his behavior.

At fourteen, a year before he would enter high school, Jacob inherited stepdad Brian, who moved the family to the same gated community where Jacob delivered papers. Having already started a savings account, which added to his sense of independence, Jacob didn't think he needed a man in his life.

Brian didn't push Jacob or his little brothers, just showed interest in the things they did.

"I would love to hear you play on a real piano sometime," he said to Jacob one day. "Your mom says you've been at it quite a while now. From the sounds coming from your room, I'd say you're really talented." An awkward moment of silence passed. "Tell you what. Let's all take a field trip."

The family piled into the SUV. In the back seat, Jacob's face showed no emotion. Brian stopped at a mall and it seemed the field trip would be mundane at best. They walked the corridors, Jacob trailing behind, stopping only when one of the younger brothers got excited by the latest this or that. Jacob ignored them as they jostled one another and kidded their way through the mall until, a half hour later, they stopped in front of a store.

Jacob looked up from his shoes and his eyes bugged. In the display window sat two beautiful pianos. Somehow his feet took him into the room; it opened to seven models on display with keyboards playing second fiddle, lining the back wall.

He had never seen so many pianos in one place. He must have sat in front of five different models listening for tone, asking questions of the salesman, finally settling on a small upright that he checked the price of three times. He sat down and began to play. His fingers seemed to take on a life of their own and the entire store turned to listen to a wonderful rendition of Billy Joel's *Italian Restaurant.*

'That's the one I will buy when I save enough,' nodded a solemn Jacob when he finished.

Brian wandered over, a stunned look on his face. "I think that is a good choice, Jacob," he said. "Let's find out how it sounds in our living room. We can try it free for thirty days."

Lacey could not keep the smile from her face as her son closed his eyes, climbed into himself, placed his fingers back on the keys and a musical piece that would do Elton John proud emerged.

* * *

The car pulled into the parking lot of the country club pool. "Little side trip," Brian called out. He walked with Jacob to the front desk and looked at the registration information. "After all," he kidded, "we're paying for it." He signed Jacob up for swimming lessons.

After several lessons, Jacob began to feed a different hunger. The country club pool became a sanctuary where he would spend hours learning to swim, all the while building strength and endurance. He loved diving to the bottom of the pool and just sitting there, holding his breath, trying to increase the time below the surface as he imagined music filling his ears. All the while, his ever-stretching frame gained mass. By freshman year, Jacob was a 6'3" specimen.

"Do you ever see him with other kids his own age?" Brian asked his wife one day as they watched Jacob slice through the water.

"I've asked him to invite his young friends over. But he doesn't seem interested," Lacy said, her worry showing in the lines of her brow.

"He needs to get into a team sport. Best way to make friends that I know of. Maybe a public high school."

"Jacob never really connected in that private middle school," Lacey agreed.

River View High School, a huge sprawling set of buildings, stood with its doors propped open like a gaping mouth ready, willing and able to swallow any student who lacked a purpose. Jacob stood on the sidewalk, watching students disappear perhaps never to emerge.

"There's no swim team," said the guidance counselor as Jacob stood with his parents in the main office, "but there are four different fall sports to choose from as well as a number of clubs. Here's a list and schedule and signup times for each."

After signing up for his classes, which included a music class, Brian drove them home, let Lacy out of the vehicle but didn't turn off the ignition.

When Jacob started to get out of the car, Brian said, "We aren't done planning your year just yet so buckle up." He fired up an Elton John CD and got back on the highway. As Brian sang along, his body moving to the music, Jacob silently banged out the notes on his lap. They pulled into the lot of a local Starbucks coffee shop.

Leading Jacob to a table, Brian went to stand in the order line. Jacob sat, muttering, "How come he didn't ask me if I wanted something?" His stepdad returned to the table with two cups of black coffee. He set one down in front of the young man who just looked at it.

"I've never had coffee before. Do you think I'll like it?"

"Jacob, I'm going to tell you a story, and I'm going to use coffee as a metaphor. Before I begin, though, I'm going to go and add a little cream to my coffee. I don't like it black. No sugar, cinnamon, nutmeg, chocolate or vanilla. Just a little cream."

Jacob watched Brian stand at a small table talking pleasantly with another customer while pouring cream and stirring his paper cup.

"I don't understand this guy," he said under his breath. "First he gets me coffee I don't drink. Then he doesn't ask me if I want something in my coffee. And how in the world is coffee going to help me decide whether to join one of the sports teams, if that's what this is about?" The coffee smelled good Jacob had to admit as he gazed into its blackness.

Brian sat back down. His coffee several shades lighter than Jacob's.

"Nothing like a good cup of coffee in the afternoon. A time when I can relax knowing my work day is done." He pushed back from the table ever so slightly. "My father was a working man, Jacob. His day began at exactly four thirty every morning, six days a week. An hour later on Sunday. Every morning he stared into a cup of coffee just like yours. Black. Every morning he drained that cup knowing the warmth in his hands was soon to be replaced with cold metal, lots of noise and extremely bright lights.

"He could have sat nursing another cup and still made it to work on time but he didn't. He put electrical components together. His job was what they call piece work. Kinda like when you delivered papers. No delivery, no money."

Jacob nodded remembering the self-motivation it had taken to get the job done every morning.

"My father, Russell, died way too young. I believe he worked himself to death. He always got to a job he hated at least fifteen minutes early. He said good morning to everyone on his way in. It was his way of bringing a little humanity to the assembly line. By the time he passed, he had lost most of his hearing and wore dark glasses everywhere but at work."

Brian looked older suddenly as if he were carrying the same weight of his dad's responsibility.

"At his funeral, nearly every one of the workers my father greeted every day for those twenty years showed up to pay their respects. That means something. They were on piece work too. This little bit of homage cost them. But Russell had touched them in a way they had to acknowledge."

Jacob raised a quizzical brow. Brian nodded and continued.

"Coffee starts out black. Most people begin drinking coffee with plenty of sugar and cream, maybe even some cinnamon. As you and your taste mature, you'll tend to add less of everything and come to enjoy the coffee closer to its naturally brewed state." For emphasis, he took a good long sip.

"My father used coffee for fortification. I'm not sure he ever got to truly enjoy it. Maybe on Sunday. What it did give him was the strength to face day after day, year after year, more of the same. He never complained, but you could see the sameness of his days slowly draining him, moving him ever closer to the bottom with another day to face." Brian stared into his own cup, lost for a moment. Then he looked Jacob in the eyes.

"He was a smart man, my father, caught up in a sense of duty to a family that never allowed him to challenge his abilities. He worked at that mindless job, at the same furious pace necessary to make a living, for twenty years." Brian snapped his fingers. "Then, in an instant, he was gone. Way too young. Dad never added sweetener or cream to his coffee. He never got to savor a lingering aroma or pause just for the pleasure of, you know, pausing. I never remember him having an afternoon cup. Coffee was simply an alarm clock sending him on his way in the morning as soon as the bottom of his cup appeared."

Tears filled Brian's eyes. He tried to hide them in the rim of his cup but failed. He wiped his eyes and looked away.

"We actually had a happy family in spite of all dad sacrificed. He came to all my school events, though it cost him plenty. He read important events from the newspaper every night at the supper table. He wanted to widen our world and show us we could be part of it. He could make a joke out of the most trivial matter. Toward the end, with his eyesight failing, I used to read to him. He'd even make jokes about it." Brian paused, "he made me who I am today.

"He was a good husband. I never saw him drink or smoke or swear. There was never time to do much vacationing but he would walk with mom, my two sisters and me on Sunday afternoons. We would find local parks and walking trails and mom and dad introduced us to a higher power through nature. *Dare to dream,* he'd say. When his heart gave out, my mother gave up herself, within the year."

"I'm a little thick, Brian," Jacob said uncomfortably. "Why am I holding this cup of coffee?"

"Okay, I probably didn't do a good job with that," Brian laughed, "but you got to meet my dad anyway. So try this. Say this cup of coffee is your life as it is now. You're at an age where a cup of coffee is permitted, so let's say we consider you grown up. Looking down into that black abyss you can't see the future. But you can see the now. Do you want to add a little light to the darkness? A little sweetener? High school is a brand new beginning. You have been pretty much a loner. Want to add a little company, expand your physical skills, maybe add others to your music? Will you dare to try something different?"

Jacob shrugged. Brian took a long gulp of his coffee and stood up, declaring, "This may require a second cup, this is important work here." He refilled his cup, added cream, sat back down and continued.

"That private middle school your mother scrimped and saved to send you to, hoping to get you to open up, was all about the individual. You've done that individual bit. As my dad said, *Dare to dream.* Take a sip of that coffee. It's getting cold. If it's too bitter, remember, you can have it any way you want it."

Jacob took a sip, grimaced, looked up at Brian and nodded in sudden understanding. He promptly scraped his chair back and took his coffee to the table to add a little sweetness and light.

* * *

The soccer coach struck the right note for Jacob at an evening for parents and prospective athletes. He spoke of soccer as the ultimate team sport where each athlete got to showcase their individual talents all the while promoting team success. When he described the loneliness of the goalie, who at the end of the day was the ultimate team player, Jacob looked at Brian and nodded his head.

Jacob, tall and rangy with the quick twitch muscles needed to respond to an opponent's attack, had found a home on the soccer team. He also blossomed in the classroom and started a band featuring his piano and a newfound deep singing voice.

He and his little band played for free at community events, the country club, wherever they could gain experience and exposure. One free concert led to Jacob's first real job.

A member of the gated community was a Starbucks licensee. He heard Jacob play, watched the charisma displayed by this tall young man with the ready smile and deep voice. He hired Jacob to play for an hour twice a week at his coffee shop. He eventually hired and trained him as a coffee barista.

Jacob's part-time job had him reflecting on that afternoon coffee with Brian. He found himself examining the face of every customer, wondering what was in their mind. Was this customer purchasing fuel for the long drive, savoring the end of a journey, just enjoying the moment, or was it simply an alarm clock summoning them to work?

Every cup he filled, from the simple black brew that started it all to outrageous concoctions, was a learning experience. That simple cup of coffee served as a daily lesson plan. The tips he received re-enforced the notion that engaging with people could

R. Wesley Clement

be as stimulating as the beverage served. Jacob was reminded daily of Brian's dad, welcoming people to a new day.

Jacob greeted customers as they entered and served them, but unlike Brian's dad he found himself enjoying every moment and thanking them again on their way out. He continued to play music twice a week and got paid for doing something that made him feel good.

When it came time to choose a career or a college, Jacob already knew what he wanted to do. He would attend a two-year community college while working and living at home. With the business skills necessary to one day open and run a Starbucks, his boss promised to provide Jacob with in-house training and send him to company workshops.

CHAPTER FIVE

1992 THANK YOU, THANK YOU VERY MUCH

Pictures and posters of the great man lined the walls in every room of the small apartment. Albums chronicling his career played constantly, even a mobile with cut out images of Elvis floating over the crib in the corner, over the head of baby Elvis, just about to turn two-years-old, who was destined to share more than just the great man's name.

Elvis lay back in the crib, sucking on a pacifier. Her hair was cut in the style of an early Elvis movie, right down to the sides fashioned as side burns. Rae Anne, who seemed too young to be a mother, stood in the kitchen, putting away a bag of groceries.

Rae Anne came by her obsession with Elvis Presley in a most natural way; she grew up in one. Her own mother planned her very life around Elvis concerts, movies, posters, magazines, 45s, LP albums and even diet. She grew up digesting peanut butter and jelly sandwiches served all hours of the day.

At seventeen, Rae Anne lost her mother to cervical cancer after a year-long battle. Elvis provided mood music for the peaks and valleys of her illness. Inheriting all that memorabilia and little else, Rae Anne was hell-bent on keeping that great man in the building.

Rae Anne was not a wild child. She was a nice girl. Maybe a little naive. Okay, a lot naive. When the good looking Billy told her she was beautiful, she believed him. After all, he looked a lot like a young Elvis Presley.

Their first time together, they went to a movie. Their second date was to the drive-in, one of the last in the state. An old Elvis movie was playing. Nostalgia Night they called it. Lots of older folks were there, rekindling their youth.

Billy had his way with Rae Anne that night in the back seat. When he found out she was pregnant, without so much as a "thank you, thank you very much," he skipped town.

* * *

On August 3, 1992, Rae Anne won a radio contest and received free tickets to a fifteenth-anniversary tribute to the Man. August 16 started out with a trip to the salon, a new dress, and nails and feet done.

"Gonna do this up right," said Rae Anne. She and two girlfriends spent that warm Sunday afternoon sipping mimosas, eating cake and ice cream, celebrating baby Elvis's second birthday, all the while singing Elvis songs. Little Elvis, born in the same month and on the same date Elvis Presley passed from this world, found her second birthday being treated as a prelude to an even bigger party.

Elvis's Grandmother Eunice had said she would watch Elvis, then backed out. Luckily the younger sister of one of the girls going to the concert agreed to sit.

"Got to be home by one o'clock.," the teenager said on the phone.

"Not a problem," promised Rae Anne. "The concert's done at eleven thirty. I'll be home by midnight." All the while, little Elvis was entertaining the girls with her Elvis shake.

The original invitation to the party was extended while the girls were taking a potty/smoke break at the concert. But when the girls arrived home at midnight and asked the babysitter to spend the night, she refused.

"I have school in the morning. Mom doesn't usually let me sit at all when there's school the next day. By the way you got a prank call that freaked me out, a lot of heavy breathing. They called three times." She shook her head. "You must have some weird friends."

"Gotta take her home," said her sister, "or it will be my neck. I'll come back we'll just hang out."

While the baby sitter's sister was being driven the two miles, Rae Anne got another call.

"You gotta come. Some great looking guys are here and lots of booze."

She should have done what the babysitter did earlier—hang up.

* * *

Rae Anne was astonished that leaving Elvis in a locked vehicle while she and her friend attended an after-concert party would be so frowned upon. After all, she'd been left to her own devices on many an occasion and turned out just fine, didn't she?

The officer, summoned by someone out walking their dog, found Rae Anne toasted while toasting the great man, having a grand old time.

Oblivious to the severity of child endangerment charges, Rae Anne didn't confer with a lawyer or try to lessen the charge. Not a reader or a watcher of current events, she had missed the reality that by 1992 society's focus on child welfare had evolved. It didn't help that she missed her first court appearance.

A lady judge with no sense of humor, and a mother herself, brought Rae Anne to her feet, then directed those feet to the county jail for 60 days along with a thousand dollar fine.

"You have three days to report to the jail. Let's see, it's eleven thirty." The judge glanced at her watch. "So eleven thirty, three days from now, I expect you to be changing into an orange jumpsuit. Do you have any questions? Something else you would like to add?"

"What am I going to do with my daughter your honor? I have no one."

"If you can't find a responsible adult, your daughter will go into foster care. The court will decide what a responsible adult looks like, so I would get right on that."

Rae Anne hung her head.

*   *   *

It was during the traumatic split with Billy and the subsequent news of her pregnancy that Rae Anne first fell under the spell of Billy's mother, Eunice.

Rae Anne had no insurance and nobody who could help. She reached out during her pregnancy and Eunice seemed sincere. In the beginning, it felt like it could work. Eunice, a single mother herself, offered to take Rae Anne and baby Elvis under her wing. Rae Anne's minimum wage job allowed no paid time off and couldn't guarantee they'd hold her job.

She moved out of the apartment she shared with two workmates when Eunice convinced her that moving in would provide an opportunity to help herself financially and give Eunice bonding time with the granddaughter she'd always wanted.

"Maybe you can even save a few bucks," Eunice said as she rocked Elvis. "You'll need to. Billy won't be coming back this way. He seeds gardens but he don't do no harvesting. Good riddance to the little prick." Rae Anne felt she'd found a kindred spirit.

The room she shared with Elvis looked out over a small patch of green with several trees forming a boundary to the neighbor's yard. Two aluminum and plastic lawn chairs and a settee that moved back and forth sat in the shadow of the two-story house situated just off a busy highway.

Rae Anne built a shrine to the King, covering all the walls, floor and surface space available. The boxes of memorabilia she'd inherited and saved from the dusty attic were put to use. The first man baby Elvis became accustomed to seeing was Elvis on the hanging mobile, accompanied by the music of the Man himself.

Sitting in her kitchen, draining her third cup of coffee, a cigarette smoldering in an ash tray—a brief respite between puffs—Eunice coughed quietly while listening to the strains from a constant barrage of Elvis tunes above the ceiling. She decided then and there that she and only she could save this child.

"Got to bide my time, be smart, make a plan, stay cool. Patience," she muttered.

Over the next two years under Eunice's roof, Elvis learned to walk, talk and sing and become very close to her grandmother. Eunice exercised her mantra of biding time, being smart, staying cool and above all, showing great patience. She had a long-term plan in mind.

Rae Anne was slow to pick up on the subtle change of roles. Two months after Elvis was born, Eunice helped Rae Anne find a job working the night shift as a clerk and janitor at a motel just five minutes down the highway. Rae Anne thought it ideal, being home with her daughter during the day and working when Elvis was asleep. She didn't factor in the upside-down sleep pattern she'd be living and soon found herself in a dazed state most of the time. She even began to resent her daughter's cries for attention.

Eunice, however, was always right there when Elvis fussed, took her out to the settee and played nice. When Rae Anne had time off, Eunice encouraged her to go out and enjoy her friends.

"Heck you're only young once. Me and Elvis, we're fine here."

Little Elvis began ignoring the hit-and-miss affection and discipline from Rae Anne. One day, when Elvis bit her while being disciplined, her mother seemed to snap back to her senses.

Holy shit, what's happening here, thought Rae Anne. The light came on.

Her daughter clinging to Eunice suddenly didn't seem like such a relief. She was losing her daughter. Rae Anne told Eunice she would be moving out and sharing an apartment with a girlfriend.

The real Eunice showed the stormy weather of her disposition.

"Have I done something wrong, something to upset you?" she asked in a reasonable barely-cloudy-day manner.

Only stolen my daughter's affection. "No, it's just time for Elvis and me to start making it on our own. Thank you so much for being there. We're not leaving the area. You'll still see Elvis."

"Who'll take care of Elvis while you work? You have to be careful, and it's expensive." A whine and approaching weather alert beginning to replace her normal tone.

Rae Anne hadn't really thought it all out but knew they had to get away, at least for a while. So she faked an answer.

"My roommate and I work different shifts so one of us will be home."

Eunice, trying to hold the lightning and thunder back, sputtered and sparked.

"If you think it will work, go ahead. I can't stop you, but I am concerned about Elvis. She needs me you know. Couldn't you just try the roommate thing by yourself first, not disrupt that little girl's routine?"

"Elvis and I will be fine, and you can see her on the weekends. It will all work out for the best," said Rae Anne smiling through teeth that now clenched with anger.

A month later, Rae Anne would ask Eunice to be responsible for her little Elvis for sixty days.

CHAPTER SIX

BLUE CHRISTMAS

Let me just say at the outset, Grandmother Eunice did love Elvis. There are all kinds of love, however. Her own son, Billy, could testify to that fact. When Billy met and set Rae Anne's life on its present trajectory, he was still in the infancy of becoming a sociopathic predator who would leave behind a trail of tears—so much for fatherhood.

Elvis, back in the care of her grandmother, was experiencing loss once again. She had re-bonded with her mother and now asked for her in a hundred different ways that Eunice didn't care for. She insisted on Elvis music being played and had reverted to demanding a pacifier on her naps or in bed for the night. She cried herself to sleep, sobbing for her mother. It almost made Eunice sorry she'd taken the initiative in getting Elvis back. Almost.

After finally getting the little girl to sleep by giving into her demand for a peanut butter and jelly sandwich, Eunice sat rocking the settee back and forth in the quiet of the night. Gazing up at the late summer stars, the scent of peanut butter on her hands, her mind whirling like the cosmos above, Eunice began planning her next move.

Sipping a coffee she'd dubbed *my pick-me-up,* a glowing cigarette waiting its turn, Eunice reflected on how she'd brought that little girl back into her life.

                    R. Wesley Clement

"Bet that idiot girl still don't know what hit her. Bet she's sitting on that hard bunk looking out at these same stars just shaking her head." Eunice chuckled. With smoke filling her lungs, she closed her eyes, her mind racing, recalling the cartoon series she'd watched and enjoyed as a kid.

"Was it Rocky and Bullwinkle? Yeah that was it, and what was that the famous line uttered by one of the characters? *And now for my next act.* I guess I'm more like my sister than I would have believed."

When Rae Anne moved out, Eunice knew it was just a matter of time before the girl would do something foolish.

"So glad I held my temper in check," she muttered. Patting her pack of cigarettes, giving thanks to their calming effect, she congratulated herself for staying cool. Showing patience. That might just have been the hardest part of the whole plan. Staying cool but ever watchful. Waiting.

When Rae Anne won those tickets, Eunice wanted to thank the King himself for answering her prayers. When asked to babysit Elvis, Eunice said sure thing, then at the last minute remembered something important so she wouldn't be available. Knowing Rae Anne would have to scramble, find some kid to babysit, knowing she'd want to make a night of it. Just knowing-knowing-knowing.

"You can't write this stuff down," she'd said, immediately putting the second part of her plan in motion. If Rae Anne was including the late great Elvis Presley in her evening plans, it was sure to be a night to remember.

At nine o'clock, she dialed Rae Anne's number. When the young voice answered, Eunice breathed just loud enough to plant uneasiness. She called twice more and the young voice took on a nervous (and on the third call, panicked) tone. That did the trick. She waited in the shadows near Rae Anne's apartment and watched the roommate leave with the babysitter. She looked up at a nearly full moon and felt like baying herself. When the roommate reappeared twenty minutes later, Rae Anne was waiting on the front steps, Elvis wrapped in a blanket.

Eunice followed at a discreet distance, heard the music before she saw the destination. The sidewalk was lit at hundred yard intervals. Rubbish awaited a Monday morning pick up. Eunice pulled to the side a block from the only home with lights glowing. She watched Rae Anne and her roommate quietly close the car doors, put their fingers to their lips, cut across the lawn, take the steps two at a time and ring the doorbell.

The call came into police headquarters at four minutes after one. An anonymous caller, a dog walker, indicated seeing a small child staring at them from the rear seat of an automobile parked at the curb near a house that seemed to be having a party. The doors to the car were locked but no adult was in the vicinity.

In fact, Elvis was sleeping peacefully when Eunice hurried by not holding a leash. Returning to her car to locate the nearest public phone at an all-night convenience store, she turned on the radio but immediately shut the damn thing off. Seemed everybody was celebrating the life of the King. Time to let the Man rest in peace.

CHAPTER SEVEN

1994 RESILIENCE TAKES A DIFFERENT FORM

"Quentin, get up! You'll be late for school!" a voice shouted up the staircase. Quentin opened his eyes, mentally ticking off all his possessions as he surveyed the room. Making sure they were in their proper place.

Encyclopedias A-Z taking up one wall, a small desk with a globe and a computer, a lamp offering the shadows he cherished. A trophy for winning a regional spelling bee with several ribbons dangling from it sat atop the encyclopedias. A small mirror, the only wall adornment, allowed Quentin shadowed peeks at his growth spurts.

"I might have to raise that mirror soon," he snarled to the glass. Mirrors were no friends of Quentin's.

It was a Spartan room. There was no curtain to offer a touch of softness, no opportunity for the warmth and light of a sun beam to get through. Just a shade drawn to its limit.

Quentin stretched and yawned. His thirteenth birthday party was just hours away. He had gone to bed thinking about it, and here it was filling his thoughts. *Been with me all night,* he thought but couldn't remember dreaming about it. The guest list—all adults—entered his head. Finally a teen and nearly as tall as his father, Quentin found no use for friends his own age.

"Wonder how she'll wreck it this time," he muttered angrily, knowingly.

In the shower, the soap on a rope swung with a certain swagger, on this special morning, Quentin noticed his emerging manhood stiffening as the soap lightly touched it in passing. This stiffening had been happening at odd and embarrassing times lately.

"Just nature giving you a nod," his father had kidded, "pointing you in a new direction. Be sure to keep your compass pointing true north son."

A full case of soap-on-a-rope, a chemically enhanced attempt to quash acne that had not caught on with his father's company, promised to lather and stimulate the lad for the foreseeable future. His father was always bringing home samples. Quentin only got to sample the harmless stuff.

His father was his best friend, not a hug-and-hold father, but a man who had been Quentin's friend for as long as he could remember. A no-nonsense man. A good if not overtly involved father.

"Always do your best, Quentin. That's all you can do," he'd answer to any and all questions and queries the boy threw out at him. A professional. Educated beyond his abilities. Wilder Spence fulfilled contracts for a pharmaceutical company. In short, he pushed pills to doctor's offices throughout the Southeast.

Wilder Spence had hoped to be a doctor himself but he simply couldn't pass the required exams. Selling the latest miracle cures, salves and placebos was the closest he got to writing a prescription. Quentin could talk to his father like a colleague, ask him anything. That might have been enough if he were home.

He wasn't home this morning; he was somewhere on the road. Four nights, sometimes a full week passed without his father's presence. He'd be home tonight though. His father's brother too. Uncle Warren and his wife Wendy, witnessing Quentin blowing out his childhood.

Quentin's mother was at the table when he entered the kitchen, a cup of black coffee before her and the array of pills she somehow washed down with the brew seven days a week.

Her eyes gleamed this morning as she pointed to the box of Wheaties. "Breakfast of champions," she offered, "it says so right on the box." She gave a fake smile, adding, "Special day requires a special effort." She popped back a pill. "You didn't tinkle on my tile this morning, did you dear?" She took a swig of coffee. "That slight reddening on your cheek, it's not another pimple about to protrude is it?"

Quentin flushed and silently fumed. No toast, no fruit, no juice. Just breakfast in a box served up the same way each morning. *For all I know that damn box was set out at midnight.* Her little daily barb had Quentin sitting down to pee like a girl. Thank goodness his classmates weren't privy to that bit of cannon fodder.

This morning, an apple sat beside his box of cereal. As he reached for his bowl in the cupboard, his mother in her grinding way said, "An apple a day keeps the doctor away. Oh that's right, your father isn't a doctor." She smiled that fake smile again."I'm sure he'll be right here to celebrate."

Dust motes danced in the morning sunlight, settling to become little dust bunnies, the only pets in the house. Quentin slurped his cereal, just to annoy. *Two can play this game.*

* * *

Truth was, Ruth Spence had no interest in anything in the house, hadn't in years. When Wilder failed to pass the exams, she gave up on the idea of a home experience. In her mind, she'd worked her ass off while he came home night after night with a superior attitude. Though bitterly disappointed when Wilder failed, it offered her a leg up in their relationship and she'd stood above the fray for the last fourteen years.

That one night, when it seemed all the work of becoming a doctor was about to become a reality, she'd let down her guard and allowed Wilder to convince her it was the perfect time to have a child. Damn fool she'd been and voiced it to herself six months into her gathering girth. But it was too late by then. Welcome to the world, little Quentin.

Never offered a tit to the little shit at least, and the bond was never formed. In the days before selfies, she became one. Those little medicinal samples Wilder always left lying around, complete with their designed purpose spelled out on the box, allowed Ruth to pick and choose her emotion of the day and her total withdrawal at night.

With no job that interested her and no inclination to be a homemaker, it was inevitable that Ruth would be out and about. She took care of one thing and one thing only—her appearance in public.

Ruth was a superficially beautiful woman. Men noticed her whether in the dreaded grocery line, department store or coffee shop. Men made eye contact with her, their purpose clear as a foghorn warning. For the first five years of Quentin's life, as miserable as playing mother made Ruth feel, it managed to occupy enough of her focus to keep those knowing looks and longings at bay.

Thank God somebody had the sense to invent school, Ruth thought on her first day of freedom, and this particular school district believed in full-day kindergarten. She smiled and waved goodbye, not to her child, but to her lifted burden.

By the middle of Quentin's first year, Ruth had taken to exploring the streets of downtown Montpelier, Vermont, the state's capital and their now-and-forever home it appeared.

It was certainly an easy little city to get around. It seemed everyone was a government employee or school teacher. Ruth sat in a coffee shop, reflecting on what those streets beyond the window glass offered a twenty-nine-year-old with three years of college and no work history for the past six years.

Wilder makes a good living, so it's not a lack of money. I don't miss Wilder at all, so it's not a lack of Wilder. She chuckled and accepted

R. Wesley Clement

another refill, watching the veteran waitress move among the tables offering good cheer along with the brew, getting smiles of acknowledgement from nearly every guest.

I wouldn't mind getting a little thanks for my efforts once in a while, she thought. *Maybe I could do something like this. Doesn't look like rocket science.*

For the next eight years, Ruth took daily stock of herself, never actually taking a job. She filled out applications in nearly every business, department store, eatery and coffee shop in the city. With her looks, she was offered employment many times over. What she was really looking for was the opportunity to sit in front of someone and talk about her extraordinary skill set.

Bright beyond ordinary, vain beyond bright, Ruth was a mess as a mother, a wife, a friend, of which she had none. She found no fault that wasn't someone else's. Quentin took the brunt of her temper, which shaped the impressionable bright-beyond- ordinary boy.

She was utterly disinterested in his school accomplishments, which emerged early. The boy was reading with accuracy and understanding when he entered school.

"My god, Quentin," she'd snapped, "of course you can read. I taught you myself didn't I."

Poor little Quentin, not yet understanding that sometimes a little white lie is the preferred prescription, piped up, "No. Dad read me all those little books that Uncle Warren and Aunt Wendy sent me for my birthdays."

Ruth looked at her son, set her countenance, and then set the compass and the course. "Well then, I think you should share with your father all the glory his efforts got you, now and in future, dear."

So from early on, the little knapsack filled with colored and graphite accomplishments, placed carefully layer upon layer. In time they wrinkled, stained and smothered themselves to death. By the time Dad arrived, tired from his trip, three or four days of papers were too much to share.

At least the boy could show proof of purpose, if ever asked; his mother's knapsack-of-nothingness offered nothing to share.

Quentin's five senses were acute. When his early elementary teacher presented the five senses as a way to become scientifically significant, starting with a rotten egg hidden in the classroom, it was Quentin who smelled it. Sounds cleverly disguised, waiting to be identified; tastes, with odd mixtures of sweet and sour, salty and bitter; touch, using a blindfold and objects; eye spy games—Quentin excelled at them all.

Ruth had begun staring down the starers three years ago. She found that, when caught and challenged with feigned disinterested innocence, most men turned red and looked away.

Caught you, she'd think, clicking her tongue.

Every once in a while, the challenge was met, and she would take a step toward the king.

Your move, you silly pawn, you. She knew how this chess game would end. Like filling out those stupid useless applications, Ruth simply wanted to show off her skill set. But offer fruit to animals with an open hand and chances are eventually you'll get bitten.

Coffee shop conversations moved on to locations that offered places to lay your head.

Still in charge, Ruth thought, the first time she shared a drink in the lounge at eleven in the morning. The airplane pilot sitting directly across from her had flown combat missions over sandy soil and was now describing Ruth as a rare desert flower that emerged just briefly following an always-in-your-prayers rainstorm.

She sat transfixed, slightly medicated and already thinking about grabbing his joystick. Not used to liquor—Wilder didn't drink or condone it in others—Ruth was warming from within. Before you could say boarding pass please, Ruth found herself following the pilot's flight plan, which he promised offered a soft landing.

Room 317 would become their flight number for the next three years. The pilot was in the city every third week. He even managed a tryst once while his family vacationed at nearby Lake Champlain.

Ruth felt entitled to a little happiness and it seemed flight 317 would be landing in Montpelier for, oh I don't know, perhaps forever.

Five months before Quentin turned thirteen, he began smelling something in the house that hadn't been there before. His nose smelled aftershave, body spray or some such thing, it was coming from his parent's bedroom. He began to use all five senses to track down the source.

During the five months the smell lingered both in his nose and his mind, he spied with his little eye. On mornings when the afternoon smells were freshest, his mother was showered, dressed and almost affable when he entered the kitchen. Same Wheaties box, same everything, but different somehow. Quentin put a mental spyglass to his eye.

The sudden appearance of the sun brought discovery. Dust motes weren't dancing on those mornings; dust bunnies were missing from their corner hutch. Mother dressed and ready for the day. Kitchen cleaned. An almost pleasant atmosphere. Eureka! A childhood story entered his mind. *Someone's been sleeping in my bed*—the line from Goldilocks, though it wasn't his room the smells were emanating from.

The thing about scientists, some discover to find a possible cure, others simply add to the knowledge base. In Quentin's case, he simply didn't like the idea that his mother was saying "FUCK YOU" to the family—a new word Quentin had heard for years but could now put to use.

If I figure this out, maybe I can get eggs and toast once in a while around here. The seeds his mother had sown and nourished with neglect and abuse since birth were flowering. Quentin was blooming into a self-nurturing narcissist.

An opportunity finally presented itself on the very day Quentin turned thirteen. Middle school kids can do some pretty

<hr>

foolish things and on that day one of Quentin's classmates called in a bomb scare from a phone booth on his way to school. The school had never received a call like this before.

The stars must have lined up, since the no-nonsense secretary, Mrs. Dyer, was home sick and the office was being manned by an honor student who suddenly saw herself as the savior of all mankind. The principal was at an administrative team meeting. The guidance director was somewhere in the building, guiding.

The girl pulled the fire alarm herself then placed herself in the hallway directing students and staff to the athletic field, just as the emergency evacuation plan carried out twice a year dictated. She forgot just one thing and it was nearly a half hour later that an English teacher approached her.

"Did you call the police or fire department dear? We aren't hearing any sirens." The ensuing confusion had middle school cleared for the day. Parents were called, buses loaded, students dispersed.

Quentin wandered the half mile home, thinking about the early birthday gift he'd just received and the book he could spend the afternoon with. He walked by a yard where spring flowers tickled his nose with their invitation to the bees. He suddenly remembered his mother in full bloom this morning and in an instant his posture changed, his brow furrowed, and Quentin put on his significant scientist face.

There was a black Ford Taurus parked just down the street from his house that he'd never seen before. He quietly entered the house through the side door of the garage using the emergency key placed there but never used to his knowledge. He immediately smelled the smell.

Taking off his shoes, he sat down at the kitchen table. Sounds seemed to echo in the house. He heard the ticking of the large clock in the sitting room. Mumbled conversation tumbled down the stairs, followed by laughter. Quentin closed his eyes and thought scientifically. He had no wish to confront; he simply needed to verify and expand his knowledge base, his power base. He scribbled a note and left it on the kitchen table.

Home early, you were busy entertaining I guess, though the living room was empty. I'd really like a chocolate cake and vanilla ice cream for tonight and maybe eggs and toast and hot chocolate for tomorrow's breakfast.

* * *

As the candles darkened one by one, Quentin took his time letting the moment last—the chocolate cake offered up with vanilla ice cream and good wishes offered all around. He sighed and smiled at his mother.

'Let's see what the morning brings,' he nodded, his smile lingering; challenging. She broke from his gaze. Quentin had become the man of the house.

The next morning, Quentin bounded down the stairs after a mock battle with his soap on a rope. The soap, used as a gentle prod stimulated him and this very morning of new beginnings he found release for the first time, quivering and quaking in the aftermath.

His hair still wet, his heart beating rapidly, he found his mother standing at the counter near the sink, relinquishing the table, staring out the window. There was no Wheaties box acting as centerpiece. A mug of hot chocolate sat steaming, mingling with the smell of fresh toast. Two filmy egg eyes stared from the plate.

His mother continued to study the backyard through the window over the sink, sipping her coffee. Quentin breathed in aroma of coffee, but along with it was another smell. It was new and foreign to this room. He sniffed deeply and opened his mind, shivering slightly, remembering a confrontation in the boys' room in fourth grade when a group of older boys threatened to put his head in the toilet. He had smelled it on himself then and he smelled it coming from his mother now—it was the smell of fear.

CHAPTER EIGHT

2014 STELLA

When Sean left for work, Stella called the hospital. She wanted to informally discuss Sean's injuries with Dr. Bronson, a trauma surgeon who worked three nights a week in the emergency room with her. He was not available but would get back to her, the receptionist promised.

Stella moved to the couch, shook out and folded the sheet and blanket, placing them on the back of the sofa. She removed the remote from between the cushions, straightening up Sean's multipurpose office.

Maybe I was a little harsh with him, she thought, *but I don't think he's being realistic.*

"Go with what you've got" had been the philosophy of her coach in high school when a starter was out with an injury. Stella had applied it to every challenge she'd set for herself. She'd conversed a number of times with Dr. Bronson, who wouldn't offer a definitive opinion without seeing Sean's x-rays and chart.

"Based on what you're telling me," he'd said, "I would agree Sean is probably not going to walk again, but I'd need to see everything before I'd say that publicly."

Stella grabbed her oversized carry bag and took out Sean's inch-thick folder held together with an elastic band. She poured three cups of water into the coffee pot, scooped out a light blend and sat down to go over Sean's records one more time.

Holding the x-rays up to the light from the kitchen window, she visualized the man who had always performed the garbage ritual making light of the challenge. Looking at the two shattered mangled images in front of her, Stella had to sit down.

Being an emergency room nurse provided all the scenarios possible a human body can come apart. Staying clinically aloof from the emotion of the moment was something Stella was proud of. But this, her man Sean, torn apart by the foolish actions of a hit-and-run driver, brought the pain and suffering home. You couldn't leave it in the corridors of a hospital when your shift ends.

Meeting Sean had added the final puzzle piece to all she'd ever wanted. She would need to be strong; she looked back to the self-discipline that had defined her. Stella had been a three-sport athlete, lettering in all three as a junior. Softball, field hockey and winter track kept her busy and focused, and staying focused can sometimes be difficult. But you couldn't have convinced Stella of that until the winter of her senior year.

She was too busy to date and boys seemed too silly, with their sexual jokes and juvenile humor, to be anything more than friends. Then lightning struck amid the smells of Lysol and liniment.

The athletic trainer who visited the school twice a week to check on injuries was simply a stage actor in Stella's life. Stella saw him around but had no injuries to report until the second week of winter track during her senior year. Stella ran the 220 and you needed to train hard for that and field hockey had intruded into the pre-conditioning part of the track season. It had been worth it though, since her school won a state championship. But it left Stella using a different set of muscles. She overdid it and tore a hamstring, ripped it actually.

Joseph Roberts a twenty-three-year-old freshly minted athletic trainer worked for the rehabilitation unit of the local hospital, which contracted with the county schools and provided a trainer for games and to service injuries. The hospital came out a winner in two ways. They filled an immediate need and formed a relationship with young people that would last a life time.

Joseph was a serious kid who hoped to become a sports medicine doctor someday. He joined the team of six trainers and was assigned to three high schools and two middle schools. Joseph was used to girls finding him attractive and shrugged it off.

"It's a cross I have to bear" he would kiddingly tell his roommate. Seems he should have crossed his heart and hoped to die as his future doctor oath of *do no harm* was suddenly in jeopardy.

Joseph had never met anyone like Stella. He had seen her as a participant, a solid athlete giving it her all in every game. They'd never exchanged more than a howdy do; the girl was healthy.

When he arrived at school that Wednesday afternoon and checked the sheet of injured athletes, he was surprised to find her name on the list. He'd been at the championship game and it was Stella who'd had a breakaway, scoring the only goal of the game. Her picture in the paper, complete with the required black liner under the eyes, could not blur that winning smile.

The attraction was immediate and mutual. When Stella entered the training room, Joseph was seated at a desk going over her injury report. Their eyes locked and the fate of their relationship was sealed. They met twice a week in that small room, subtle flirtation adding a nervous energy to their conversation. Obviously they touched in an innocent way as the injury slowly healed.

It was as if two ships traveled the same route side by side in the same body of water, felt the same waves carrying the same cargo, yet were not allowed to communicate about anything more than the weather. The only words left unspoken were the ones that mattered, words that would have moved the relationship into forbidden waters. Like those two oceangoing vessels, they bobbed and weaved, watched islands of opportunity pass, too self-disciplined to stray from their destination.

R. Wesley Clement

Stella knew she had never felt like this with anyone. Her heart raced whenever she saw him or thought about him, which lately seemed like most of the time. Stella steeled herself for the Wednesday that would end their official school-sanctioned meeting time. Both Stella and Joseph had their game faces cemented in place as she was officially released to return to the track. She cried for a solid hour in the girl's locker room on her way to practice.

In the end, the inner strength, the self-discipline required to become a star athlete and the arduous path needed to become an athletic trainer, kept the relationship from becoming physical. With Stella's injury healed, their conversations returned to "howdy" in the hall. The only injury that remained was a broken heart—truth be told, two of them.

Stella shook her head, smiling, and returned her gaze to Sean's injury report. Both legs shattered at knee level. The pickup going through a red light and making a wide left turn struck the jogging Sean at a sideways angle. The injuries shattered both knees laterally and the bones directly above and below them. Stella shook her head again, this time not smiling. Sean was thrown away from the path of the truck, which probably saved his life. Landing in a water- weed- and debris-filled ditch well to the right of the graveled roadside, Sean would have drowned in the filth if another early morning jogger hadn't heard his moans.

The driver sped from the scene only to be caught three days later when he sought an estimate for the significant damage to the right headlamp, bumper and fender of his 2004 F150 with mag wheels and oversized tires. The custom paint job that had attracted admirers became an attraction for the investigating officers. Word went out; information came in.

The driver, a nineteen-year-old with a long rap sheet for traffic violations, was operating on a suspended license with no insurance. Sean's lawyer, his cousin Braden, was going after the parents' homeowner's policy since their son still lived at home and was a student at a local community college. Right now though, he was serving a two-year sentence for habitually offending traffic laws, personal injury and leaving the scene of an accident with injury.

Even now, the painful memory of that early morning brought tears to her eyes. She could still hear the moaning of a semiconscious Sean arriving by ambulance in her emergency room. She had clocked in a short time earlier, called to service without even knowing it was Sean.

It was a rare morning shift. Normally she ran with Sean before she went to bed after finishing her midnight-to-seven shift. She had just worked a four-to-eleven shift the night before and was sleeping when Sean left the house. Even through the tears, shock and shouts of recognition, she had responded professionally and given the support needed for the attending doctor to get Sean stabilized. She felt guilty about Sean lying there in pain, no matter how irrational the thought.

Brought back once again to the charts before her, Stella gave the manila folder that steely-eyed determined look she'd given her husband this morning and dialed the doctor's number again. As the phone rang on the other end, Stella walked to the bookcase. It held a picture of a happy bride and groom, the end result of a chance meeting one workout morning. She had looked up from her awkward position—one leg thrown over a metal bar, head down, her workout tights stretched to the max—into a pair of liquid green eyes framed by a furrowed brow and a smile that showed intrigue, not treachery.

"Yes, he did get the message." The receptionist's voice broke into her thoughts. "He'll call when he's free." *Click.* Holding the framed photo, Stella returned to her reverie. As she removed her leg from the bar, stretching her 5'7" frame upward towards the blinding early morning sun, a stocking-capped silhouette appeared before her. Her vision cleared as she moved from the spotlight.

"How do you do that?" he asked, bringing a smile to her lips. Not your usual pick up line.

R. Wesley Clement

They sat on one of the many metal benches, each one placed beside a workout station designed to tax a different group of muscles. An informal introduction and handshake became the ingredients for a relationship. Sean asked if they could meet for coffee after a morning workout in the near future, and they settled on a day and time. Coffee would play a strong part in moving the relationship along. He suggested a certain coffee shop, and Stella agreed.

"They make the best coffee in the city," she said.

Sean smiled. *This is just might be the longest game of baseball ever,* he mused. After a month, second base still hadn't been reached— their relationship was not an instantaneous collision of hormones that demanded closure. Just like Sean's running style, it moved forward only one step at a time but found strength in the distance traveled. It took a month of twice-weekly coffee meetings at a competing cafe before Sean revealed he was a manager in a local Starbucks in another part of the city.

Stella, not one to rush into anything, used the informality of coffee talk to peek into Sean's life. She learned what his family had meant to him, the loss and obvious love for his father, a mother no longer in the state and distant even if she lived next door, two sisters busy with their own lives.

The first time they exercised together, their compatibility and competitiveness, unknowingly sealed the deal. They became friends first. Not necessarily a bad thing.

Sean was always exclaiming at all the angles Stella could exercise in. Stella found Sean to be a straightforward one-foot-after- the-other athlete who liked to do sprints while showing great endurance and seemed to finish workouts stronger than when he started. Their taste in food was similar, favoring fruits, nuts and veggies with an occasional fish thrown in. Neither would turn down a burger or a dog if the setting dictated it, and at least once a week a square box of pizza would serve as centerpiece.

Their favorite time with one another was set on those early morning meetings, coffee and an occasional Danish. They moved in together six months after that chance meeting. Suddenly, they were sharing their favorite time of day gazing into one another's eyes across the kitchen table.

"Never did play the game by the rules," said Sean. "Just hit a home run." With their photo in hand, Stella mentally agreed and cheered from the stands.

CHAPTER NINE

1992 COFFEE CLIQUE

Rae Anne had served half her sixty-day sentence following all the rules.

Eunice would bring baby Elvis to visit once a week for an hour. Lethargic and unfocused when she arrived, fifteen minutes in, her eyes would begin to reveal the beautiful little girl inside. Together they would sing *Love Me Tender,* Elvis's favorite lullaby, and soon the mood in the entire room improved. Other prisoners and their visitors smiled, while some even joined the music. By hour's end, *Blue Christmas* would have the entire room lamenting their own failed holidays as baby Elvis sang every word in her affected Elvis Presley voice.

Just a month to go, Rae Anne thought as she heard the clapping for her daughter's singing. Promising herself she would be the best mother in the world when she got out, and squeezing her daughter one last time, she returned to the daytime cell that housed twenty other inmates, feeling renewed and resolved to turn her life around.

Eunice waved to Rae Anne, swept up Elvis and went to introduce little Elvis to Elvira, her twin sister. Eunice chuckled as she buckled little Elvis into the car seat, *wonder what the little girl will make of her.*

Growing up, Elvira kiddingly or maybe not so kiddingly was told her name had been misspelled at birth and she should have been Evil-ra.

Her father watched her set the cat on fire when she was nine. Sure, maybe he shouldn't have left his lighter laying around. Other disquieting episodes saw Elvira suspended from elementary and later junior high. The belt came out when her transgressions caused him the inconvenience of missing work. Laying in the same bed at night for their first eight years, the girls had no way of ignoring one another or the sounds and smells in the night. Eunice wisely called her twin sister Ellie, never Evil-ra or the evil twin. She was simply Ellie.

Many a night the evil twin entered the bed smoldering with anger. They had long conversations about their parents; Eunice mostly listening. They touched and explored their growing bodies, tried out what kissing felt like and shared their hatred of school and dickhead boys. Ellie would turn from her side of the bed, drape an arm over Eunice's shoulder and begin. The quiet way Eunice channeled her own anger seemed to soothe if not quell Elvira's tirades.

"Did you know daddy was married once before us?" asked Ellie one night in the heat and dark of their small room. "We have an older brother somewhere. Betcha he's a firecracker, dontcha think?" The silence that followed had both girls staring at a newly arriving moon peeking over their window sill.

"I heard mama complaining," continued Ellie, "when they got a letter asking for child support. A registered letter, she called it. Had to be signed for. Boy was daddy pissed. He thought he'd won something." Elvira always seemed to enjoy her father's rants; they fueled her own anguish. "After calming mama down, 'cause she didn't know he'd ever been married before, he said it was pretty much a one-night stand and a two-month marriage when he was in the army."

She shook Eunice, making sure she was still awake hearing this. She was.

"When he got transferred, he'd left with only his duffle bag. Said he didn't know about no kid, and he wasn't paying jack shit

    R. Wesley Clement

after all this time." Elvira paused but still got no reaction. "Are you even alive over there?" She pinched her sister. Eunice shook her head, the only reaction to the newest chapter in this house that was not a home.

"Mama agreed," Elvira continued. "She said *you can't get blood from a stone,* whatever that means. I think it means our brother-from-another-mother won't be getting any of daddy's coin of the realm."

Eunice just listened. Most of Elvira's tirades did not call for conversation. Eunice learned by listening, and while she was not an active participant in her sister's deviltry, she got to quietly revel in the stories and end results. Her own anger seemed to gather fuel even if it didn't burn so publicly. Elvira never asked Eunice to take an active role in her evil twin act. There was only room for one star of the show.

The girls got separate bunks when the family moved to Ohio to live near an uncle's small home construction company. Eunice and Elvira started at the local high school; a new beginning, their parents assured them. Right.

November can be a cruel month in Ohio. Cold rain and dark skies accompanied the girl's right to the glass doors and into the main office where they were left to fend for themselves. Daddy had dropped them off out front, throwing up a dismissive hand, all the while bitching about how there was no way in hell he was going to work outdoors today, no matter what his brother said.

The two girls, both overweight and acne-ridden, looked like battered bookends as they sat on opposite ends of a wooden bench. Well above average height at 5'8" with long stringy forgettable brown hair hiding as much of their faces as possible, they sat draped in tired sweaters and skirts waiting to be directed to the guidance office.

Other students entering the office stared. "They look like two oversized stuffed chairs" was a description carried back to the corridors. One boy farted and the secretary admonished him. The girls were left to endure the smell. The boy left laughing and holding his nose as if blaming the sisters. He gathered a couple of friends outside the glass, pinching his nose and pointing as if they had caused the stink. He was the carrier of that critical disease called first impression.

These giant twins of forgetability knew they'd just received the bad beef label. *Like wildfire,* Elvira thought nodding to her sister, knowing their existence and fate would soon circulate throughout the school.

After fifteen minutes of being left on display like one of the many trophies that lined the hallway, Elvira stepped to the glassed-in cubicle and cleared her throat. One of three secretaries lifted her head and came to the window, apologized for the wait, assured them the guidance director had an early meeting but they would see her soon.

Elvira returned to her seat but not before seeing an evergrowing crowd of boys and girls glancing their way, holding their noses, making remarks that were surely not flattering.

Well fuck a duck, thought Elvira, taking a deep breath as if getting ready to begin a marathon, *this ought to be fun..* And she meant it.

* * *

Mediocre grades that had nothing to do with ability or intelligence dictated the classes the girls were placed in and suddenly their high school agenda had been entered into the ledger. Eunice quietly seethed at the indignities cast their way while Elvira fought everyone and everything tooth and nail.

Poor Eunice could be mistaken for Elvira even when she subtly tried to become her own person by a change of hairstyle or clothing. A sudden elbow in the ribs or even a whack behind the head let Eunice know Elvira was still in the fight and she, Eunice, was going to be collateral damage long term.

Daddy and mama survived the move but hated feeling beholden to a brother they couldn't stand. The girls, with bigger

---

R. Wesley Clement

beds but still sleeping in one room, listened to a different version of same old, same old, night after night.

Cigarette smoke and complaints poisoned the small house. The girls never let on what was going on at school for two reasons: one, nobody gave a shit and two, nobody really gave a shit—not in their house, at least.

The girls did whisper in the night though, Eunice mostly listening as usual; she was becoming a little concerned about her sister. They were juniors in high school now and their acne had cleared up. They had dropped some weight as adolescence seeped out of them, an even deeper anger ushering in adulthood.

Elvira had adopted a gothic look that actually quelled some adversaries. With her height and black-frocked body seemingly daring people to fuck with her, they started leaving her alone. Truthfully, she scared the shit out of them.

"Bastards are going to pay, just wait, just watch," she mumbled more to herself than her sister. Even when Elvira experienced a rare feeling of hope or acceptance, it seemed the cosmos was aligned to punish her. "Serves me right for thinking I could be part of something I might actually like in this fucking school."

What had Elvira so worked up was an English teacher who had encouraged her to take part in the school's Junior Prize Speaking Contest. Every student in each classroom had to select either a passage from literature or a poem to learn and recite. The six Junior English teachers would pick two winners from each classroom and a reading for the public would take place.

Elvira, thinking it was bullshit, changed her mind when she discovered William Shakespeare. *This man must have known me in a different life,* she mused as she read a brooding passage from *Macbeth.*

"Love those witches," she chuckled. The darkness generated in the lines held special meaning for her. She cut and pasted various lines from the play to fit the time allotted and her personality, giving her the opportunity to tell all mankind to take a flying fuck in a public setting.

Eunice could almost recite the passage word for word as well; she must have heard it at least twenty times. As her sister continued to rave on and on, Eunice revisited her sister's words that publicly spoke of revenge and murder.

"Double, double toil and trouble; fire burn and cauldron bubble. By the pricking of my thumbs, something evil this way comes. Open, locks, whoever knocks! A deed without a name. The raven himself is hoarse that croaks the fatal entrance of Duncan under my battlements. Come, you spirits that tend on mortal thoughts! Unsex me here, and fill me from the crown to the toe top full of direst cruelty; make thick my blood, stop up the access and passage to remorse, that no compunctious visitings of nature shake my fell purpose nor keep peace between the effect and it! Come to my woman's breasts, and take my milk for gall, you murdering ministers. Nor heaven peep through the blanket of the dark, to cry, 'Hold, hold!' I am in blood, stepped in so far, that, should I wade no more, returning were as tedious as go o'er."

Elvira, standing at the front of her class in gothic black, really feeling the lines she spoke, mesmerized the room. Who knew? This outrageous young woman put a spell on her audience. When Elvira was asked to perform along with the other class winners for the six teachers, once again, she held them spellbound as her inner anger added to the powerful passage.

Elvira went home that night and had actually smiled when she confided in her sister that maybe she could be an actress.

"I'd probably only get the black hat roles, but that suits me just fine. I'm actually having fun with this."

So on to the public, right? Not so fast. One of the teachers objected to the line *unsex me,* and *woman's breast* and *mother's milk turned to gall* could not be allowed. "We educators understand the context of the passage, but the general public will be up in arms," she argued.

The teachers huddled, argued, stewed, stirred, hemmed and hawed—much like the witches over the cauldron—after the

     R. Wesley Clement

students were gone from the building. And all they really wanted was to get home to their lives and families.

Credit Elvira's teacher with trying to defend her student. She explained this was the first time the girl had shown any interest in school. In the end though, with five o'clock looming and no vested interest in Elvira and most of the teachers knowing the girl's reputation, she held a minority opinion and was left with the task of encouraging Elvira to change some of her wording. Elvira refused, and that was that.

"Who needs this shit? You're as pathetic as the rest of them!" she said on her way out the door.

Having one more insult added to her perceived injuries, Elvira began to plan her revenge. Even gave herself a deadline. She would lie on her bed, nodding as the plan became clear, speaking in a hushed yet animated voice. Eunice, staring into the blackness of the night, could almost see her sister's face twist and contort into the hag over the cauldron, pouring potions into a steaming abyss.

* * *

The first day of April dawned brightly, the skyline lit up with more than a normal shade of red and orange. It being April Fool's Day, the call into the police department was not taken seriously until the caller heard all the penalties he would incur if this was a joke. No joke, he assured the dispatcher, and the fire department was summoned to the local high school. It had flames emerging from every corner and the roof.

The street was cluttered with vehicles, their doors left open and engines running as residents ran to help put out the flames. Several teachers had to be restrained from trying to enter the building to retrieve their important papers. By nine o'clock, the front doors blew open and glass littered the walkway all the way to the street.

In the end, all the firemen could do was keep people from acting stupid as hoses sent arcing streams of water into the mouth of the unquenchable thirst. The fire raged for four hours then took up smoking for several days, little flare-ups emerging as reams of paper and old books sought enlightenment.

The school died of its burns and smoke inhalation on April fourth. It would be left to the city to decide where the charred remains would be buried.

Investigators determined it was arson, started with good old gasoline, no attempt to disguise its origin or intent. Teachers and students were interviewed as they tried to glean who could have such a serious grudge against the school.

A tip line was established and both Eunice and Elvira were mentioned.

"Why do you think we were given your name, Eunice?" the investigator asked. He was an arson expert and member of the state police.

"It just might be that everyone in this school hates us. Could that be a reason?" Eunice offered with raised eyebrows.

The investigator nodded, jotted something into a spiral notebook and asked his next question. "Have these kids made you mad enough to want to hurt someone or take your anger out in some way?"

Eunice looked at him suspiciously. "Why isn't my dad here while you question me? I'm a minor, you know."

"Your mother and father said you were old enough to speak for yourself. So please, answer my question."

"I keep my anger to myself," she said, her face turning red and hot, as if falling to her death and every slight she'd endured was passing before her eyes. "But yes, if I could wave a wand, all the assholes in this school would disappear, which by the way would leave the hallways pretty empty."

"So you have no knowledge of how this fire got set?"

"Nope, sorry, but not sorry the damn place burned."

The investigator jotted another note then dismissed the girl. When she reached the door, he said, "Your sister."

 R. Wesley Clement

Eunice turned back. The investigator was checking a list from the inside cover of his notebook.

"Elvira. Would you send her in on your way out?"

Eunice chuckled at that, shaking her head, and muttered, "You're in for a treat."

Elvira strolled in as if without a care in the world. The investigator shot her a confused look, as if Eunice had returned in a different outfit.

"Do you mind if I smoke?" Elvira asked. She was already rummaging through her purse to capture her cigarettes and a well- used lighter, which had a history of its own.

"Probably would be better if you didn't light up in here. Are you even old enough to smoke?"

Elvira held her lighter up turning it over in her hand examining it, before flicking the hinged top open and closed.

"You know if I didn't smoke I'd probably have smoke coming out of my ears."

"Why's that?"

"I've been told I have a short temper." Elvira gave him a sultry look..

"Is that true?"

"Is what true?" She gave him a shit-eating grin.

"Do you have a short temper?"

"I'm sure you've done your due diligence. Probably says so right there in your notes."

"Actually I do have a little background on you and your sister. Didn't know you were twins, though. It appears you've both had a difficult adjustment in the three years you've been here. I would be a poor investigator if I didn't look under all the beds, wouldn't you agree?"

"So if you know all about the dust bunnies in my past, what questions are left to ask?" Elvira leaned toward the investigator. "Can you keep a secret?" she asked, licking her lips and pausing a moment. "I think my sister, Eunice, did it."

The investigator jerked back in shock. "Why do you think that?"

Elvira laughed. "Nah. I'm just kidding yuh. My mousey sister has let everyone beat on her for years. She wouldn't say caca if she had a mouthful of it."

"How about you? It would appear you suffer no slight without retort."

"Why that's a nearly poetic way of saying I don't take any shit from anyone, mister investigator. I'm impressed."

"We're nearly done here." said the investigator, obviously frazzled. "I have one final question. If you were going to seek revenge for all the slights and wrongs committed against you, would you have considered burning down the building?"

"Absolutely."

* * *

The school had no place to send the high school students in the meantime. It was decided the seniors would graduate on time without attending the last two months of school.

It was a little more complicated for the underclassmen. They also got the next two months off, but call it your summer vacation, they were advised. When the area schools dismissed in June, the remaining three classes would attend school at the junior high for the summer. In the fall they would share another area high school on a split-day basis, starting their day at four o'clock. Clubs and sports would have to schedule as many contests on the weekends as possible.

Elvira decided she was not going to attend any stupid summer school and on her eighteenth birthday, joined the army.

Eunice, ever the sufferer-in-silence, hung on and eventually graduated, got married, had Billy, got divorced and had a generally shitty life right up until Baby Elvis entered the picture. And then Elvira showed up. Even Eunice wondered how the kid would survive her sister.

R. Wesley Clement

CHAPTER TEN

1992 BEWITCHED AND BEWILDERED

Strapped in the back in a child seat looking into a mirror tilted and turned to reveal a portion of Eunice's face, Elvis struggled to understand what she was being told. Wind noise from the one cracked-open window offering exit to blue smoke, the radio touting the best new car offer ever, the front headrest adding muffled mystery to what Eunice was saying. A sister. Elvis clearly heard the word *sister.*

Elvis, just two years old, her face streaked with dried tears, nose clogged with snot, was clearly bewildered. Why had all the women in the room been dressed like her mama? And why when they all seemed to be enjoying her singing and dancing was she suddenly whisked away while her mother stood there crying? It was all just too much. An exhausted Elvis fell asleep to Willie Nelson singing about blue eyes crying in the rain.

When she awoke in her crib, her grandmother was standing over her. Then her grandmother came into the room and joined her grandmother looking down at her. Elvis looked from one to the other, clearly baffled.

Grandmother Eunice spoke quietly. "Elvis this is your great aunt Elvira. She's my twin sister, and she's going to live with us for a while."

"Hello Elvis, you're a little cutie aren't you! We're going to help you grow and get ready to face this rough old world." Elvira reached down and picked up little Elvis giving her a big hug while continuing to offer soothing words. Her sister stood there shocked to hear a voice that seemed calm, almost caring.

Twenty-two years had come and gone since the school burned and Elvira joined the armed forces. She had written to Eunice asking if she could stay with her awhile.

The letter was brief and to the point. She was looking for a fresh start and missed her sister. If it was not okay, she would understand. A telephone number was given where she could be reached for just three more days. Then she'd be on the road again.

Eunice, curious to hear her sister's life adventure and lonely herself, had called and left a message: *awaiting your arrival*. Elvira had arrived in the early morning hours and was still asleep when Eunice packed Elvis into the car for her weekly visit to her mother.

Sitting at the kitchen table across from one another, a coffee cup in one hand, a cigarette competing for attention in the other, all the while Eunice balancing and dawdling little Elvis on one knee, the sisters played catch-up.

Eunice told her life's story first, ending with, "and that's how I ended up with little Elvis here." Elvira, after asking if she could hold Elvis for a while, told of lasting three months in the military and then being deemed unfit to serve. She found herself in Texas, joining a population of conservative Christians who showed little tolerance for the gothic girl Elvira had reverted to.

She wasn't gay but was labeled it, didn't steal but was accused of it, wasn't a witch but was called one. Finally, Elvira found a job as a second cook in a retirement home and saved enough money to get the hell out of there. Little Elvis watching from across the table took it all in like a sponge.

From Texas, Elvira took a bus to California and ended up in Bakersfield. "Don't ask me why Bakersfield. The name, I guess, warm smell of fresh bread and all," she chuckled. "Good a place as any as it turned out." She pointed to her cup and Eunice rose to refill it.

Elvira waited until her sister was seated, took a sip and continued as if reading a story. "Nobody harassed me out there at least, plenty of freaks to go around. Lots of flower people, tolerance talk and anti-this-and-that marches and such. I came to consider myself almost normal."

Eunice got up to warm her own coffee. The word normal from the lips of her sister was cause for a pause.

After another sip, Elvira pointed to the note on the table, the one left by Eunice on her way to visit Elvis's mother.

"I did me a couple of short-term jail vacations for doing drugs. Every time, I had to undergo counseling, which filled the hours but didn't change who I thought I was."

She shifted in her chair. "You know what changes you? Time on your hands. Sitting in one of those little cells, listening to every excuse known to man, sixty days at a time. I finally realized you don't have to take any crap in this life, but maybe you shouldn't spend your life in a toilet either." A cigarette was lit in celebration of her enlightenment.

"I've become a little less angry over the years and I've come to accept that I was a screw up as a kid and probably still am to some degree." She blew blue smoke away from Elvis, sucked in another lungful and sent the smoke up into the kitchen light fixture.

Little Elvis sat quietly on her grandmother's knee and continued to watch, first her grandmother, then her grandmother across the table.

It was over coffee and cigarettes that Eunice enlisted her sister's help in keeping Elvis under her roof for the long term.

"I've spent enough time in jails to know there's always someone willing to do most anything for money. You got any? Looks like I'm about to step back into that toilet with my twin sister, hope it's a two-holer."

———

"I could come up with maybe five hundred. What are you thinking?"

* * *

Jailhouse coffee isn't exactly a gourmet brew. Purchased in bulk for a dollar a pound and served with a sneer not a smile. Rae Anne grabbed a metal cup and placed it under the half-glass wall that separated the food servers from the time servers.

The girl behind the glass looked her right in the eye, smiled, half filled her cup, then with a deliberate motion, poured boiling coffee on her hand and wrist. Rae Anne jumped back and flung coffee on her neighbor in line. The girl shrieked, her cup flinging into the crowd. She pulled back her fist and punched Rae Anne in the face and on her arms, landing three good solid blows, while around her all hell was breaking loose.

When the melee was finally quelled with batons that were not there to lead a parade, Rae Anne was singled out as the catalyst. Sitting in the office of the jail administrator in cuffs and leg irons, Rae Anne tried to tell her version of events.

The administrator sitting across the desk from Rae Anne actually seemed to be enjoying his own cup of coffee. He took a sip, placed it on a coaster and looked Rae Anne in the eye.

"You know I tend to believe you, Rae Anne," he said sympathetically. "You haven't caused any trouble while you've been here. However, my dilemma is this. I have people to answer to. I have damages to pay for and injuries to explain.

"Someone has to pay the piper, as they say and I'm afraid it's going to be you. When you were sentenced, one of the stipulations was that, if you caused any problems while serving your time, I have the right to lengthen your stay without going back to court. This morning, I'm afraid I have to do just that. I am adding on another ninety days as well as asking for damages of a thousand

R. Wesley Clement

dollars for both equipment and medical attention provided, including your own scrapes, burns and bruises."

A last sip of coffee revealed both the bottom of the cup and the bottom line, Rae Anne wouldn't be spending her winter outdoors.

These little slip-ups in Rae Anne's life continued to happen and before you could say shit on a stick she'd been returned to the same courtroom and the same judge she'd met six months before.

"You say someone's out to get you. Would you care to reveal who this someone might be and their motivation?" asked the judge.

Rae Anne thought maybe she had it figured out as she glanced to the gallery and viewed Eunice and her twin sister Elvira making pretty with her daughter. *If I tell the judge I think my daughter's grandmother is scheming to keep Elvis, she maybe gets put in a foster home or worse.*

"I don't know, your Honor. All I know for sure is I'm standing here as God is my witness and telling you I have a daughter who I love and want to get back to. I am not the cause of all that's landed me back here in front of you." She looked straight at Eunice and her sister.

When asked if the living arrangements for her daughter seemed to be working, Rae Anne nearly bit her tongue in half as she said through gritted teeth, "Yes, your Honor, my daughter seems well fed and clean and happy."

"I'm of a mind to change your address, Rae Anne. There's a facility in the northern part of the state that offers counseling, parenting classes, even job training opportunities and college credit. I think a year there could help you plan for the future for yourself and your little girl. It's either that or I am going to let you see what the prison system looks like. Unlike your local lock-up, it's not a very friendly environment. But it's your choice."

Rae Anne served her time, taking advantage of every program offered. She was healthy, her life full of promise as she stepped off the bus expecting to reach out for a little girl who would surely rush into her arms. Elvis hadn't been brought to see her in a long time. Her phone calls hadn't been answered. She was out now. It was time to reclaim her little daughter.

When nobody showed to pick her up she thought it must have been a mix up, though a bitter-tasting bile was rising in her throat from her churning stomach. A cab ride to Eunice's house, looking freshly painted and landscaped, she wasn't surprised when a stranger answered her knock at the door.

"We bought this house six months ago," the woman told Rae Anne, with sympathy in her eyes.

Over the next few weeks, Rae Anne reached out to anyone and everyone who might know where her daughter had been taken. She even called Billy.

"I've really missed you, Rae Anne," was all he would offer. "Maybe we could hook up and go looking together. Yuh think?"

R. Wesley Clement

2009 MEANWHILE BACK AT THE COFFEE SHOP

Still stiff from the plane ride and the last two hours of meetings, Sean was doing deep knee bends and stretches in line while he waited his turn at the trough.

"You run?"

Without turning his body or stopping his repeated efforts, Sean muttered, "Yup, you?"

"I do indeed, and hope to do some while I'm here. Care to join me." A hand extended. "I'm Jacob."

Sean stood up, his eyes continuing the prolonged climb up to the face of a long-haired giant. Sean offered his own hand in return and noticed *State of California* on the paper badge.

"I'm Sean from Maine. Pleased to meet you, Jacob from California. Always from California or a transplant?" After getting their food trays, the two found a table and sat across from one another.

"You kicked butt in that state capitals contest. You a geography nut or what?"

Sean smiled. "If I were, I'd have come by it genetically. I have my dad to thank for winning. He took us all over this country. A little credit goes to a couple of teachers I had in school. So, you're a native Californian. That's one state I haven't been to."

Jacob nodded. "Yeah. Actually, this is my first trip out of state. Can you believe it?"

"How long you been with Starbucks, Jacob of the Redwood Forest. And can I add? Man you are huge!"

Jacob just smiled as he wolfed down a sandwich. He swallowed his bite and offered, "I started with them while I was in high school, playing a keyboard a couple times a week. The manager liked me and I became a barista, then got more training while I took classes in college." He sipped his drink. "Just a year ago, I got promoted to an assistant manager's position and, voilà, here I am representing all those redwoods."

The banter continued, the two taking an instant liking to one another. Sean was fairly new to management too.

"Graduated from Thomas College in the city of Waterville, Maine, then left for a while after I graduated. Got hired as a sales rep for a wholesale food distributor in Massachusetts. One of our clients was Starbucks.

"Their stores were beginning to multiply and I did some research. I decided to go back to my neck of the woods. No redwoods though," he chuckled. "Quit traveling up and down the East Coast and settled into the nicest little coastal city in the U.S. of A., which would be Portland. And here I am."

The men continued to talk as if they had known one another for years and made plans to meet at the hotel and possibly a run before dark. Three runs later, the conference was winding down. The speakers had been motivating, the coffee was hot and available, the goals for the company were encouraging.

On the third day, God spoke; well maybe not God, but certainly an influential messenger. Howard Shultz took them on an imaginary Disneyland-like ride—a high-in-the-sky ride with a panoramic view of the Earth, showing where Starbucks fit in.

"Coffee, that ubiquitous brew shared around the campfires in all those western movies and used as a setting in the most sophisticated company, has established an identity," he said.

     R. Wesley Clement

They came away with an understanding that coffee was a metaphor for relationship building, a kind of foreplay That shared morning cup of coffee with a spouse. The thermos riding shotgun on the way to work. The preamble to a group meeting. Toasting a job well done. You felt better about everything and everyone after a good cup of coffee. Simply by changing price point and advertising the uniqueness of a blend and yes even establishing a little stature by your choice of brands, set you apart.

All across America and around the world, Earl Grey and his entire family of teas were making room at the table. The supermarkets, where for years two or three brands of coffee held sway, were creating top-shelf choices for the first time.

After a pause, a new white baby grand was rolled out.

"Now, I've heard some high praise about the talent of one of our own from California," Howard's voice boomed. "Jacob Morrison. Come on down!" Jacob walked with some reluctance, then shyly sat down. But when his hands hit the keys, the room filled with the strains of a Billy Joel tune. Twice the applause forced Jacob to continue.

Invigorated and inspired by Mr. Shultz and the impromptu performance and ready to preach the gospel, Sean and Jacob shook hands, reluctantly saying *nice meeting you,* not wanting to say goodbye.

Promising to stay in touch, but knowing that likely wouldn't happen, Sean made a decision to share his own dream. He made his new friend an offer of Assistant General Manager in Portland, Maine, if he ever cared to explore a different coastline.

"You know, I might just take you up on that, Sean. I'm too young to put down permanent roots, and I don't have a love-of-my-life like you do."

"Well, I'm going to continue bugging you about the idea. Not going to let you get into a rut when you get back. I've got another business idea that we can discuss if you make the move. It even involves your musical background."

"Intriguing."

———

"You wowed 'em Jacob. We could do big things together."

They boarded different flights, heading in two different directions. They had no idea what that future would look like. They thought they did but, just as your taste in coffee changes over time until you find the right blend, your future has a mind of its own.

R. Wesley Clement

CHAPTER TWELVE

1993 A FLEA MARKET FUTURE

Elvis turned three while her mother was away and for her birthday, her two grandmothers decided it would be fun to go to Disney World in Florida. Every little kid should meet Mickey and Minnie, the only happily married couple in America, according to Elvira. What they didn't tell Elvis, or anyone else for that matter, was they wouldn't be coming back anytime soon.

Knowing Rae Anne would try to find her daughter, they sold Eunice's small country home, held a yard sale, packed what they could in the little green Dodge and left in the dark.

Heading east, they picked up Interstate 95 in Virginia then promptly jumped on 85 south towards North Carolina. They spent a night outside Raleigh and found Route One the next morning. Route One was the favored route before Interstate 95 offered a faster more direct ride north and south.

When they got below St. Augustine, they found nothing but wilderness on both sides of the road. The two sisters had spent nearly six months exploring their options. All of the discussions had one theme in common: sell the house, find a place to live under the radar and raise the little girl they'd both come to love.

In a way, little Elvis had a weird effect on the sisters. The self-centered direction they'd taken with their lives, blaming all misfortune on others, had kept displays of affection at bay for years.

Elvis changed all that and the two sisters actually seemed to enjoy one another's company.

When they had disciplined the little girl for the music her mother had instilled in her, Elvis simply sang quietly to herself in her room. She didn't fuss or throw temper tantrums. She always looked her grandmothers directly in the eye when they scolded her, as if asking, "Is this really necessary?" The little girl slowly changed the frown lines that had taken over the sisters' features. It seemed they finally had a purpose in life.

Twenty miles or so below St. Augustine, they encountered a sign that spoke of a new community taking shape. Palm Coast. An infrastructure of roads, canals and house lots laid out in the 70s was finally coming to fruition. Still rural enough to be invisible. They followed the east-west road that took them into the slowly developing small city.

The two sisters saw the possibilities, located a realtor, conversing in whispers, blue smoke blazing, they bought a lot from a builder. He promised he could start almost immediately on a small home *with a backyard facing the jungle,* as Elvira aptly described it. Elvis was still two years from kindergarten. "I think we'll homeschool her, anyway," said Eunice. "Look what school did for us."

They found a small beachside motel south of Flagler Beach on route A1A to stay at for as long as it took to have their house built. Elvis had never seen the ocean.

In the sleepy little town of Flagler Beach, they took her to the shore where she splashed in the waves with wide eyes. She chased the little birds to and fro, shrieking when they ganged up on her.

Without prompting, Elvis hugged each grandmother in turn, and the two sisters watched a different child emerge.

"I guess maybe this little beach town might be just what the doctor ordered." They sat smoking and sipping coffee from a thermos, a blanket thrown down that seemed to be claiming this little patch of beach as their own.

"Did you see the way she perked up when those little birds teased her? And the waves around her knees? Never seen her laugh like that," Eunice cooed.

"She hugged me, all by herself," said a suddenly choked up Elvira.

"Hell, this little burg is just as remote as the lot we bought, once you get off A1A. I got some ideas from all those shells she picked up and hand-delivered like they was gold nuggets."

They discovered a lot three streets back from the ocean and in Daytona Beach they found a ready-built house called a double wide. They backed out of the contract with the builder in Palm Coast and two weeks later they were in their new home, a two bedroom, one and a half bath, brand spanking new beginning. No mortgage to pay; no banks to fuss with.

"We're free and clear," declared Eunice.

The sisters took the master suite with a half bath and were back sharing a room again. Little Elvis had her own room. When they asked her how she wanted it decorated, it was a no brainer. "Elvis everywhere. I just love him don't you?" Elvis beamed. "And seashells and birds, too."

So Elvis grew up in Florida. The two sisters never spoke of her mother, Rae Anne and before long Elvis didn't either. What Elvis did was cast her own spell on the two witches, turning them into harmless spinsters who doted on her every request. Little Elvis, just like her namesake, touched a place the sisters had never explored—their hearts.

After they had been there for a while, visiting the ocean every day, languishing in the kitchen at night, blue smoke climbing the walls, the cribbage board between them, the coffee pot on, getting a little bored really; the two sisters bandied about what sort of work they could do that would allow them to include Elvis.

"I got into leather crafting when I was in jail one time. This Indian gal taught a class, said she sold a ton of her creations and made good money." Eunice perked up. "Maybe we could find a place to sell stuff we make right here at home. You make those bracelets and belts you're always wearing?"

"I did indeed. Never had no reason to brag on it but I liked doing 'em."

The two sisters researched the leather and tools they'd need and took Elvis with them to the local library in Flagler Beach. The little girl sat quietly looking at children's books as the women enjoyed being in a library for the first time.

They decided to use local shells Elvis could help pick up on the beach as accents for their leather craft, and so their little company was founded. They named it *Triple E Leathers,* the fifth letter of the alphabet tying them together in their new business venture.

They set up a stand along the A1A, marketing their belts, necklaces and hair accents. One of their customers suggested a ready supply of visitors could be found at the Daytona Flea Market. The two sisters wandered the grounds on a Saturday and fell in love with the atmosphere of the place. So in October 1993, the little company was open for business two days a week.

Elvis was cooed over by everyone stopping to gawk or buy and it wasn't long before she was entertaining fellow vendors and visitors alike with her Elvis Presley music. Eunice found a bunch of Elvis Albums and memorabilia for sale in one of the booths and soon Triple E Leather's popularity soared as Elvis worked a little bench creating bracelets, necklaces and lots of music.

The Twins lived this beach-town life for ten years. Elvis as brown as a chestnut her blue eyes bright and inquisitive. The Flagler Beach museum and the town library became her classrooms as she wandered from exhibit to exhibit, learning to read, write, cipher and speculate on the wonders of the natural world. The books she chose mirrored her ever-increasing reading ability.

R. Wesley Clement

The two sisters dropped her off and then went to the beach to drink coffee, craft belts and trinkets, smoke and generally *shoot the shit*. No libraries or museums for the sisters—anything with the written word as its focus brought back bad memories.

Two life changing events took place in the summer of 2003.

The first was a birthday. Elvis, who was born on the date of Elvis Presley's death, turned thirteen on August 16. After a small cake and ice cream celebration with the make-a-wish-blow-out-the-candle flourish, Elvis asked about her mother for the first time in a long time.

"No idea where she could be," said Eunice straight-faced. "I've lost all track of her in recent years. I heard she got married and has two other kids. No idea where she lives though."

"Maybe I could find her on the computer," said Elvis. "I'm learning a lot at the library. Mrs. Jackson has been great to me."

Suddenly, seemingly overnight, her body and voice matured into an almost surreal reincarnation of the great man himself. Visitors started commenting on what a future the girl could have, suggesting everything from making a record to getting into the movies.

Some days later, in the darkness of an August night, tree frogs in full voice, rocking back and forth on a settee, their ever-present coffee cups and cigarettes bearing witness, the sisters found they had to make a decision.

"We're doing awfully good here," said Elvira, "but I'm a little worried Elvis is gonna get us caught. She's a talent and word travels. I'm sure her mother has an ear to the ground, not that many kids named Elvis. I think we gotta sell out and find us another less-traveled place. Elvis is getting way too much attention."

"Now, let's think this through," cautioned Eunice. "She's bright and going to want a say in all this. We don't want her digging in her heels."

Elvira grabbed a cigarette with an angry flourish, went through the light-up ritual and inhaled deeply, her eyes watering. When she exhaled, she was surrounded by a cloud of poison residue and for the first time in years, Eunice thought she looked like Evil-ra, the evil twin.

The sisters continued to rock silently, sipping and puffing. The moon made its way up above the trees.

"What if we let her tell us where she would live if she could move anywhere?" said Elvira. "You know, those are the same stars I watched from my backyard in Ohio. Same moon too. We'll remind her how things will be the same even if the place is different."

"It could work," Elvira said, taking another drag. "Bet she's going to demand a seashore with lots of birds and shells."

The other life-changing event shows how difficult it can be to keep a villain from returning to a story when his whole life's intent has been self-serving.

CHAPTER THIRTEEN

2003 A YOUNG COWBOY NAMED BILLY

A week after Elvis turned thirteen, Elvira sat in her booth at the Daytona Flea Market, putting the finishing touches on a new snakeskin belt. A man in his thirties wearing a big old Stetson hat, jeans, denim shirt and pointy toe cowboy boots stopped to examine her leather goods. The smell coming off him was jasmine meets foot rot—with the feet surely in the lead.

Elvira turned to answer a question of price and the man became wide-eyed.

"Well I'll be a son of a bitch. That you, mama?" When Elvira just looked at him blankly, he added, "I was told my momma had a twin sister. If you ain't her, well then, bite my tongue."

Elvira's lips pasted on the fakest smile on the planet. "Don't tell me I have the pleasure of meeting my nephew for the first time, right here in sunny Florida!" she gushed, offering her hand. "Don't know as your momma would appreciate you calling her a bitch, though."

Billy, who had continued his quest to bust every broad worthy of his attention the way a real cowboy breaks broncos—*"ride 'em hard leave 'em wet"*—showed every one of his gleaming white teeth in return. He removed his Stetson, revealing lots of hair on the sides but a noticeably thinner top.

"This is my first time in Florida. Pretty steamy by noon. My momma's down here with you, maybe my daughter too. That's a cool looking rattlesnake belt you're building. Can I take a look at it?"

You little fucker, you have no idea what you just got yourself into. Elvira stood silently for a moment, caressing the nubby skin of the rattlesnake she'd killed in the backyard with a spade, feeling her blood rush. She smiled and handed Billy the belt.

"This one's special; I put his rattle to rest. I don't suppose you've ever faced something that means you harm just because you occupy their space."

Billy gazed at the belt abstractedly. "Yeah, heard you guys might be down here. One of my old girlfriends. Ever heard of google? Anyway here I is. This place is huge, had no idea. What you asking for the belt?"

"No idea what that google gob you're spouting might be, but you sure came to the right place. I pretty much run the booth. Your mother and daughter help make the stuff, and I sell it. We don't live together, but I'll tell her you asked about her. If you're interested in that belt, you can have it for sixty bucks. That's family price by the way." Elvira smiled showing too much teeth.

"She don't have a phone," she continued, "but if you plan to be around for a while I'll tell her you'll be here next Saturday. That work for you? Think you'll recognize your daughter? Oh yeah, you've never seen her have you? She just had a birthday. Thirteen this year. Maybe you look around one of these booths, you'll find the perfect present." Elvira put away things as she spoke gathering up her earnings.

"She writes everything down in a little book, maybe you can find her one of those. Kind of quiet today though, think I'll close up. Anyway, pleased to meet you." She took the snakeskin belt with her when she left.

 R. Wesley Clement

Rubbing the skin of the belt, as if casting a spell, Elvira located her car, got in and slouched in the seat until she saw Billy leave. She sat there, thinking of her sister. *Oh she is not going to be a happy camper.* Still roiling, she snuffed out her cigarette and glanced at the serpent riding shotgun. *Oh she is not.* She opened the door and went back into the flea market.

* * *

Being one of the permanent vendors at Daytona Beach Flea Market for a number of years, Elvira, Eunice and certainly Elvis had established strong ties within what was really a small village. Elvira wandered among the rows of booths giving a shout out to waves, clouds of blue smoke and raised coffee mugs. The tune of the song *Alice's Restaurant* played through her mind.

"*You can get anything you want at Alice's restaurant,*" she crooned. Alice Jordan ran a small booth that sold postcards to anywhere and everywhere. She sold cards with sayings, she sold cards which featured images that go without sayings and, for the right person in the right financial situation, she sold time with a live version of one of six different *Babe on the Beach* postcards that were always selling out.

Elvira sat with Alice, smoked with Alice, accepted a cup of coffee and came to terms with Alice.

* * *

Saturday morning, Elvira and Eunice opened their booth as usual. It was already hot. A small fan moved the air listlessly above their heads. Elvira suddenly smelled the unmistakable blend of jasmine and foot rot and without raising an eye, left the booth.

Eunice sipped her coffee and waited. Her sister would take care of this just like she always took care of everything else.

Billy stopped at the booth and looked at the woman sitting in the shadows.

"Momma, that you?" Suddenly he looked a little less sure of himself, seemed to shrink in his clothes. He no longer looked like a cowboy about to break a bronc, but rather a cowboy who was having trouble finding his horse.

Eunice, who in all his growing up years had never seen anything but a skinny kid who failed at everything except being pretty, thought, *He hasn't changed a bit, still the spitting image of his asshole father.*

"Hey Billy, so you decided to be a cowboy. You're living the dream are you?" She offered her hand if not her heart. "I was lost but now I'm found, as the old hymn goes. So what can I do for you that I haven't already done for you?"

Billy stuttered, "R-r-rae Anne g-g-got a hold of me." He paused, trying to catch his breath. "Sh-sh-she a-asked if I mi-mi-might have an idea wuh-where you'd gone with her child. I-I-I mean I don't-don-don't blame you or nothing bu-bu-but she's married now her husband wuh-wuh-works for a k-k-chemical company. She says he's got some money and sh-sh-she she'll give me ten grand ta f-f-find her daughter," he rushed to finish, "no questions asked."

"I'm surprised you even remember her name," Eunice sneered. "You lit out before there was a bump on her belly. I see you're still having trouble putting words in your own mouth. You sound like a mosquito buzzing with no place to light." She let that last statement raise an emotional welt. Billy's eyes returned to the ground as they had in all the one-sided conversations he'd endured as a kid.

"So you're not claiming emotional ties," Eunice continued. "Just in it for the money right? That's the boy I remember. Want a cup of coffee? Elvira's around here somewhere. Said you might want that snakeskin belt. Have a seat."

Billy sat a spell, warmed his hands with a mug of coffee, well doctored with sugar and milk, still looking rattled. When Elvira showed up, Billy nodded but said nothing. He was noticeably

R. Wesley Clement

sweating. The mug cooled in his hands, but he continued to sip the only sweetness present.

The two sisters went on about their business, yakking and sputtering about everything and anything, ignoring the cowboy until Elvira said, "You really ought to do something about the smell coming out of those boots Billy. Ain't enough jasmine, lilac and rose water in this whole state to quash what you got riding on the wind."

Billy nodded his head but said nothing, already deciding he'd made a terrible mistake in coming down here to confront his mother. Trouble times two was what he'd found. He was just about to think up a graceful exit when a gorgeous young thing walked up to the booth.

The girl looked over the merchandise, gushing over the necklaces and bracelets, completely ignoring Billy. She bought a seashell necklace and moved on, her hips swaying a farewell. "

"Maybe I can salvage something out of this trip yet," Billy muttered under his breath. He tipped his hat to the twins and without a stutter in his step walked in the direction the girl had taken.

Elvira and Eunice lit up cigarettes, refilled their mugs and toasted one another.

"How can he not smell those boots?" asked Elvira.

Billy was found a day later, on a deserted section of Daytona Beach, badly beaten, his two front teeth missing and oddly, without his boots. A little seashell necklace dangled around his neck like a noose.

CHAPTER FOURTEEN

NORTH BY NORTHEAST

Elvira nodded to Alice, who gave her a coffee cup salute. She moved on in this maze of booths under skies that were threatening rain. Just a quick peek at a small piece of sun gone into hiding for the last several days.

"Just a tease," chortled Elvira. Rain is not a flea market friend, and the only noise emanating from tinsel town the entire weekend had been rain on the roof. Coffee, lots of coffee and the blue haze that seemed part of the ambience accompanying the ritual hung over the sisters heads, adding to the dreariness. The few customers seemed to be in a funk as well. Didn't buy. Didn't smile. Didn't want to be there. Just a place to be out of the rain.

Even Elvis's cheery chatter couldn't perk up the grandmothers. Truthfully the weather was just a small part of the gloom that seemed as ominous as the lightning and thunder that was making its way to their booth. The patter of rain was already drumming up support for what would be a spectacular light and sound performance.

"Oh did you hear that!" exclaimed Elvis, her blue eyes sparkling with excitement. "Did you see that?"

The sisters had spent the wet weekend sending Elvis to every booth imaginable, giving them time to firm up the newly minted action plan. They had broached the subject of moving with Elvis, and just as they thought, her conditions involved a shoreline, birds and a newfound interest in climbing way up high. "So it probably won't be Florida," advised Eunice.

"That's okay," Elvis had assured her. This rapidly maturing young lady took the lead in finding a new destination, calling it The Great Adventure.

She reviewed the past she could remember, all recorded in her little book. She was amazed at all the Elvis tunes she'd memorized since that first song, Blue Christmas, sung at the county jail. When she went to the library in Flagler Beach, the librarian introduced her to the internet. With instruction, she learned how to investigate communities in states with a shoreline. She decided she would like a state with both a shoreline and mountains. New Hampshire and Maine became finalists.

"We want to be able to sell our crafts to the tourists, don't forget that," said Eunice.

In the end, the little town of South West Harbor in Maine on a coastal island, Mt. Desert Island, poked its head up like the sun did earlier and now the sisters sat putting the devil to the details.

"Since we'll be traveling North and East to get there, and settling in a town with the other two directions as part of the town's name, that ought to confuse anybody trying to find us," Eunice kidded.

"Let's not forget we're gonna be on an island, to boot," Elvira added. "This compass of confusion would stymie old Christopher Columbus."

"We should be able to keep Elvis's singing under the radar for a while longer, give us time to plan long term. That article she printed out says there's an elementary school but no high school, which is fine; she's educating herself anyway and she won't be around boys with their tongues hanging out." Eunice offered her sister a high five. "They hold flea markets and farmers markets throughout the spring, summer and fall. Plenty of tourists around exploring this island, so we'll at least make a living," sighed Elvira. She lit up another coughing candle.

———

"I think we ought to hold onto our place in Florida for a while at least, maybe rent it out for the summer if we can. Things work out we can winter here, do our thing, bingo, best of both worlds," voiced a nodding Elvira, reaching for her own pack of plague.

A week later, Elvis was spending one last day at Flagler Beach, saying good bye to all the creatures she'd watched, studied and commented on for the last ten years. A little ghost crab emerged from the sand and appraised Elvis as if it knew this would be the last concert. A squadron of pelicans passed directly overhead in salute, much like the famed Blue Angels Elvis had seen at an air show.

"I won't sing Blue Christmas," Elvis told the little crab, "my grandmothers are planning to be what they call snowbirds so I'll be back for Christmas."

Gazing out over the water at a darkening slate colored sky, Elvis suddenly thought of the last time she'd seen her mother in that same drab colored building. She looked the little ghost crab straight in his protruding eyes and shared a secret longing that she hoped to someday make a reality.

"I can't tell my grandmothers this, they would get upset, but as sure as I'll see you at Christmas, I will find my mother." This pronouncement and the promise that followed brought her own party at the beach to a screeching halt, tears flowing. Suddenly The Great Adventure had lost some of its luster.

The trip north was uneventful, though stressful for the sisters. Elvis would not let them smoke in the car anymore so, between stops to smoke and reload their 24-ounce coffee mugs, they couldn't wait to get to Maine. Eunice seemed to be catching a cold; she was irritable and out of sorts. She coughed almost nonstop, her head in the passenger seat constantly in motion as she tried to calm the spasms.

Elvis was the radio, and it seemed any new little sighting of anything from an Elvis Presley lyric would spark a song. Cotton in South Carolina, tobacco plants near Raleigh, the inner city areas of neglect, the mountain vistas, rivers, sunsets. Elvis created her own playlist of the famous man's hits.

They arrived in South West Harbor just as the leaves were turning all the shades necessary to signal surrender to what was becoming a brisk early fall.

The cooling winds of Flagler Beach were a distant memory as the three ladies emerged from a Salvation Army store loaded down with winter apparel. Elvis was the only one making a sound that could be construed as happy.

"The colors are so rich they don't look real, with the blue water in the background and the mountains on fire. How can you two be upset about anything?"

The sisters simply mumbled, swallowing the complaints of numbing cold along with their stale coffee. They knew the two colors that would follow this fire on the mountain.

They left the water, the mountain view disappearing and followed a poorly maintained tar road for half a mile. Referring back to their written directions, they took a left on a dirt path, passed two what appeared to be hidden driveways, took a right and the little trailer they'd rented appeared gleaming in the late afternoon sun. The 15-foot totem pole sporting a sea gull, a fish and a warrior's head, standing sentinel. Elvis looked up, registering each carving and a big smile broke loose.

"I think I'm going to love it here, grandmothers."

Ten-by-sixty with a bedroom on each end and a single bath, Elvira looking skeptically at the well-worn furniture thought, *The things we do for this kid. At least it doesn't smell terrible.*

They lugged in the clothing and groceries they would need for a week and looked around. The forest peeked into every window, the little gravel driveway offering the only visual break. During the time necessary to put things away, no one spoke, though Elvis was humming to herself.

* * *

———

A pattern of sameness developed that lasted for the next three years. Green summers and lots of rain followed by apple-crisp autumns and finally the sound of the furnace kicking in every ten minutes or so.

Eunice had changed though. Her energy lagged as her coughing jags began to compete with the timing of the furnace's rumble. So, autumn in Maine, winter and spring in Flagler Beach. In their fourth year in Maine, when Elvis met a boy and fell in love, the sameness ended and the bottom of the sisters' plans dropped out.

At sixteen, Elvis had reached her full height and development. She was indeed a beautiful girl, with blue eyes and black hair. She had continued to study anything and everything and was well spoken. She had also continued to master the sound emanating from the vinyl records of her namesake.

In a very subtle way the sisters let their guard down and now it was going to be hell to pay.

"How did we not see this coming," exclaimed a distraught Eunice who had continued to cough in ebbs and flows since their original migration to Maine. This summer, she had lost weight and appetite but refused to see a doctor. Autumn brought color to the leaves even as Eunice's color began mimicking the November gray that would send them south.

"Maybe because at her age, you and I were a mess in every way imaginable. Boys didn't want to meet us, just harass us. Remember I was just a little older when I left school and joined the military. We were not exactly homecoming queens, as you recall. We weren't trying to attract boys, the little pricks."

"Okay so what do we do?" (cough-cough-cough) "We can't have her dating, maybe getting pregnant like her mother did or like me for that matter," she paused for oxygen, then continued, "and remember this girl is smart, perceptive and not easily dissuaded when she sets her mind on something." Finishing that many words without a spasm was becoming a marathon of effort.

"Let's meet this boy and size him up. Maybe he's as delusional as your boy Billy. Might give us some idea what he's got in mind. We've got to be smart about this, help Elvis be the one sends him packing, that's the only way—unless he just disappears, which probably ought to be a last resort." Wheels turning, a blue haze of smoke circling her head, Elvira slammed her coffee cup down as if to emphasize what a last resort might sound like.

The high school, which was not located in town, serviced several island communities. Elvis had announced the first week of October that she'd met a nice boy and would like to go to the Halloween dance at the end of the month. Three weeks later, just after six o'clock on a night in late October, the seventeen-year- old senior from Bar Harbor knocked on their trailer door. Nick Morris had come to dinner.

The sisters had spent the day cleaning—mostly Elvira these days—and promised Elvis they would smoke outside on the small attached deck they had paid to erect.

"At least those damn mosquitoes and black flies have cleared out," said Elvira.

By seven thirty, the two kids were on their way to the dance. The sisters filled their cups, put on heavy sweaters and went back to the deck to smoke and try to figure out their next move.

Not ready to discuss the visitor quite yet, Eunice wondered aloud if Elvis meant for them to be taking all their smokes outside from then on, remembering how she was now deprived of smoking in the car.

"She sure gushed about how nice it smelled all clean and aired out in there, didn't she?"

"Hopefully, she'll forget about it. She looks like her mind is filled up right now anyway."

"He seemed nice enough," coughed Eunice begrudgingly.

"Yeah it would be easier if he was a little shit box. Mayor's son at that. Let's take the long view here, do the math. I'll refill these cups," offered Elvira.

———

With two hands full of hot mugs, she deftly used a foot to start the door's arc. It slammed behind her as she placed a steaming cup of caffeine in front of her sister and sat down.

"Elvis is sixteen. If we interfere, she's going to rebel. Her hormones will blind her to anything we say. So this kid is seventeen. He's a senior going to college next fall. Maybe just wait it out. See if it ends naturally. We'll be leaving for Florida soon anyway."

Eunice studied her sister. *Hmm, the middle ground. My sister who's normal approach to problem-solving mirrors the Red Queen in Alice in Wonderland is not suggesting lopping off heads. Amazing.* She broke into a spasm of coughing. These days, even her thinking brought on a coughing fit.

"That might actually work sister," she finally managed to say, "but someone's going to have to have a sex talk with the girl. We don't want to add yard sale-ing for a baby seat to our itinerary."

Eunice coughed into her cup, spilling a little of the hot liquid on her hands. It sparked a memory of Elvis's mother serving extra time for her own little coffee spill years earlier. She shook her head, trying to remove her guilt.

"She probably knows more than we do on the subject," continued Eunice now on a roll between coughing jags that echoed Billy's stuttering, "but I'll fill in the blanks about throw up, constipation, back pain, labor pain and basic pain in the ass pain, and that's all before the little shit is even born."

"I'll be plain as day with her," a smoke-exhaling Elvira weighed in. "Men want what they want, say what they need to say, do what they need to do and then, once they've done the evil deed, cast you to the winds." Elvira looked to her past to share. "Oh yeah, she'll get the straight scoop from me. I had a man once, you know, right after the military. I might have been nineteen, still with the smart mouth and poor-me attitude, looking for a reason to damn someone."

After a chuckle of memory and a long sip, Elvira slid into an all-too-brief hour glass of happiness. "He caught me off guard is what he did. Slid onto a bar stool, ignored my carrying on for the sake of carrying on and when I finished, asked me to dance a slow one." She swayed in reflection.

"He said I sounded like a wounded blackbird and he just thought he ought to hold me for a spell." Her eyes widened. "Sister, you know I'm not at a loss for words, but the sincerity coming out of that boy's mouth was like an opiate. I was hooked." She raised her arms as if in surrender.

"Maybe it was all those years of hearing nothing but hatefulness, or," she laughed, "maybe it was that third margarita kicking in. Anyway, I cried in that boy's arms and let him have his way with me for a solid week." That brought a smile to her face. "One hell of a week if I'm being honest." She lit a cigarette as if to light her way to the exit.

"Just when I had quit pinching myself and stopped imagining the worst, he out-imagined my worst." Elvira sucked down half a cigarette and finished with a song about cheating, about being already married, about little children to consider—in the end about nothing, which was all she was left with.

CHAPTER FIFTEEN

2009 DREAMS AND NIGHTMARES

Stella was waiting at the Portland jet terminal for her man. Arriving early, she parked the car in the short term lot and wandered to a spot to watch the planes landing and leaving. It always amazed her how a couple hours in the sky could change environment, circumstance and situation. Mai tais at midnight. Sex on the beach. What was even in that drink?

Stella the nurse, ever the realist, got to see the downside when some of these vacationers arrived in her emergency room in the wee hours of the morning. A hard landing indeed.

Sean, who could live out of a paper bag it seemed, took the stairs down, backpack in place, eyes sweeping the escalators on either side.

That's how he runs, too, thought Stella. *More interested in smelling the roses than reaching the finish line.*

Then Sean turned his head and their eyes locked. He grabbed the rail and vaulted the last four steps, meeting Stella in full stride.

"Oh babe, did I ever miss you." Their lips met, and a hug that sent the truth of his statement rattling through them both went on and on. It wasn't Sean's head moving side to side it was their collective bodies swaying in unison, the puzzle parts fitting together perfectly.

"You're the one with the luggage," said Stella as they walked to the parking lot, not letting go of one another. "Fill in the blanks for me. How was the conference? You're not a phone freak, that's for sure."

"Sorry. I did call and tell you I love you, every day— true? And I brought you something."

"Yes, there's that," she chuckled. "Tell me about this friend you made and that gift, better not be free coffee forever."

"He's amazing, talented, tall, tanned. A gifted athlete. If he was a woman, I'd snag him for sure. Your gift is in my backpack. You get it later."

"Well thank the Lord for small favors. I get to keep you all for myself. This gift, are you bribing me for a past action or a future one?"

"Past action involving two women and my Dad." Stella's eyes widened. He laughed. "I'll tell you all about it. And I invited Jacob, the big guy I told you I met, to come here and join me at Starbucks, possibly be part of the little venture we've been discussing."

"So both a past action and a future action. Wow. How did he break through your crust of distrust? Your mantle of morbidity? Your words, not mine."

Sean laughed again. "Do I really use those words to describe suspicions of my fellow man?"

"Yes, you do."

"Hopefully he'll come. I promised to send him pictures of the area. Jacob seemed ready to see another side of the world. Well, continent, at least. We'll get to know one another first and see if we're as good a fit as you and I." Sean squeezed her hand a little tighter.

Leaving the jetport, they got on to the highway, and minutes later familiar running routes emerged. Sean's thoughts leaped to their favorite route.

"Let's get home and change. I'd like to run the Back Bay, get a coffee like we used to. Sit there, all sweaty and stinky and I'll tell you about the exciting things Starbucks is planning."

———

Stella reached across the seat and patted Sean's thigh. "Before you tie those sneakers on, I believe a run around a different area of geography will fill you in on what you've been missing in Maine. And you can give me my gift."

Three hours later, the young couple were finally sitting in a coffee shop, enjoying the final stimulant to a day of exploration. Stella looked at the new gift on her wrist, a sports watch that offered more information than an emergency room monitor.

Sean returned to work the next morning. He called for a meeting with the two assistant managers and the lawyer who had made a lot of money in an industrial accident case and diversified his portfolio by opening a Starbucks.

They'd met through the lawyer's sister who went to Thomas College with Sean, and the two had become friends. Long story, ending with the two meeting and liking one another, Sean having the business background, the lawyer having the bucks and the company being agreeable to the location. They were going to open a second Portland Starbucks.

At home that night before Stella headed in for her eleven-to-seven shift, the two studied material on the Old Port.

"I believe a working man's bar that doesn't cater to the typical party crowd would do very well down there. On your next day off, let's just walk the area one more time. There are two locations that seem ideal—room for us at the bar, so to speak."

Stella nodded. "Now's the time, before we do something foolish like start a family"

"We didn't start one yesterday, did we?"

"No, but when we do, that's the kind of energy I want to put into the effort," laughed Stella.

Sean smiled wickedly. "Maybe we should go practice, yuh think?"

* * *

  R. Wesley Clement

Six months later, Sean stood with a guy named Freddy Levine, Stella and newly arrived Jacob in an old warehouse on Fore Street.

"I know I showed you a couple of other places, but honestly, for what you're trying to do, I think this is it. Not the biggest, but not the most expensive either. And there's a brick wall you could tear down that hides the old furnace room. Too small by itself for any purpose. And beyond that, a ton of floor space with entry on Union."

"There's only a single window to the street and only one exit. That'll limit capacity, right?" Sean cupped his chin.

"What I can do," Freddy announced, "is make that window an emergency exit. We'll blacken the pane, remount it in a way that lets it swing out if you unlatch it. Put an emergency exit sign over the top, bingo, two exits."

"Pretty small window Mr. Levine. Am I going to be seeing people in the emergency room with collapsed lungs because they got caught trying to get out that window?" asked Stella.

"Call me Freddy. Mr. Levine was my old man." Freddy chuckled like that was the first time that line had been used; he didn't notice Stella rolling her eyes. "I checked city code already or I wouldn't be suggesting it. Reality is, with the size of this place, one exit is plenty. Anyway, there's nothing hazardous near the entry door. Trust me on this."

After a pause and one more walk-through, Freddy asked, "So when you going to open? I'm thirsty."

* * *

On March 23, 2011, *Troubled Waters* opened its doors. Every table and chair had been bought on the cheap at yard sales or through for-sale ads. Stella was the interior decorator.

The 20-foot bar was created from the headboards of a dozen full size beds that Jacob mixed matched, cut and pasted so to speak. The end result was pretty cool.

"More than one patron will be laying their head down for a nap here, I'm thinking," said Sean surveying the finished piece. "You play that skill saw like a keyboard, Jacob." He admired the varnished grains of wood.

Freddy was there for the grand opening and nodded in satisfaction.

"My old man was right. Give creative people willing to work an opportunity and good things will emerge." He raised his glass of Bud Light in a toast.

"And happy birthday to my old man," said Sean. "Seems an auspicious date to open a bar."

Sean and Jacob sat in the little two-man booth they called their office and looked around with satisfaction. Stella was manning the bar, said she'd always wanted to do that "once."

Word of mouth was the only advertising, the team deciding a soft opening would allow them to get their feet under them. By nine o'clock the soft opening was history and the bar was packed. Even Freddy was pouring beer as Stella delivered drinks to the tables. Sean and Jacob glad-handed everyone who entered and when Jacob sat down at the keyboard to introduce Billy Joel, he had a standing room only audience. Seems *Troubled Waters* was on everyone's mind.

* * *

Sean had hired Jacob as an Assistant General Manager at Starbucks, and they scheduled themselves so one of the two would be free to open the bar every afternoon. Braden, Sean's legal advisor and cousin to boot, was there for the opening and his secretary Shellee became their first employee.

Sean had Braden help him throughout the licensing and legal mumbo jumbo. Shellee, a paralegal as well as secretary, was just at an age where being part of the bar scene sounded cool.

Jacob continued to stay in the spare bedroom of Stella and Sean's rented apartment on a hilly street named India. There was only one bathroom so the awkwardness of the arrangement had Jacob looking for a place of his own.

"Love you guys but I need some space. I don't intend to join the priesthood either, so keep your ears open."

Freddy the Fixture as he came to be called sat at the bar on a Thursday afternoon. First in and often first out, which didn't always mean he'd left the premises. Jacob was running the place, and they were alone with one another. The bar had been open for business since March. It was Columbus Day, October 12, 2011. Freddy was pontificating on the holiday and the hype.

"He must have had the first public relations guy ever. Didn't even make it to here. Other guys did the heavy lifting for this country, Columbus gets the credit. Go figure. I prefer to celebrate the fact that it's Thanksgiving Day in Canada. I love Canadians. Spent a lot of weekends in Lac-Mégantic and St. George. Those people know how to celebrate."

Jacob just listened as Freddy segued from one topic to another, pointing to his glass that seemed to have a hole in it. Jacob plugging the hole with amber liquid.

"You wouldn't know it from looking at me but I played on some really good softball teams. Right field. In softball, not a lot of action in right field." He chuckled, remembering the good old days. "Anyway, we played up in Lac-Mégantic one weekend. The field was surrounded on three sides by a lake.

"We were a good team a lot of former college baseball players. The Canadians threw fast pitch, and I mean fast pitch. Windmill. We played what you call modified pitch in our league. No windmill. Their mound was two feet closer to home plate too," Freddy paused and shook his head. "Their pitcher was in a suit and street shoes, I kid you not.

"Warming up, he had that catchers' mitt popping. We all stood in our dugout, blown away, nobody making wiseass comments either. This guy could throw! Anyway, the first bat around, we all either struck out or popped up. They scratched out two runs and in the dugout we talked, set our minds. So in the fourth our baseball genes kicked in, and we batted through the order," Freddy toasted the inning. "By the time the fifth ended, that lake was bobbing with little white spheres."

Freddy cackled. "Funny story. I was in Old Orchard with my buddy Steve, one of our power hitters from that team. By the end of the weekend in Lac-Mégantic, he had been dubbed Babe Ruth by the other team.

"So, were sitting at a bar and notice a table of guys eyeing us and pointing in our direction. Trouble we think, but turns out these guys in unison point to Steve and shout, "BABE RUTH!" We couldn't buy another drink the whole night. True story. God's honest truth."

Freddy downed half a glass of Bud Light as if to punctuate the ending. Jacob decided this might be a good time to see if Freddy had a rent or knew of one in the area.

"'Course I know of rents, it's what I do, Jacob. Are you asking me if I have one I'll rent you, course I do, Jacob, in fact a rent just surfaced so to speak that will rock your boat," Freddy laughed and toasted his sense of humor. Jacob just looked at him blankly.

"It's a boat, Jacob."

"What's a boat, Freddy?"

"Why your new apartment, of course. It's just up the street too."

Jacob decided this was another occasion to just listen, so he poured Freddy another beer and poured himself a cup of coffee.

"I bought a sailboat, Jacob. A 42-foot three berths with a toilet and shower. Small kitchen, but you can cook. It's got a diesel engine so you don't have to sail it unless you want to or know how to, which I don't, on at least the last count. I bought it on account. On account the guy couldn't keep up with his lease." Freddy toasted his own wittiness.

When Jacob simply smiled, Freddy got back to business. "Anyway, it's at Chandlers Wharf and you can rent it if you want.

I lived on it for a week or two, but I don't need to be rocking back and forth, I do that to myself." He laughed.

"I'd kinder like having someone there anyway. No idea what kinds of problems pop up owning a boat. Maybe we can learn to drive this thing. Some beautiful island spots just off the mainland. Been there, never driven there, or nautically speaking Jacob, sailed there." Freddy laughed and toasted what he considered a done deal. He was right.

* * *

Life in Portland was good, life on Fore Street was really taking off and life on Chandlers Wharf was just getting under sail.

On March 23, 2013, the bar had been open exactly two years. Sean and Jacob had left Starbucks in the last month, after training their replacements.

"All our eggs are in one basket now, Sean. It seems like it's working out the way we planned."

"Life can turn on a dime, Jacob, but barring a flood, famine or major misfortune, I think we're good."

On March 24, 2013, at five twenty-seven in the morning, Sean turned out the light in the hallway, quietly closed the door not wanting to wake Stella who had worked a rare four-to-midnight shift because of a staff shortage. She was due to go in early that morning as well.

A half hour into his run he looked at his illuminated watch, Stella should be scolding the alarm clock about now. He chuckled. *I love that woman,* and just thinking of her warmed him. He had run his route in reverse this morning, since darkness had welcomed him and there were still patches of snow and ice from a freak storm on the hilly roadway.

The Back Bay, officially named Back Cove Park, was flat and lit at intervals that allowed him to track his footing. He entered the darker city's streets after daylight.

———

"Got to get my hill work in," he said aloud as if convincing himself it was a good idea. So after twenty minutes circling the bay, morning just opening its eyelids, he hit the streets of the city.

He was just coming off a steep downhill and hanging a left that still had some pitch to it, staying just on the edge of the tar to avoid the frozen slush, when he heard an engine noise. Lost in the rhythm of his heartbeat, he neither saw nor sensed the headlights before a roaring crunching sound reached his ears.

Suddenly, he was buckling, horrific pain just beginning to register, and he was flying sideways through the air, folding like a jackknife. A raised piece of ground still snow covered dislocated his shoulder while his arm instinctively tried to soften his collision only to break itself on the unforgiving turf. He bounced once, skidding only a matter of inches before rolling painfully backward into a water- and slush-filled ditch.

R. Wesley Clement

CHAPTER SIXTEEN

SAIL ON

Jacob was still asleep on the boat when Freddy hollered down the hatch. "Sean's been hurt!" Stella had called Freddy as soon as his office opened.

"Can you get word to Jacob? His cell doesn't come in for crap on the boat!"

Jacob ran his hands through his long hair as the dream he was having left him, a hoarse voice replacing the soft sexy bed partner he'd dreamed up. He rousted himself and looked at the silhouette framing the opening at the top of the stairs.

"What are you saying Freddy?"

"Sean's been hurt! Seriously, I think. Stella called. Get dressed. I'll drive you."

Two cups of coffee were setting in the console of Freddy's Ocean Blue Lincoln SUV. "Thought you might need this, Jacob," he said, pointing to the cup. "Doctored it already. Two creams no sugar."

Jacob nodded his head, still trying to take it all in. Freddy had no details. Stella, in her nurse mode, laid out just enough to let him know it was serious.

They arrived and asked for Stella. She ushered them to the cafeteria. "I need a cup of coffee. You guys want anything?" Both men shook their heads.

Stella, wide eyes rimmed red from crying, told them what she knew. "He's in surgery now. I saw him when they brought him in.

Both legs are broken, hopefully no head or internal injuries. He was semiconscious when he arrived."

They sat quietly after that, thinking their own thoughts, listening to the morning rituals of others with their own problems, all conversation seemingly hushed with heads shaking.

Sean spent two weeks in the hospital then was transferred to a rehab center for another month. When he was finally allowed to go home, his upper body had been strengthened for a reason—his legs would probably never bend properly again.

Stella talked of finding a different place to live. Their street was hilly and their driveway, steep. Though they lived in a first floor flat, their bedroom was up a flight. Sean said not yet, he wasn't ready to give in to any changes until he had exhausted his efforts.

"Remember, I get stronger the longer the run." He flexed his newborn arm muscles. "These puppies might, note, I say might, have to be my new legs, so I have to work the hills so to speak." They sat on the couch, sweat still in his hair, his forehead glistening from the climb up the driveway he had insisted on doing, his aluminum crutches carrying his weight as he swung himself forward.

Jacob arrived a short time later with a piano stool that swiveled and could be raised or lowered. He'd attached rubber castors to the bottom of the legs. Two shortened ski poles with rubber bottoms completed Sean's new bar transportation.

"I've been working the bar long enough by myself. Got you on the schedule for two nights next week. I cleared everything that could get in your way, so you'll be free wheelin'."

No sympathy, which was Sean's mantra, dating way back to his father's family of fifteen. He looked the equipment over already trying to figure out how he could expand on Jacob's creation.

He thanked Jacob and sent him off to the bar with an affirmative. "I'll be there on Tuesday, three thirty, to try out my new ride."

<hr>

When the door closed, Sean pulled Stella close and cried silently for his loss. She held him, knowing this would be Sean's last look backward. When he had emptied himself, she took the lead.

"I think it's time now for me to test your new ride." She pushed him backwards, stripped him naked, licked him alive and mounted herself. She moaned into his ear, "This new ride, Sean, it's definitely going to get me where I need to go."

Sean with eyes wide open as he found his release thought, *Thank you Lord for that,* the aftershocks still driving him upward. They stayed in that position, Sean finally melting from the connection, and slept.

———

CHAPTER SEVENTEEN

SMOKE ON THE WATER

Elvis was sad to leave for the winter for the first time in her life. Nick promised to write, that he'd be waiting for her return in the summer. The sisters were just glad to leave. It didn't appear any lasting damage had been done, though the wailing Elvis could not be consoled once Nick left the trailer on their last night in Maine.

"I don't remember that much heartache," said Eunice. "It was all hormones for me, then a kid, then nothing."

"I might have wailed, but balling my eyes out was rooted in anger. Never did sort out my feelings for that boy," muttered Elvira.

On the way back to Florida, the girls decided a little cheering up was in order.

"I know how much Elvis Presley means to you honey, so we're going to take the scenic route on the way south and stop in Memphis. Sister says she went by it in her earlier days, but I've never seen it, and I know you'll be thrilled," said Eunice, riding shotgun with her head turned toward Elvis in the back seat. Elvira was doing almost all the driving these days since Eunice's coughing jags rendered her nearly helpless when under attack.

In the quiet of an evening just before they left Maine, Eunice had confided in her sister that she thought something was wrong with her body. "Fatally flawed" she termed it. "I feel like I'm spitting up body parts. My head hurts. My back aches. I hate the taste of those damn cigarettes but I still can't put 'em down."

As if to emphasize her words, a nearly three-minute coughing spasm had Eunice heading to the bathroom to spit up. When she returned, her eyes were rheumy, red and running. She told her sister she believed this would be her last trip to the sunny south.

Elvira knew in her heart that the words were pure truth. She'd seen this woman who mirrored her image become a distorted reflection at best. Jagged edges, fading colors, she could even smell a scent that was new; it was the smell of death, almost worse than Billy's boots.

"I want to see Graceland once myself. All these years of having his spirit and sounds consuming a good part of the day and Elvis truly blessed with his talent. I need to pay homage before I maybe meet him in person." As a parting shot she added, "I'm not afraid to meet my maker. Can't be any worse than this old world has been."

They did the tour not as your typical tourists but rather as truth seekers. Every piece of memorabilia, stick of furniture, photo, sound, sight, smell, touch or taste seemed to linger and attach to their collective memories as firmly as a deer tick.

Elvis sounding as she had when thunder and lightning provided entertainment at the flea market was constantly uttering, "Did you see that, did you hear that, can you believe that!" The stop at Graceland became the fuel that got them to Florida. Elvis knew something was seriously wrong with her grandmother, but no one wanted to talk about it. Elvis Presley was kind enough to fill the silence.

* * *

It was cold that winter in Flagler Beach. Elvis found herself wrapped in a blue plaid blanket, the wind whipping off the ocean, clouds scudding by not even pausing to wave. Elvis saw animal shapes of all description moving rapidly across the sky like they were escaping a wildfire. When they reached the forest's edge they combined and morphed into an old gray-haired lady with an extra-long nose.

The sun's only mission it seemed was to provide light; warmth was somebody else's business. The month of January brought a rare killer frost that found foliage throughout the neighborhood wrapped in blankets and tarps, dogs wearing designer sweaters and the snowbirds chattering like crows arguing the reason they hadn't left the cornfields in the north this year.

Eunice was dying at home and it seemed mankind, plants and animals were all wearing funeral shrouds.

Elvira looking harried and haunted herself, walked on tiptoes, trying not to wake her sister. Without her sister's knowledge, Elvira had asked Elvis to find some final days assistance. The last month had been difficult, Elvira and Elvis holding Eunice up as she made her way to the toilet and back to her bed, not even bothering to get dressed these days. When they got trapped in a corner of the small bathroom by a falling Eunice, they knew they needed help. The pain was becoming unbearable and the agonizing noises that escaped her sister finally brought an organization called Hospice in to help. The ever-helpful librarian had given Elvis the number she needed to call.

By the time help arrived, Eunice was no longer lucid for more than a few minutes a day. Miraculously, two days after Hospice became involved, she woke up as if cured. She smiled, asked to have her hair combed and chatted away like old times. She signed her portion of the home over to both Elvira and Elvis.

"This place is about all I have in the world. The trailer in Maine, well you two figure that out. I want coffee and a big breakfast this morning and yes I'm going to want a cigarette. Maybe you can help me outside. Wrap me in a blanket, I need some sunlight, open those damn blinds, will yuh? And Elvis, no more sad songs.

Let's hear something with a little life to it!" Even Eunice's cough calmed in quiet celebration.

R. Wesley Clement

Elvira and Elvis just stood there in disbelief. Was it possible Eunice was recovering? Eunice continued to bark orders, the home springing back to life with sounds, sights and healthy-cooking smells.

By evening, Eunice was asleep, exhausted. Elvis who had gone in to sing a nightly lullaby came out confused.

"What do you make of it grandmother? Is she going to be alright?"

"The hospice lady will be here in the morning, maybe she has an answer. Maybe we're witnessing a real miracle. I've been praying. If it's true and she's cured, I'm going to have to rethink my thinking," said Elvira. "I don't take much stock in miracles and God and all that, but I confess I prayed for my sister to get better. Made all kinds of promises," confided the former evil twin.

"I pray every night for lots of things, not for myself, but I pray for both of you guys," said Elvis.

When darkness found the kitchen table, Elvis and Elvira continued to ponder life and its mysterious ways silently with all the lights off, the glow from Elvira's ever-present cigarette offering a visual ebb and flow to her addiction. In this moment of optimism Elvis had allowed her grandmother a rare indoor smoke.

Morning brought the hospice lady. Coffee, fresh and hot. Elvis stood over the stove, humming. She had freed the Pillsbury dough boy from the cold and proceeded to raise his expectations, only to cut and bake him into tasty little biscuits she was just now putting jam and butter on.

The hospice lady listened to what Elvis and Elvira had experienced the day before. She sipped her coffee and bit into a biscuit. When they finished, she cleared her throat and explained.

"They call what you witnessed yesterday, a burst of life. It can last just a single day or two and occasionally three. There is mystery to it, but in the end, it's the final pages of a life trying to get the ending right. Your sister and Elvis's grandmother is at peace now.

"Eunice has had to come to grips with her existence. She might wake up clear-eyed again this morning or she might just have moments where she has clarity of thought. She might not wake up at all. If she does wake, listen carefully to what she has to say in those moments, both her mind and body are purging themselves of any toxins. She will be speaking pure truth. Usually only several days remain before they pass."

"She did seem to be on a mission yesterday. She signed papers and gave orders," said Elvira.

Elvis heard this lady explain things in a way that was beautiful in its simplicity, she too hoped for one last bit of clarity from Eunice, a time when Eunice might tell her something of her mother. Two days later, Eunice passed from this world.

Twin brothers in Daytona offered cremation services that included pickup and delivery. Eunice's final wishes were carried out and her ashes were deposited along a stretch of Flagler Beach in the first two hours of nighttime with a quickly rising moon and stars bearing witness. In the dim light, reflection coming off the water, Elvis thought she saw her little ghost crab friend standing tall, as if at attention.

*　*　*

Elvis was old enough to take care of herself and be by herself. She continued to walk the beach, sing to the birds and read stories she borrowed from the local library while lying prone just below the whip of the wind, a blanket above and below. At night, she wrote letters to her boyfriend Nick. She did all the cooking and cleaning now, continuing to sing while she worked.

Elvira simply crafted her wares in slow motion, wrapped in Eunice's favorite blanket, sitting outside during the day, talking and sharing cigarette smoke with a sister who was no longer there. In the morning, she poured a cup of coffee for both herself and her sister. Elvis poured out the untouched cup every day without a word. Elvira became restless and agitated and began leaving in the evening. At first, Elvis had no idea where she went.

Elvis invited her to go to the beach, but Elvira showed little interest. Losing her sister seemed to raise a permanent cloud over her head, a fog that would not dissipate, a cigarette that never reached its filter. Elvis began to smell alcohol on her grandmother when she wandered in after ten o'clock three nights a week.

They continued to attend the flea market on the weekends but three days became two, then finally just on Sunday.

Elvis missed her grandmother Eunice and now Elvira was not around either. During one of the last moments of lucidity, Eunice had told Elvis the truth about her mother, that it was really all Eunice's fault her mother was not in her life. She begged forgiveness and Elvis did not want her grandmother who she had grown to love to suffer more than she was.

"I forgive you grandmother," she'd said. "Rest in peace." With that forgiveness, a new steely resolve entered Elvis's eyes.

Elvira went off the deep end of the pool and started not coming home at all for days at a time. When she came home after being gone for a week, she had a man with her. Not a nice man, Elvis surmised, when he went immediately to the refrigerator looking for a beer, set it on the kitchen table like a centerpiece and then stretched out on the couch as if testing his new digs.

He sighed, smiled, got up and grabbed his beer, moving to the recliner, working the lever that changed position. This man reminded Elvis of the neighbor's dog, always peeing in a different spot and sniffing to see if its territory had been violated between walks. Upon finishing the beer, still without uttering a word, he went back to the couch and fell asleep. He did not introduce himself. Elvira said nothing either but went straight to her room.

Zorro was what Elvira called him "cause he's such a great swordsman," she sniggered. Elvis was not very pleased. Zorro stayed with Elvira a week before the arguing began. Between fighting— the man did find his voice—and swordplay, the squealing noises sent Elvis to the beach where she walked the uneven sand, allowing the cold water to just reach her bare feet then scooting away.

Elvis, with time on her hands and nowhere else to go, spent lots of time looking for an elusive rare sand dollar in mint condition. The little ghost crab had yet to make a spring appearance— except maybe that night when Eunice's ashes were scattered so only the seabirds and snowbirds witnessed her ever longer days at the beach. When the sun rose over Flagler pier to twilight, when even the wind seemed to realize enough was enough and calmed its engine for the night, Elvis would call it a day.

* * *

It was April Fool's Day when Zorro was finally sent packing. Another bridge burned. Elvis sighed with relief. "There!" Elvira nodded her approval. *Maybe now Grandmother Elvira will rejoin thefamily,* thought Elvis.

The relief was short-lived, however, and Elvis's approval turned into being appalled. Elvira began bringing home a different bridge to burn every night, like when she had bought a new outfit at Bealls Department store wore it once then took it back for full refund. "Gotta kiss a hundred frogs they say," was the only explanation given to Elvis as another burning bridge stumbled off in the morning.

When one of these night crawlers found Elvis's end of the trailer, she hefted the small leather sap she'd purchased at the flea market for just such a purpose and pointed to the front door, never said a word just pointed.

Later that morning, with Elvira sitting at the kitchen table, her head barely an inch above her coffee cup, Elvis had a sit down with her grandmother.

"I've been doing lots of thinking at the beach, grandmother. I do my best thinking there," Elvis took a deep breath. "I'm leaving here today."

R. Wesley Clement

Elvira barely raised her head.

"There's nothing more I can do for you, grandmother, you're wallowing in misery and that's just not me. I know I own half of this place, but for now, if you can just give me bus fare and a little money to tide me over for a month or two, I'm going to find my real mother."

Elvira who seemed hell bent on following her sister on a fast track, nodded her head, barely, her hair reaching into her cup as if for a sip.

"I knew this was coming. Sister told me just before she passed she'd confessed her sins." The words found their way through the kitchen table. She looked up then. "In a way I'm sad, but I am who I am. The only time in my life I've been happy has been on this journey with sister and you." She finally made eye contact. "You have to start your own journey now. I'll see to it this place is properly signed over, before I either smoke, drink or frolic myself to death. There's money in my undies drawer. Take what you need."

Elvis hitchhiked and caught a ride on A1A South, her sap snug in her pocket. Her last clear look at the Atlantic Ocean from this part of the world was from the back of a Harley driven by an old man with a bandana and a beard like Santa.

I think I saw your sister's face in the clouds recently, grandmother, thought Elvis, her face flushed and red from the wind.

CHAPTER EIGHTEEN

A FORMAL EDUCATION

*F*ull scholarship, Vermont local makes good, Middlebury College recipient of first graduate in Montpelier history to achieve better than a 4.0 average. The local paper had sung his praises wished him well and honestly, forgot all about him.

When Quentin arrived on campus, his father helped carry the few possessions to the dorm he'd been assigned to. They met his roommate who had staked claim to the bed with a window. Quentin had come to know himself quite well by now and shadows were his friends.

"Oh I don't mind, you were here first. This little table lamp will get me by nicely."

The window wasn't the problem between Quentin and his roommate; it was the constant strumming of that damn guitar and a voice that would be of use at Halloween to scare children. Quentin went to his advisor in October, by then several of the freshman boys had departed and he got a single room with a view he wouldn't use. Quentin placed his bed as far away from the window as possible, pulled the shade and put a lock on his door. Though it was frowned upon, he did it anyway.

He attended no social mixers, preferring his own company. Besides, the classroom interactions were mixers enough to turn his stomach. Though lecture-based and Quentin loved lectures,

R. Wesley Clement

the informal organization found the ways and means to tease, flirt and on one occasion copulate, behind a lab table. The lecturer, none the wiser, spewed his version of the way and the truth from the safety of a lectern. Quentin quietly fumed at their sophomoric action.

Quentin did have needs, however. During a rare trip home during his junior year, after a lot of introspection, he had a talk with his father.

"Do you have some samples of some of the prescriptions you peddle?"

"I do, though I keep them in a safe place now-a-days. Your mother has been acting strangely in public lately. I know your mother always acts strangely, but strangely enough to get a policeman involved this time. She convinced him she must have taken too much of her prescription medicine, but they called and I happened to be home. I had to retrieve her from police headquarters. She's taken to her room. Withdrawal, I expect."

"I'm really having a hard time getting to sleep. There's so much work, and I need to sleep."

And so it began.

* * *

The girl was attractive, if a bit overweight. They shared a second semester class and knew each other's names from the professor's roster call. Colleen was a true Irish girl, crinkled red hair and a splatter of freckles that gave her a wholesome look.

Quentin was in the library doing research on his favorite author, Charles Dickens. His last term paper would compare women characters of evil intent and show how various authors used them to drive the narrative. Miss Havisham, a character from *Great Expectations* raised her ugly head in a passage he was reading. Quentin was drawing a comparison to his own mother and scowling when Colleen spoke.

"You seem always on firm ground," she said. "I admire the way you offer your opinion in a very scientific way." Quentin, whose praise had mostly come from his professors, blushed. He could smell her. Ivory soap, 99 and 44/100 percent pure.

Quentin invited her to sit down and found she was a good listener. In a round-about unusual for the straight-ahead thinker, he told her about himself—the cliff notes version that didn't call for follow-up questions.

Colleen seemed as socially awkward as he was, but somehow they managed to make a date of sorts. *A meet-and-greet,* they kidded. Coffee house for starts, then see where it went.

Quentin had little packets of protection in his room thanks to good old dad. He had practiced on himself and the restrictions didn't seem to affect the outcome. What he had no practice with was getting a real live girl beneath him and convincing her this was a natural outcome of caring about one another. Quentin had difficulty caring about anyone but himself.

They had coffee and a sandwich at the coffee shop, feeling their way along and it went well enough that Colleen agreed to go to Quentin's room for just a beer or two. They had a beer, listened to some music on the computer, hugged and began to neck innocently. When Quentin got a bit bolder, Colleen didn't say anything, just removed his hand. He backed off, rose and returned with a second beer. Colleen accepted it and sipped lightly. Some sips and lips later, with the two hugging, Colleen went limp on his shoulder.

He laid her down, studied her momentarily, then slowly removed her clothes, starting with her sandals. He carefully folded each garment after smelling it; everything was a new experience to be savored. His breathing accelerated, his pulse raced and he became fully aroused. He touched her, the first girl he'd ever touched. Her arms were covered with a light red down. He smelled her, licked the soft down, then nuzzled her nipples.

He placed her limp hand on his hardness. He couldn't help thinking, *Gollum,* the name he'd given his penis all those years ago when reading the *Hobbit.*

"I should be using his favorite line about now, *Come my precious,"* he chuckled.

Then he opened a packet, slipped it on, and placing pillows strategically, took advantage of his sleeping beauty. Shadows thrown off by the lamp bore witness.

He had imagined what it would be like but was shocked by the warmth that wrapped around him, all of Quentin's senses acting in concert, intensifying the effort and his release. He lay there gasping, the reward surpassing his expectations. When he finished, he removed the latex and left the room. Returning, he dressed Colleen as he'd found her and laid on the floor, a blanket beneath him. He couldn't sleep, but used his significant scientific tools to analyze the experiment.

Let's start with touch, he thought. *She was warm, pliable, wellmuscled beneath a layer of softness.* He smiled. *I would like to ask her how it felt for her, but I'm sure she'd misunderstand. Pity, I could use the feedback, perhaps improve my delivery.* He chuckled in the darkness, checking each of his senses, feeling how they'd been stimulated, each bringing a smile to his lips.

Quentin's moral compass was profoundly lacking—no sense of shame, guilt, remorse, betrayal. He found himself humming a tune they'd shared from the computer earlier; he rather liked it. On this night in this place, the song, *It's All about the Bass,* had entered his head. He changed the last word to self. *It's all about the Self.*

"Catchy," he whispered.

Morning follows nighttime and the sky lightened the sides of the shade. Quentin rose and turned on the table lamp. Colleen O'Connor was looking him straight in the eye. He backed up a step. She sat up, squinting her eyes in pain, pointed at him and said, "Don't move a muscle. I have to pee." When she returned she continued, "I'm pretty sure you put something in my beer. I'm pretty sure you violated me."

Quentin began to speak, but Colleen held up her hand. "Don't speak. Don't you dare speak. I have half a mind to call my three brothers. They'd end this conversation in a heartbeat. They live close by." Quentin remained quiet. "I made a mistake with you and that's on me." She looked him up and down with contempt. "I'm usually a good judge of people, but you fooled me. Score one for the bad guys." She stood up, nose to nose with Quentin.

"I'm leaving now and if you see me on campus, go the other way." She squeezed his bicep and smirked. "I think I could kick the crap out of you myself." She walked to the door, saying, "You need help, Quentin." Turning back, she added, "At least you helped me discover something. I make a better advocate than a victim." She pointed at him, "You best remember that," and left the room, slamming the door as forcefully as possible.

A normal person might have taken this as a phew-thank-God-that's-over moment and changed course. Quentin just sat on the bed and laughed, pumping his fist in the air. Then he ran around the room, taking a victory lap. None of what she'd said registered; he was already thinking of how to better mix his medicine and methodology. *Dad can help me with the medicine part.*

Colleen never returned to the class they'd shared.

For the next episode of *drugged delight,* Quentin went to Montpelier and picked up a long-haired local barfly. He used the encounter as an opportunity to improve his knowledge base of how lust and laudanum, a derivative of opium, mixed in different measures could give him a better result. The methodology was the same.

He deemed the experiment a failure when the girl sat up the next morning, saying, "Just another fucking delightful day. Headache in place. Sour stomach. And asshole in tow." She too slammed the door of the rented room but not before adding, "Welcome to my world, weirdo!"

* * *

Quentin applied for graduate school and was accepted into the famed Bread Loaf School of English in Ripton, Vermont, located a dozen miles from Middlebury's Campus. He visited and was taken by the mustard colored buildings that dated back to the late 1800s.

There were magnificent white colonials as well, but the mustard yellow was a color Quentin could fill his eyes with, his mind with. He gazed out over meadows toward the mountains in the distance from a wraparound porch harboring innocent rocking chairs seemingly eager to assist a sitter in conjuring up an original line or idea.

He had just one semester to complete at Middlebury, and he would be well on his way to gaining a Master's Degree in English Literature. There were rocking chairs and wraparound porches standing sentinel at each building, centerpieces for stimulating ideas and opportunities. Quentin returned to the last semester at Middlebury filled with hopes and dreams and hopes.

Unfortunately, life can turn on a dime or, in Quentin's case, a failed experiment, a dime with a doll's face. He blew up the lab.

When conducting an experiment, there are always variables you do your best to anticipate, plan for, consider and control. The variable in the spring of Quentin's senior year was a fifth-year senior who was finally getting her degree—one of a slew of celebrators at a bonfire.

Quentin chose her because she was a beauty, a specimen really. *Let's get superficial here.* He nodded his red solo cup as if waving a red flag. The girl responded and the deed was done.

"Unfortunately there must have been a misunderstanding," Quentin said to the Dean of Students after she reported him. There was scant evidence, though plenty of suspicion. The nature of where and when the act took place mitigated the mess. In the end, Quentin was put on notice. Whatever the hell that meant.

The real punishment came in the form of a letter, received at his dormitory room just a week before graduation.

Sorry Quentin, the deciders have decided there doesn't appear to be a rocking chair available for you in Ripton. You'll have to bake your bread somewhere else.

Quentin, angry but with no recourse, packed his belongings and left one mountainous state for another. He got accepted at a small school in Montana, the school eager to have a 4.0 graduate from a well-regarded eastern college. He flew under the radar got his degree, got accused but never charged and was sent packing anyway.

He became a nomad of knowledge. Never got to be a professor. A lecturer of learning however, seemed always in demand somewhere. Quentin, a fountain of insight regarding English Literature, landed a job at Bowdoin College in Brunswick, Maine, to assist in writing a curriculum for English majors. It was just a half hour from Portland where he decided to take a room.

He vowed to himself to stop messing with medicines. Then he met Elvis.

CHAPTER NINETEEN

2009 HEARTBREAK HOTEL

The trip back north was an eye-opener for Elvis. The bus stopped in virtually every little town, passengers, each one with a unique back story, being greeted or waved goodbye to.

Elvis had never felt so alone. *Who will be there to greet me?* She hadn't received a single letter from Nick in the last two months. She had continued writing, but the letters, originally as colorful as an autumn landscape, turned as bleak and cold as winter's demands. The last was a single page giving Nick the news of her grandmother's death.

Not one had been returned to sender like the tale of woe sung by Elvis the man. She didn't even have the emotional baggage of a lover's quarrel. Numb is all she felt. Numb all over.

The hum of the wheels and the monotony of movement had her thinking the worst. A world without a voice passed before her eyes as she rested her head against the glass.

A stop allowed her a brief respite and she sat nursing a cup of coffee, her first, in memory of her grandmother Eunice. She added enough cream and sugar to turn it into a warm frappe. She toasted the ceiling and the memories flitting through her mind, like the clouds she'd reshaped at the beach, were mostly good.

The banter of others sitting on stools at the counter offered white noise to her mind adrift. Laughter and conversation eventually seeped through her reverie and Elvis looked around, watching the people interact and connect.

Sighing deeply, she tried to put a positive spin on things. *I'm feeling just the way Elvis did in a lot of his songs. That should help with the emotion I bring to my performances.* The thought brought a sudden smile to her lips and a new resolve to make this trip a learning experience.

Elvis re-entered the bus with a different outlook. *Hmm, maybe there's something to this coffee pick-me-up my grandmothers always touted,* she mused and began to sing the Elvis songbook quietly to an audience of one.

She arrived in Portland, Maine, just as old man winter was whispering a sad tale to a tearful April spring. It seemed the tale being told was woeful indeed; the rain poured down for four straight days.

Remembering lines from one of the little poems that Eunice recited every spring, Elvis hoped April would quickly step aside and usher in pretty little May. Something was coming by gum, though she couldn't remember what. She laughed out loud and suddenly spoke to no one and everyone. "Elvis is in the building!" she fairly screamed, covering her head with a magazine offering beautiful houses on the ocean, as she dodged puddles.

She located a small café. She needed to think and maybe one of those coffee concoctions would help. She needed to dry off too. Elvis took inventory. She had the money Elvira had given her but that wouldn't last; Portland might offer her the best chance to find housing and a job. Nick was still away at school for another month anyway. No sense heading to the island.

What a job would look like was anyone's guess. She would be seventeen in August but looked older. *As long as I don't attempt to take up drinking*—Elvira's recent escapades certainly discouraged that—*no one should be interested in my age.* Job descriptions entering her head were filtered and filed away or discarded. Elvis ordered a second cup of coffee and reworked the color and taste. Without realizing it, she was working her way toward discovering frappuccinos and lattes.

She picked up various tourist literature from the metal bins at a bus stop, sat on a bench and started reading. Real estate magazines, community newspapers, restaurant and business flyers, it seemed Elvis had stumbled into a busy tourist area.

"With all this to offer I should be able to find something," she said.

"But I have to stay under the radar. The grandmothers always said its best to stay under the radar." No official jobs that require birth certificates or background checks.

"If you see something you want to try, just knock on the door," Elvira had said as her parting words. As far as finding her mother, Elvira had little to say except that it would not be easy and to be careful what she wished for.

A map of the city was laid out in front of her. It was a business brochure, really, but helpful; it showed the streets and businesses, including where she now sat. Just off the major road near the ocean, Commercial Street acted as a buffer for the many wharves, piers and warehouses that dotted the area. Several high rise condos had the Atlantic looking directly into their living rooms.

She perused a corkboard of business cards, lost pets and apartment-for-rent ads and found a rooming house on Spring Street that sounded promising.

Three of my guests have been here for seven years. We share space, a place at the table, conversation and above all compassion. Wont you join our family?

The ad seemed to beckon Elvis, who had no family, to the nondescript two-story home that would never make it in any house-beautiful brochure. The location was good at least, near many Old Port restaurants and small businesses that appeared to be owned by the occupants.

———

Elvis had never lived in the lap of luxury and liked the hope offered by the name of the street. Spring Street. *It's coming, by gum.* She sighed looked up and mounted the six steps, all begging for paint and complaining about it. She hesitated and then knocked.

A tiny elderly lady with blue hair and a warm smile answered the door. Elvis had to look down to meet her eyes. She ushered Elvis past a stairway to a kitchen that was sparkling clean but had not borne witness to any modernizing in the last four decades.

The metal table and chairs were in good repair, though they would never shine again, faded to a dull green. The sideboard held a shiny silver toaster and a percolator. A single geranium begging for companionship sat just to the left of a slate sink. An old gas stove was just that: an old gas stove. Tin ceilings reminded Elvis of the little tin-covered booths at the flea market.

The walls sported a different wall paper pattern and color in the rooms she could see from the kitchen. Porcelain knickknacks that obviously held memories dotted the window sills. A cookie jar sat to the right of the sink just above a rack that housed a floral dishwipe. Elvis smelled molasses.

The kitchen fairly shouted the words from the flier: warmth, compassion.

If this lady cares for her tenants like she's cared for her kitchen, I think this just might work, she mused.

"Tell me a little about yourself dear," said Mrs. Waslowski as she sat across from Elvis. "By the time you've finished, I will make a decision on whether to welcome you into our family."

Elvis told her story, holding nothing back, quickly surmising this lady could see through subterfuge.

Mrs. Waslowski never took her eyes off the girl even as she stood and moved about the kitchen, offering coffee with a nod and a grin, or grimacing with concern while bringing sugar and whole milk and molasses cookies to the table.

Elvis interrupted her story to bite into a cookie, and her eyes grew wide.

R. Wesley Clement

"Oh my gosh, what are these?"

"An old family recipe, dear. I can't give away any family secrets just yet."

By the time Elvis had finished her story, and a second cup and a second cookie, Mrs. Waslowski had washed and dried the dishes, wiped the table and added water to the geranium. But all the while the proper inflections of her body language showed that she was really listening.

"You're an old soul, Elvis." Then the old woman smiled. "You'll fit in nicely here. Let me tell you a little about our family members and you listen this time. If you find my story as intriguing as I found yours, you'll have a home here."

Elvis listened. The woman's words were as soothing as the nicest day she'd ever spent on Flagler Beach. When Mrs. Waslowski finished describing her life and how she viewed the other tenants, Elvis realized she would be breaking bread with four really old people, three women and one man who was in the middle stages of dementia.

"He's harmless, but it can get a bit odd around here, so be prepared and keep a smile in place. Sometimes that's all you can offer."

Elvis met Kate and Sarah, seventy-year-old identical twin sisters, full of the devil and quick to laugh.

"We enjoy our afternoon toddy's," said Kate.

"Only one though," giggled Sarah.

They were former teachers in "what seemed like another life—" insisted one.

"—in the same school system," finished the other.

The sisters had lost their husbands within the same year and joined Mrs. Waslowski's family in 1998.

"We love it here and we love Portland—" insisted Sarah.

"—there's so much to do," offered Kate.

Short and thin, the ladies finished one another's sentences then pretended to be aghast that the other would know what they were thinking, laughter following like punctuation. Elvis felt like her head was on a swivel.

Arthur, well, he was a story that was ongoing. He met Elvis at the kitchen table on the first night they shared dinner. Saturday night beans, hot dogs, biscuits and coleslaw were on the menu.

Elvis kept quiet, content to let conversation drift like the fragrant smells to her side of the table.

The shopaholic sisters discussed their latest purchases at TJ MAXX, advising Elvis that, whenever they shopped, it was at least a two-for-one purchase.

"You see dear—"

"—we're the same size." Laughter followed. Mrs. Waslowski gave Elvis a look that said *I told you so.*

Topics at the table included bingo, the weather, their children, food prices, *Days Of Our Lives*—the one soap opera they allowed themselves—and daily shopping for bargains. The only caveat at the dinner table was "no politics and no pretending allowed," they announced early in the meal.

Arthur didn't say anything until dessert was offered.

"Jell-O wouldn't have made the menu, back in the day," he said calmly. All heads turned.

"Well, fart in a bottle," it was the closest either sister would ever come to really swearing, "here it comes—"

"—another tale of the old west."

Elvis looked at these two vibrant ladies and couldn't help drawing a comparison to her two grandmothers. Other than the splitting of eggs at conception and an observation that they clearly loved one another, there was no comparison. She shook her head, shaking away thoughts of her grandmothers and the little they had accomplished in life other than loving her. *I guess that was enough for them,* she thought and gave her full attention to Arthur.

"Did I tell you I was born in Montana, big sky country? Had a ranch with a couple of hundred head of cattle, a small herd of buffalo and a string of horses I broke myself." A blank look suddenly entered his eyes and tears watered the vacancy. He wept openly. "I'm seventy-nine years old and live in one room, and I can't remember how I got here. What's your name again young lady?"

The sisters whispered conspiratorially, "He's actually eight- one—"

"*a*—you know."

Arthur wiped his eyes on a napkin and immediately forgot why he was sad. He polished off his Jell-O without complaint and asked if there were seconds.

* * *

Over the next few weeks, as Elvis looked for work, she wandered the area called Old Port and beyond. She found a museum a short walk from her room. A library, one of her favorite places to spend time, sat just above the next major artery running east and west called Congress Street.

She found herself returning to the ocean every other day, drawn in by the smells. She was never disappointed by the mighty Atlantic, which played hide and seek all along Commercial Street, but she was a little wistful that she could not find a beach within walking distance. No place near to gather shells either.

Still no word from Nick. Remembering the island she had spent summers on, a line she'd heard somewhere about love and loss hit home: *that ship has sailed.*

Elvis searched for a week but found no job offers—no experience, no need. The message was the same everywhere. She was lying in bed, thinking of expanding her search to include dog walking, when a feverish knocking rattled her door.

"Arthur is missing," Mrs. Waslowski said, clearly agitated. "He didn't come down for his early cup of coffee and the paper. He always plugs in the percolator I prepare before bedtime and, when I smell coffee, I get up and we share the paper. My goodness, it was seven o'clock when I woke up and realized my sniffer alarm didn't go off." She grabbed Elvis's hand. "He's not in his room. His wallet is there, though. We need to find him, can you help?"

They scoured the immediate neighborhood, but no one had seen him. When they returned to the house, Elvis suggested they call the police.

The dispatcher listened, and the mystery ended. A patrol car had discovered Arthur wandering aimlessly at three seventeen in the morning. It seemed odd since he wasn't wearing a jacket and what with spring nights still harboring some of winter's resentment, temperatures were in the low 40s. He couldn't remember where he lived but he knew he lived with four women. All nice ladies, he'd insisted.

Arthur, sitting on a bench in the hallway outside the desk sergeant's office, lit up like a Christmas tree when he saw Mrs. Waslowski and Elvis.

Mrs. Waslowski drove her ten-year-old Buick as if it were a Bentley, barely able to see out the windshield. Arthur sitting in the back seat had already forgotten the need for a ride but remembered he'd already had coffee.

"That nice sergeant. When you can, could we stop, I need to pee."

Mrs. Waslowski sat across from Elvis, nursing her first well-needed cup of the day after getting Arthur to his room.

"I have power of attorney for Arthur," she said in a kind and thoughtful voice. "He has no one else."

"Five years ago he came here to board. Two years later, he began forgetting things. After seeing a doctor, he was diagnosed and, while he was still clearheaded, we met with a lawyer. Arthur has lots of money, I write his checks and buy whatever he needs."

Mrs. Waslowski rose and turned to warm her cup. Elvis nodded yes and pointed to the cookie jar when Mrs. Waslowski raised the percolator in her direction. The smell of fresh-brewed coffee and the comfort of a molasses cookie seemed to warm the air and gentle the direction this conversation was about to take.

After they were both seated once again, Mrs. Waslowski studied Elvis as if looking inside the girl's soul.

"Right about now, I think Arthur needs a companion. There I've said it!" she exclaimed as if closing the lid on a package she was about to mail. "Would you like the job? It means doing his hygiene, getting him dressed properly, going out every day for exercise. Walks to the museum. He loves the museum.

"Lunch. He'll eat anything but really likes his beef. Walk the Back Bay. He enjoys all the runners. He stops at those exercise stations and just watches people. You can use a cab or city buses to go wherever you want. He loves your voice. Sing to him a little, he'll love that. He used to do a lot of karaoke when his wife was alive."

Elvis raised her eyes and, thinking ten steps ahead, smiled.

"That was their social life back in Montana. He's only here because he has a fifty-year-old daughter who thought the displeasure they felt in one another's company might have dissipated with age." The old lady huffed and drained her cup, sitting it down with more force than intended. "They lasted under the same roof less than a month. Haven't seen or heard from her since Arthur moved here. He's all ours now, Elvis. The good and the confused. So what do you think?"

Elvis sat there as if she were back at Flagler Beach, holding a silent conversation with the little ghost crab. Deciding, she nodded her head yes. Finding her mother would have to wait. Arthur needed her for a time.

Elvis included all the suggested venues and added more. She took him to the beach using public transportation. They walked the waves and sat on large boulders sharing sandwiches. She sang Elvis songs, many that seemed to spark a memory in the old guy and he would weep. She also found an Elks Lodge that offered karaoke and managed to get Arthur singing. He could still read and nobody forgets the beat. Arthur appeared happier than he had been in years.

Elvis did a little research at the library and found the tunes that Arthur would have grown up listening to. When Arthur heard himself singing the music, his whole body loosened up and he appeared a much younger man. Elvis was getting a musical history lesson as well.

Memories from the past would leap out sporadically when they found a catalyst. Arthur had two huge dogs that helped him on his cattle ranch. This half-hour tale was told after a lady with a small dog passed the bench they were sitting on.

When Arthur tried to repeat the story every time he saw a dog—not remembering yesterday or twenty minutes on a bad day—Elvis found creative ways to change the subject.

She had grown to love him.

* * *

Elvis lived in Mrs. Waslowski's home for four years. She had indeed found a home. Mr. Arthur as she called him became the father and grandfather she never had.

During the time she lived on Spring Street, Elvis came to know Portland in a very intimate way. She came to understand the public transportation system, cabs, local artists and frequent city celebrations. Cozy little eateries were tucked away, some with just three tables and a few of the large restaurants. And the coffee shops. Arthur loved his coffee, and Elvis continued to explore the many creative ways coffee could be served.

She researched Arthur's affliction, wanting to be the best caregiver she could be. She learned when to take the lead and when to just let him amble physically and mentally. Doctor's visits competed with their fun excursions, and she found out firsthand as a caregiver, the need for insurance, Arthur had Medicare, and additional coverage as well.

"Good thing too," said Mrs. Waslowski said, and she showed Elvis all the receipts, charges, prescriptions and copays. "It's a paper trail of misery if you're not covered."

One day, that paper trail finally ended at a cement marker in the local graveyard. A simple marker revealed two things about Arthur—he had been born and he died. He had decided the engraving years two ago, according to Mrs. Waslowski.

"I can't remember anything in-between any way," he'd said matter-of-factly. Everything in-between was left to the memories of those who had known him.

One organization benefited, and they hadn't known him at all. Arthur left nearly his entire estate to an Alzheimer's research foundation and nothing to his daughter. In a lucid moment years ago, he'd shared that he didn't know his daughter back when he didn't have remembering issues.

Elvis was left with the gift of good memories and the realization she'd need to find a new job.

After the positive reviews, and hoots and hollers from old people at the Elks Lodge, Elvis activated a plan that had been building since she was born. She wanted to be an entertainer.

My mother will act as my motivator, she thought. *Maybe if I'm good enough at this business, she'll find me.*

CHAPTER TWENTY

ELVIS IS IN THE BUILDING

The largest city in Maine, Portland is really a series of small towns. One such area, the Old Port, is unique in that it sits below those hilly streets and for decades was looked down on in ways that had nothing to do with geography.

In the early part of the 1900s, *down at the docks* meant entering a world with its own language, rules, rewards and punishments. The men of the docks, warehouses and sailing ships were hard men. They worked with their hands. They fought with their hands. Tinkers and tailors, captains and sailors, makers of goods and thieves in the night—the brick warehouses and factories muffling the sounds of good and evil within.

The revival of these streets and buildings paid homage with nautical themes, old photographs of sailing ships and artifacts from warehouses put to utilitarian purpose, anonymous men pictured doing the heavy lifting, their lives as empty as the lack of identification below the photos. Anonymous men in literally hundreds of pictures who lacked a voice, they were the silent witnesses to history.

Two days after Arthur was laid to rest, Elvis, in the year 2013, stepped out the door on Spring Street and headed towards Chandlers Wharf. She checked the address on the business card once more and the directions on the back to an office located nearby. Passing the Cumberland County Civic Center after crossing Spring, she paused briefly, uncertain.

In Flagler Beach, every cross street was simply a number either north or south of Route 100 that ended its life where it intersected A1A, an easy way to figure out where you wanted to go compared to this city Still musing and following directions, she found herself on Fore Street and headed north then east onto Dana Street and then Commercial.

If you get to Dimillo's Floating Restaurant, you've gone too far the directions read. She looked up. Staring her in the face were the condos that led to Chandlers Wharf.

Freddy Levine had offered her a job. He had come to a karaoke night at the Elks Lodge with an elderly uncle. He heard Elvis sing and this forty-two-year-old man fell head-over-heels in love. He invited Elvis and the old man she was accompanying to have a soda with him and his uncle. Freddy had a Bud Light.

The old guys shared memories while Freddy got to meet Elvis without interruption. After that night, he brought his uncle to every performance and continued to share his knowledge of Portland and the opportunities it offered. Elvis told him of exploring Portland with Arthur and even shared some of her dreams.

When Arthur died, Freddy and his uncle attended the simple graveside ceremony and when he hugged her to offer condolences, he handed her a card.

"If you ever need a job," he said, "contact me at this number."

Elvis found the office. A ground floor nondescript office in a warehouse just to the right of the paid parking lot used by condo owners, boat owners and their guests. Chandlers Wharf was one of many properties that Freddy had a stake in. Elvis knocked and entered the office.

An elderly gentleman heard the nautical bell over the door and slowly turned his head.

———

"You're Freddy's uncle. Pacey, right? We met the other day." Elvis gave him a bright smile.

"Elvis!" The old man beamed with pleasure. He moved around the desk and gave her a hug. "Freddy had to run out for sandwiches. Let me call him. He can get you a lobster roll."

"I'd never say no to a lobster roll," laughed Elvis as Pacey dialed up his nephew. While they waited, he showed her around the office. Pointing out artifacts gleaned from various local buildings, describing their role in production of some sort.

The view from the window covering the entire eastern wall was pure Atlantic Ocean. Elvis gazed out over the water, trying to see her own little beach and tears came to her eyes.

It all seemed so long ago, she thought, *and here I am, just a kid. Chapters,* she decided. *One chapter done with; today, maybe I start a new one.*

Pacey's hand on her shoulder brought her back and she heard him telling her about a boat ride he'd taken that landed him in this country when he was just a toddler.

"You're too young to know, Elvis, but this is the greatest country in the world for reasons that escape anyone born here. This is a nice city built by people whose mothers and fathers came from somewhere else. That ocean out there, and more recently its kissing cousin on the west coast, was the only way to get here." His eyes looked misty, too.

At that moment, Freddy set the bell to ringing, arriving with lobster rolls, Cape Cod chips and pickle spears of course and three bottles of Cherry Dr. Pepper to wash it all down.

"I don't do cans," he tossed out. "For me, they ruin the taste. It's like the fizz does a disappearing act."

"News to use," offered Elvis, and they all laughed.

After lunch, Freddy showed Elvis around. They walked through the basement garage used by condo owners and strolled onto the wharf itself, where a dozen boats were moored. There were boats on the water; some being motored, others under sail.

R. Wesley Clement

It was so very different from her past life. It seemed that here you had to tickle the ivories to hear the music while on her little beach in Florida the water lapping your toes was the stimulation. Two different worlds, people adapting to what was being offered and finding enjoyment.

Mentally rejoining the tour, Elvis asked, "What will I be doing?"

"Everybody pays for this view in one way or another. They pay at the gate I'll show you or have a sticker that shows they are here for a longer time. Your job is to collect money when they enter. If they have a sticker, you check the date to make sure it's current, then wave them through. This is a gated area, not a lot of free parking in this part of town. You get twelve bucks an hour, and you don't do nights. We get our share of wackos when the sun goes down, so we let the guys who enjoy being in the-right-and-the-fight man this area at night."

Elvis looked at him quizzically.

"You are an innocent, trust me. You'll meet people who actually enjoy beating people up or getting hit themselves, mostly nighttime, thank heavens."

Elvis signed on to start Monday, reporting first to Pacey who'd help her fill out paperwork.

"I don't have a social security card or any identification papers, or even a birth certificate. I'm just Elvis."

"Pacey will help you with all that. He'll figure out the best way for you to be employed with the company."

"Will I get insurance? Mrs. Waslowski said everyone needs insurance."

Freddy chuckled, looking at his uncle. "Make sure she gets top-notch insurance when you sign her up, Uncle Pacey."

"I guess I should go, then," said Elvis.

"Can I offer you a lift?" asked Freddy.

"No thanks. I'll walk. I'd like to get familiar with the area."

"When will you be singing again?"

———

"Sunday afternoon. There's going to be an open mike at the Elks Lodge."

"See you there, then." Freddy and Uncle Pacey waved, smiling, Freddy's gaze growing wistful as she went through the door, the bell ringing on her way out.

CHAPTER TWENTY-ONE

JACOB'S ARK

Jacob left the boat at ten o'clock each morning, as if his body was rigged to some inner alarm. Wearing black shorts and a tan tee shirt, a San Francisco Giants baseball cap keeping his mop out of his face and sporting aviator sunglasses, rain or shine, he silently asked himself the question that preceded nearly every event in his life: *Are you ready to do this?*

Living on a boat had changed his routine a bit, like finding himself before these morning runs, looking out over the water and seeing his life in the waves and chop. He had never thought of himself as the philosophical type—more a doer, a worker. Living on the water, slowly, subtly, had him thinking about things in the quiet of the morning, sitting with a hot cup of homebrewed Starbucks warming his hands.

The smoke on the water this morning was wispy, not the socked in pea soup that wets your skin like a lapping puppy. He stared through it, seeing all the people who had helped shape his life, and thanked them. He sang a song to his father—one of his dad's favorites. An old Eagles song. *Hotel California.* Jacob hadn't known him before he'd gone to war, but the number of people who sang his praises at the funeral revealed a much different man than the troubled-yet-loving father he remembered.

Miss him, every day. Jacob nodded in silent acknowledgement.

Brian, the man most responsible for who he had become still called weekly. "Just checking in" was his opening line, whether Jacob answered or he was leaving a message. His mother called every so often, but, from the time Brian entered the picture, he had done the heavy lifting. Both Jacob's younger brothers had responsible jobs and were hard-working guys with families now. He toasted them, knowing he'd helped plant the seeds of doing a job well.

A sudden wave, a rogue wave higher by half, struck the mooring, and the boat snapped him back to the present, spilling a little coffee on his shirt. *Good thing this shirt is brown,* he kidded himself, brushing it into the fabric.

The wave changed his introspection into taking a tally. He'd been working seven nights a week since Sean got hurt. He went below and refilled his cup.

I feel so bad for him, running was his religion, cleared his mind, purged his poison he always said about four miles into the run. Jacob laughed to himself remembering how Sean would scream something, and suddenly gallop like a horse excited to be let loose, shouting, "I'm cleansed, Jacob! Poison free!" then return to pace, laughing like a fool.

"We'll make it work, Sean," Jacob uttered aloud. During this morning's reverie, the cat sat silently watching him. How a cat had taken up residency was anyone's guess. But this white Persian piece of royalty with a single eye was sitting in the captain's chair every morning when Jacob emerged from below deck. Jacob was still at the *ignore it and it will go away stage,* though it'd been aboard a solid week now.

When Jacob lowered himself to do fifty pushups on the wooden pier just off his boat—gazing at the water through the slats—the white queen softly hoisted herself aboard Jacob's back like a captain in the bow bobbing up and down with the waves. Startled at first, Jacob chuckled, *this cat don't know what I've been lifting, lately,* and decided to ignore this trespass as well.

R. Wesley Clement

A half-hour run through several streets and part of the Back Bay brought him full circle. He climbed aboard the *Last Tango* to shower. The cat was gone.

"I've got to ask Freddy about this cat," Jacob said aloud to himself.

An hour later he walked through the parking lot, freshly showered and hungry. He stopped a short distance from the gate, his body responding to a voice.

Wearing a Red Sox baseball cap with short black hair peeking beneath the edges, a yellow nylon wind jacket and jeans, Elvis was all business. "Good morning, sir," her company-issued greeting bouncing off the pavement.

Not sure if it was a man or a woman from the distance the greeting covered, Jacob threw out a unisex response, "Good morning to you as well. The birds are singing."

When he covered the short distance and looked into those liquid blue eyes, he felt like he'd been punched in the gut and it was clear that more than just the birds were singing this morning.

"Are you the new employee? Freddy told me he had hired a new security person but he didn't tell me you would be you," he fumbled.

Elvis smiled, her full lips parting and a winters worth of snow revealed itself. She didn't speak.

Jacob wanted to speak but was afraid his words would fail him so he too stood awkwardly silent. Finally he managed, "Hello, I'm Jacob of the Red Wood Forest."

Elvis smiled again extending her hand. "I'm Elvis. Freddy told me he had a guest on a boat down here. Is that you?"

Losing her small hand in both of his, Jacob found his voice. "I'm going to get a breakfast sandwich. Can I get you one? Maybe a coffee? I'd like to show you the view I wake up to every morning?"

"I suppose I can take an early lunch. I'll call security and ask. Maybe they can cover me." Elvis looked deep into Jacob's eyes.

They were a warm brown, matching the color of her coffee these days. "Three creams, three sugars, I'll mix it myself, no meat on that breakfast sandwich and a packet of mayo. See you in a few." With that she walked off to do what security people do.

Jacob stood watching her go, feeling he'd just run a marathon. He couldn't catch his breath. He sat on the fender of one of the parked cars to regain his bearings. He was still in a daze when he arrived at *The Home Plate,* a breakfast eatery just across from the Wharf. After ordering, Jacob stood against the wall, watching the late morning's activity.

The long bar was full and the tables, nearly as busy. Several heads turned when he entered—Jacob's size seemed to inspire that. One guy, a grizzled growler as he called them, had egg leaking down his chin. Jacob was reminded of comfort food served in many places all hours of the day and night. People starting their day here or ending their day at a bar. Some of these patrons would both start and finish their day sitting on a stool, toasting a good day's effort or simply trying to forget.

He would be singing to some of them tonight. His name was called, and his thoughts returned to the here and now. He checked the takeout bag to make sure everything ordered was there.

Don't want to begin this voyage in choppy waters, he thought, chuckling.

Returning to the parking lot, a different security guy stood in Elvis's spot.

"Have you seen Elvis, Stan?"

"She called in for someone to cover her spot, then she got a call from Freddy. I think she's at his office." Eyeing the brown bag, he asked cheerfully "Hey! Did you bring me something?"

Jacob gave Stan the meatless sandwich, a packet of mayo and a coffee with two creams and three sugars.

"I don't need that cream and sugar, I drink my coffee black man, but thanks," he winked. Stan, a sixty-year-old black man, retired from Brunswick Navy Shipyard after an earlier career serving the U.S. Navy. He laughed at the disappointment he saw in Jacob's body language. "You're listing to the left, my man."

Jacob who usually enjoyed bantering with Stan merely nodded, turned and headed to the view that wouldn't be quite as wonderful this morning.

* * *

A new ritual began for Jacob once he became the legs for Sean. Hoisting himself on the back of Redwood Jacob, Sean dubbed his giant friend. Each step taken was seen as a challenge that he would soon navigate himself. The driveway was so steep Jacob parked as close to the door as possible. He sat Sean in the seat of his newly acquired Dodge passenger van. Sean had added some money to the trade-in value of Jacob's twelve-year-old jeep.

"I know this rig is not the ultimate pick-up line, Jacob."

"Don't worry about it, Sean. I think I just found a gem a stone's throw from the water." No follow up was offered.

None needed, decided Sean when he looked up and saw the light in Jacob's eyes.

* * *

Elvis, while courteous and always smiling, had not returned the interest that seemed to spark their very first conversation. Jacob wondered about that, fretted to himself over that, talked to Sean about that.

Sean paddled his canoe behind the bar, serving up the brewskis and the liquor, Jacob and Shellee, working the tables. Shellee was becoming quite the little cook as well, offering up burgers, soups and chowders.

Freddy, now part of the frequent flyer club, was sitting at the bar, the beer part of his night a dim distant memory when he heard Jacob and Sean discussing a girl who seemed to be put off by his approach.

———

Raising a glass of Jameson, he appeared to look through his glass as he offered up a toast.

"Here's to me, a rare Jewish Irishman whose wise council is offered, though not often listened to."

Sean and Jacob had no idea Freddy was addressing them and continued muttering back and forth. Freddy, usually ignored until a nugget of wisdom left his lips changed course.

"Elvis is the topic of conversation this evening, I see. Well I have insider information that could raise your stock, Jacob."

Both Jacob and Sean looked up from their little table to see a glass of amber held up, beckoning them to invite a third party to their conversation.

"Do you mind if I join you lads," offered Freddy affecting an Irish brogue.

"Okay, Freddy, tell us a story, not a distant past story please. Recent history."

Freddy sat in the wooden booth as if in church about to offer confession.

"Cross my heart, this is the long and short of it. First things first though," he said, taking a generous sip of whiskey. "Jacob, the morning you first met Elvis, and she called in to be relieved for an early lunch, I was sitting in my office. She came in to freshen up a little before you got back." Freddy shook his head slowly from side to side. "Like that girl needs to freshen up." He smiled.

"She was animated, antsy even, never seen her like that. I think she was smitten a little bit." Freddy took a healthy pull on his Jameson, seeking the courage it would take to continue. He sighed long and deep. "I love Elvis. Stupid, yes. Helpless, yes. Harmless, most definitely, but still, I love the girl and don't want to see her hurt." He paused.

"When we met, she had an old guy she was responsible for, and I had Uncle Pacey with me. They talked; we talked. I know Elvis's history, and it's been anything but normal." Freddy drained his glass and signaled for more Irish reinforcements.

R. Wesley Clement

"I have come to know both you guys, and I wouldn't frequent your place or rent to you, Jacob, if I didn't like you. But this is Elvis we're talking about and I told her that morning, 'Let a little time pass. See if his intentions are honorable.' I actually had an errand for her to run that morning so her absence was legit. Here's the deal. I would like your relationship to grow organically."

Jacob had a strong urge to tell Freddy to butt out, using his pewter mug as a point of emphasis. The look on his face spurred Freddy to quit with the discourse and get to the ticker tape.

"Final revelation, Elvis is named Elvis for a reason. She can sing like the man himself. I have watched her perform dozens of times. I want you guys to hire her to work for you. She's bright, personable and she'll compliment Jacob's nightly act.

"Don't thank me now. In a month, you'll beg to kiss my ring, guarantee it." Reaching for his wallet, he added, "I'm going to put my money where my mouth is men. I will pay her wages for the first month. If this works out, you reimburse me with a small interest charge we can discuss after a week." Laying a swath of green along the table sealed the deal in Freddy's mind.

Sitting back, Freddy seemed pleased with himself, kind of puffed up, and continued like an anointed matchmaker. "Jacob, you get to know Elvis in a natural way. If things click, there's always time for coffee on the boat." With that, Freddy rose and moved back to his stool. "Not tonight. Give me your decision tomorrow when I first come in. Let's involve Bud in the decision, he's a clearer thinker."

As Freddy's drinking moved him ever closer to claiming his nightly office space, Jacob broke into song at the keyboard and tonight his voice seemed as light as his heart.

CHAPTER TWENTY-TWO

X-RAY VISION

Stella received the manila envelope with a solemn nod. Dr. Bronson was not smiling either. "The pictures are just as you described, Stella. The damage is done, I'm afraid. I've never seen knees shattered at quite that angle before."

Stella stared out the office window of Dr. Bronson's clinic as a plastic grocery bag soared by like a hot air balloon. The sun warmed her face on this late afternoon even as what had to be a twenty-mile-an-hour wind cleared the air from the recent late season snowfall. The reality that Sean would never walk, much less run, hit home in that moment.

We move on then. Sean seems ready. He loves that bar, he loves me, we move on. Stella nodded this time with purpose.

Armed with Dr. Bronson's professional analysis, Stella entered the law office of Braden Danner, Sean's cousin. Shellee, who was Braden's secretary when she wasn't moonlighting at the bar, greeted her and the two swapped light banter.

"Heard you've become quite the cook, Shellee."

"Crazy right? I never cooked for myself, but now I'm finding new ways to dress up store-bought. I even made a soup the other day out of leftovers in my fridge." The two high-fived. "Sean is amazing, Stella. Course you know that. He can make a joke out of the simplest thing. I just love the whole job," she gushed.

"And Jacob," she whispered, "I was kind of hoping there, thought he was just shy." She sighed. Then she put on her game

R. Wesley Clement

face. "But clearly, he's an Elvis fan." Both ladies laughed and nodded their heads. "I have to admit I'm a fan too, what a voice, and she's as nice as she sounds."

Stella held up the envelope; her eyes, smiling. "That's why I need to speak with Braden. I want his approval on an idea I haven't even shared with Sean."

Braden entered at that moment.

"Stella what blew you in on such a windy day." He reached for her hand.

Stella ignored the hand and gave Braden a big hug, winking at Shellee in the process. She knew Braden was not a hugger and wanted him back on his heels for a moment. It worked. He stumbled behind her to his office, a shade redder, then he invited her to sit behind his desk.

"Have my seat," he said, gesturing, "I think you'll be taking the lead on this meeting." Stella laughed and did just that.

Braden reached across the desk and buzzed. "Shellee hold my calls unless it's Chief Justice Roberts wanting my opinion on the Health Care initiative."

Stella sitting in this chair had a whole new perspective. She looked around at an office that could only be described as restrained yet whimsical.

Braden, recently a new dad, had placed a nautically themed mobile on his desk. Dolphins, sea turtles, colorful fish and one giant shark bobbed up and down, above and below the surface when stimulated by a wave of the hand.

"My son has one of these above his bed so when I set this bad boy in motion, I can see him in his crib sending me messages."

Law books lined one wall, but they bore covers that were anything but traditional. Braden had played college basketball and his law books were covered in colorful NBA wrappings that had a sequence and meaning that only Braden could understand. One wall offered residence to the various degrees that certified Braden's right to counsel.

———

Stella knew she'd made the right decision by coming here. She rolled her chair out from behind the desk and right up to where Braden sat and began without preamble. "Braden we need to settle with the insurance company soon. I have an idea that's going to allow Sean to regain control of his life and maybe change the lives of a lot of people in the process. The little bit Jacob shared with you was exactly that, a little bit."

"Jacob mentioned busting through a wall taking over a furnace room, he didn't get into specifics. Said you just wanted him to know and get his okay."

"I didn't have it all fleshed out, but now I do and I could use your help in a hundred ways. Freddy's aboard. His only comment was 'You gotta love this country.'" She took Braden's hand in hers; he could feel the strength of Stella's commitment.

"So here's my idea."

CHAPTER TWENTY-THREE

JACOB AND ELVIS JUST DUET

Sean called his Aunt Loretta, and she answered on the first ring. "I have been waiting for your call, I know you aren't a phone person, but as I said in my message I've been doing research."

"Good morning Aunt Loretta. If you're excited, I'm excited. What's up?"

"It's experimental and insurance won't cover it, but they're looking for volunteers for a trial. It involves using your own cells to grow bone. From what you have shared with me the bones above and below your knee were shattered, correct?"

"Like a light bulb exploding."

"And that is why you can't have knee replacements, correct?"

"That's what they tell me."

"From what I'm finding and from a call or two I have made, this project is about growing your own bone using cells from your body then fusing it where you need to, attach knee replacements." She paused. "Exercise and eat right, we'll have you back on your feet."

"Give me that site you visited. I'll have Stella do some digging. So how's everything in Skow Town? All the aunts and uncles?"

"Be skeptical if you want Sean, but this sounds like it offers hope. I'll email you the site. And everything is fine here, though we're thinning out, wilting on the vine," she chuckled.

"If you and Uncle Pat get down here, come visit our little bar on Fore Street. We have people playing the kind of music you guys listen to and a great burger to boot. Say hi to everyone. Tell them I said, Come to the big city, see the lights."

"I know an exit line when I hear one nephew. Love you. Let me know what you discover. Hope it helps. Bye now."

It was still early, a couple of stools occupied, one being Freddy. Jacob and Elvis were going over the music they had planned for the night. Sean was wiping film off the liquor glasses when the door opened and the new latest odd ball regular entered. He'd been coming in at the end of his shift for the past month. His penchant for sitting off to the side at a table muttering like a brooding bird, along with his bill-like profile had garnered his nickname, AFLAC. Not one they shared with officer Armand Giroulx.

Sean paddled his way to the table, knowing already what the man drank all time every time. "Good evening, officer, what can I bring you this evening?"

His message, though muttered, was decipherable. "Let's mix it up tonight."

Sean looked at him in surprise.

"Let's make it tonic and gin. Yeah, let's mix it up."

"You're in rare form, Officer Giroulx. Let me make sure I have the order of your order. Tonic then gin, correct?"

"You are indeed a Mensa Sean." He gave a rare grin.

"Did you write that down, Sean? Can't afford to get customer orders wrong," quipped Freddy.

Meanwhile Elvis and Jacob were speaking in their own language, a language Jacob was teaching her.

"You have a gifted voice, Elvis, but you might not want every song to carry the man's signature. Helping you understand the different keys you can tap into and changing tempo can make every song you do your own. Plus didn't you tell me you kept a little book with thoughts you had at the beach and the flea market? And on that island? Maybe you can put some of those experiences into songs."

Jacob, sitting here with Elvis at his side, their mutual interest sparking their conversation, suddenly raised his mug and hollered to Freddy.

"To you Freddy for knowing the ways of Portland and being a truly gifted organic gardener."

Never at a loss for words, especially when receiving rare praise, Freddy raised his early evening Bud Light.

"A rose appears in the tangled overgrowth of our imagination. A rare occurrence indeed."

"What did he just say?" asked Elvis.

"I think he said he needs his bushes cut," laughed Jacob.

* * *

Stella stopped in and was sitting with Sean in the little booth used as an office. *Troubled Waters* was packed with troubled people, those in trouble or those soon to be in trouble if they didn't get their asses home.

Freddy shouted over the noise level that was beginning to rise, "I may need that space an hour from now, so don't get too cozy you two!" He grinned, pointing to his empty whiskey glass. "Not before Elvis and Jacob sing my new favorite song though."

Jacob upon hearing Freddy's raised request, lightly touched the keys.

"Uncle Freddy what night cap can we offer you?"

"I heard you guys play it the other afternoon when you were practicing. Elton John singing about a train that don't stop somewhere, anymore, something like that."

Stella and Sean, knowing their time in the booth was waning, finished up their conversation.

"I have a surprise for you," Stella said, in closing, "It concerns our future. So tomorrow, by two o'clock, be shaved, showered and shampooed. We're going shopping."

Sean looked across the booth at his beautiful wife and was totally in the dark. "O-kay …" was all he could manage. Stella rose waved goodbye to a series of exit lines tossed her way and made her way through the din to the door.

Jacob and Elvis side by side on the piano bench sang, *This train don't stop here anymore* to the man they now called Uncle Freddy. Elvis had decided she wanted a relative.

* * *

By two o'clock, Sean had accomplished all he'd been asked to do. The shower was the biggest challenge but a plastic lawn chair allowed him to sit and using soap on a rope, he wasn't slipping and sliding his way to good hygiene.

When Stella appeared from the garage, he was in his office, wearing a tee shirt and shorts, which were much easier to maneuver over his lifeless legs. Stella looked stunning and Sean was quick to tell her so.

"You look all squeaky clean and handsome yourself. Ready for a road trip?"

"I am, though I have no idea what road we're talking about."

Stella brought the wheelchair to the bottom of the two steps leading into the garage and Sean—using the same technique employed at the bar with a similar stool—paddled his way to an unknown future.

They stopped first at a Starbucks. Answering Sean's quizzical look, Stella held up two fingers. "For two reasons. Number one. I love their coffee. Number two. This was your old career. Today you start a new one. Here's to your new day." Stella emerged with Sean's old career in two paper cups. She handed them through the window, got in and they toasted with cups of *Pike's Peak*. One cup knowing the answer to the question; the other merely enjoying the coffee and the company and the whimsical way this road trip was starting.

<hr>

  R. Wesley Clement

As they passed *Troubled Waters,* Sean raised his cup in salute. Stella took a left on union and almost immediately another left into a garage door opening. Sean suddenly sat up. Standing there were Freddy, Jacob, Braden and a man Sean didn't recognize. Stella, put her finger to her lips. "All will be answered during the next hour, Sean. Then, the decision is yours."

CHAPTER TWENTY-FOUR

BRINGING BALANCE TO THE BOAT

Spring moved to summer, the hardwoods leafing out, soothing the winds coming off the ocean. Flowers appeared in window boxes dotting the apartments above the restless energy created by a season of tourists ogling the Old Port. The rooming house on Spring Street had been freshly painted, a flag flying, window boxes blooming and a new tenant finally replacing Arthur.

Mrs. Waslowski introduced Mr. Quentin T. Spence at dinner on the third day of July, 2014. Mrs. Waslowski kept accurate records both in her mind and on paper. She would later need to refer to her uncanny skills of observation. The two sisters were in attendance as well as Elvis and of course, Mrs. Waslowski.

Mr. Spence, a thirty-seven-year-old Professor of English Literature, had joined the teaching faculty at Bowdoin College in Brunswick, a half hour up the pike.

Dinner offered fresh Maine grown peas.

"The first of the season," beamed Mrs. Waslowski. "Our first mess of beet greens too."

As the sisters sliced into cold ham and spooned potato salad onto their plates to join the seasons new picks, the ladies started their innocent interrogation of their new house mate.

"Mr. Spence is it—" asked Kate.

"—will you be with us a while?" finished Sarah.

Since Arthur's death, the two sisters had been working on separating their thoughts, but their attempt had merely forced a listener to move their head north or south where they now held positions at opposite ends of the table.

Mr. Spence seemed flummoxed by the question.

"Call me Professor, as my students do," he smirked, pipe-stained teeth teasing his lips. "I am part of a grant the college wrote to completely revamp the way students are taught English literature. It's a shambles. I will enlighten the entire campus, I predict." He daintily severed a pea. He was at his lectern now, never looking up.

"I will be at the college for two years at least. This summer, I am looking at the present curriculum, along with two colleagues brainstorming our approach." A pause for a bite of beet green. "We have until the second semester to offer the first course to seniors." Each sentence ended with a self-satisfied smirk, his body as rigid as a UPS cardboard. A small sigh left his lips when he had finished, the smirk transforming into a rectangular grin that would do a puppet proud.

The two sisters, overwhelmed, unimpressed and not giving a hoot about this billboard advertisement for pomposity reached for closure on their simple question.

"HERE PROFESSOR, in THIS house—" said Sarah clearly and distinctly as if he were deaf.

"—HOW LONG will you be in THIS house?" finished Kate.

Professor Spence looked south then north, and a crack in his façade appeared, a lecturer with no lectern suddenly exposed to a question that forced brevity.

Elvis, who had spent years watching birds, ghost crabs and crabby people at the flea market noticed it. So too did Mrs. Waslowski who had let the man into her home.

"Well, well, I certainly hope I made a sound decision in joining *yourfamily,*" said the professor rather tartly, using the words from

Mrs. Waslowski's advertisement as he surveyed the table. "But I'm sure we'll get on, as they say. Would you pass more of those delightful peas, Elvis, is it? Odd name for a girl, I'm sure I'll hear the story." His gaze lingered and probed.

The sisters exchanged glances that seemed to finish one another's thoughts.

Proudly pompous— —

and he never did answer the simple question.

Elvis's favorite dessert, molasses cookies, was absent this evening as a biscuit smothered with strawberries and blueberries, and topped with whipped cream paid early homage to the nation's birthday. Dessert was taken in silence and, with the briefest of goodnights, the professor retired to his room. The sisters followed whispering.

Elvis stayed in the kitchen and helped clean up. Mrs. Waslowski hummed quietly to herself as she washed and Elvis dried the dishes. Elvis was about to go to her room to get ready to go to work at the bar when Mrs. Waslowski called her back.

"Have a cup of coffee with me. We might be able to manage half a biscuit with the fixin's. I would like your impression."

"We've been around Kate and Sarah too long, Mrs. W. We may not be finishing one another's lines but we share the same unspoken thoughts."

"He didn't need dinner that's for certain. He appears quite filled with himself," voiced Mrs. Waslowski.

"He's no Arthur."

"He's certainly an oddball. I fear I let down my guard when I interviewed him. Cracked under the credentials, it seems."

Elvis the optimist, swallowed the last drop of her coffee, finished her last bite of biscuit and offered her opinion.

"We all have different schedules and lives, so mostly we'll just see a light under his door. By the way I haven't told you, I'll soon be working full time at the bar. They're adding an addition.

 R. Wesley Clement

You'll have to come to the grand opening around Christmas time," adding as an afterthought, "Kate and Sarah too."

* * *

There never was a light under the door, but odd noises sometimes drifted from the professor's room, traveled throughout the upstairs, creeping out the twins in their sanctuary and wafted into Elvis's room. The sounds refused to descend the staircase and it was impossible to describe them accurately to Mrs. Waslowski.

"A low hum and a sound like you'd hear in your own head—" offered Kate.

"—if you ground your teeth at night," said Sarah.

The four ladies sat at the kitchen table one morning a full month into the tenancy of Quentin T. Spence.

"The Propisser—" snickered Kate getting down right daring in her language.

"—is a certified nutcase," judged Sarah.

"Arthur was easier," they announced in unison.

Mrs. Waslowski rose and returned with fresh-baked molasses cookies, offered as an apology for letting the man into their house.

"What's that word I hear with politicians all the time—vetted—yes. I should have vetted him better."

The coffee was hot and harsh. Perfect for the mood in the room, but the molasses cookies brought a comfort that seemed to calm the situation. Within a bite or two, the ladies were discussing what stores they might frequent today. The sisters pushed back their chairs and left the table to go up and assemble themselves, as they liked to describe their morning duties.

Elvis, who up to now had listened in silence, dunked a molasses cookie into her coffee, savored the melting flavor and washed it down with a long swallow like she was fortifying herself for a journey.

"I went to the library, went on the Internet and googled him."

Mrs. Waslowski who didn't know Google from gobble did just that, her cookie disappearing as her eyes widened.

"He is a professor, and he does work for the college like he says, but I couldn't find where he's ever spent more than a year anywhere. He's been all over the map, from Alaska to Florida. He spent a year in Iowa, and six months in Georgia. I couldn't find any real information, just a road map of movement. Something's not right with him, like the sisters said." Elvis closed her eyes.

"I remember one of my grandmothers had a speech she memorized for school. It described herself back then she told me. *Something wicked this way comes.*"

Mrs. Waslowski nodded. "We have to find a way to get him out of this house. I can't stand the stress. I'm an old woman."

CHAPTER TWENTY-FIVE

HAMMERS AND SAWS AND LOTS OF COFFEE

Sean immediately fell in love with Stella's idea, with the whole concept of expanding the bar to not only include the handicapped but offer a place to celebrate any small victories they might never get the opportunity to give voice to.

He thought back to when he was finally able to pull on a pair of long pants, the perspiration running along the sides of his ears, his breathing as loud and ragged as a ferry announcing its arrival across the waves. Remembering brought a smile to his lips and he raised his coffee mug to himself.

This is why I'm doing this. He silently toasted all the small victories taking place in a hundred different places.

The sounds this morning, a full month after Stella's surprise road trip to Sean's future, were hammers and skill saws, muffled chatter, the inevitable smell of dust, history and stale coffee brewed three hours earlier still on the burner. The game plan, blue prints and pulled permits dictated the order of construction.

Freddy had lent his architect to the effort. The warehouse with the exit on Union Street was stripped to the brick walls. A stage was being built that would allow Jacob and Elvis to perform in front of a hopefully larger audience. The first fifteen feet looking out from the stage would be free of tables and chairs, space for wheelchairs and any other conveyance needed to give the VIP treatment to greater Portland's physically challenged. Ten tables accessible to wheelchairs would fill the middle space.

A small card room or meeting room was emerging with studs already in place. The small furnace room with no direct exit would be Sean and Jacob's new office. A big screen TV, area for darts, his and her bathrooms and room for a slightly lowered pool table would complete the expansion. All liquor would still be served from the bar in the original space.

Freddy liked that idea.

"Finally some peace and quiet when I lay down my head." Sean, who was a big picture person, had already expanded the idea in his head to include a handicapped bus service that would pick up and deliver this new audience. He sat behind the bar now, calling various organizations who worked with or provided support in some way to anyone with a condition that would keep them out of the mainstream. He sipped on his own freshly brewed and dreamed the dream.

Cautious seemed the key word, which was the one consistent message emerging from various groups when Sean mentioned what would take place at a bar. *Baby steps,* he was urged. He didn't back down, though, explaining the need for social contact that reminded a person they still belonged to the human race. They could still laugh, sing, commiserate, argue, cuss and complain with the best of them. Dammit, they could do all this in a place designed to do all of the above.

Further, he reasoned, was the need for the man who has the means to stand on his own two feet to acknowledge his brothers, maybe gain a little perspective.

When he sat that day in the empty warehouse and heard Braden explain the settlement being offered by the insurance company, he was a little baffled. He had heard low, very low six figures being thrown about every time he visited his lawyer. This morning Braden announced half a million was the final offer.

"What changed their mind, Braden?"

     R. Wesley Clement

"The lady you live with. She made them an offer they couldn't refuse," grinned Braden.

Sean looked at the lady he lived with the same look that had asked the fateful question of an exercising beauty on the Back Bay, *how do you do that?*

"I numbed them with numbers," Stella said simply.

"What numbers would those be honey? I can work with these numbers. How did we get here?"

Freddy looked at this couple playfully probing one another, watching real love subtly overtake the room; his eyes were suddenly wet and he couldn't explain why.

"Well as you know, boys and girls, I'm a nurse. I get to see the beginning of the aftermath, lights flashing, screams and moans, relatives arriving or, in many cases, nobody claiming ownership. We keep stats on all this mayhem. I simply did the math and showed your insurance company how many of you there are in the greater Portland area and what needs they are going to be paying for the rest of these victims lives." She cleared her throat.

"I thought of you, Sean, how hard it is even with a support system. I saw how resilient you are and thought of how you always finished your runs stronger than when you began." Stella teared up but continued.

"I talked with some of the doctors who treat trauma victims long term, and the words *resilience* and *stress* popped up over and over. Some of them, it seems, are looking beyond pills and probing. They're reading the research that suggests socialization and focusing on the future, imagining what can be rather than what is. Bringing these people together, letting them challenge themselves to get back all they can, could save lots of money in mental health fees, pills, you name it." She looked at Sean's cousin and lawyer.

Catching the cue, Braden offered, "After I talked with Stella, listened really, I did my own math and showed the insurance company how they could save millions in billable hours and maybe raise the images of both lawyers and insurance companies in the process. I talked with my boss and got his perspective.

"Bottom line, lawyers don't get paid till the fat lady sings. Insurance companies need a better model than deny-deny-deny. They actually listened, hence here we stand in an empty warehouse, asking you, Sean, can you see your future, cousin?"

Freddy spoke for the first time. "You know, I am a businessman first, Sean, and if I didn't see how I could profit as well, we wouldn't be here. I did my math too and bringing life to this old building makes good business sense. I can offer very favorable terms, and I will do my part in bringing this place up to code."

Sean, his mind racing well ahead of the conversation, was thinking of his trip to Seattle and the five-year plan that emerged from those three days, simply nodded.

"Let's do this."

Jacob, who had been part of the Starbucks experience and was perhaps making his own mental road trip down memory lane, was even more emphatic, offering high fives and breaking into an old Beatles classic. *We can work it out*, he sang, *we can work it out.*

R. Wesley Clement

CHAPTER TWENTY-SIX

SQUEAKS AN' SQUAWKS

Quentin T. Spence checked his schedule for the day at the small table in his room. He did not shower in this house, preferring the privacy of a faculty facility which was seldom used. The bathroom of his youth was filled with painful recollections, every sense assaulted at one time or another. He still found himself at times looking deep into any mirror he might pass trying to find an emerging pimple that would provide ammunition for a verbal assault, though the antagonist was long gone from his life.

Quentin lived in half-light; he loved shadow lamps projecting a larger than life appearance on the walls and ceiling. A canvas tote lay open on the bed, toiletries, socks, underwear, a simple tee shirt and jeans. His iPad in its leather cover lying just beneath a red-and-white striped towel folded exactly four times from two directions.

The noise the ladies reported was in fact a small electric massaging tool that Quentin used to stimulate himself. Employing his scientific approach, he used the vibrating head to find the most sensitive parts of the human body—behind his ears seemed to rank near the top. Perhaps the added sound of the motor increasing in proximity to his ears added to the stimulation.

But nothing compared to the human encounters he involved himself with. The tool was mostly used as a simple massage to calm nerves that the three old women were frazzling.

Looking in the mirror, his unshaven face creating its own shadow, Quentin looked exactly the way he felt—menacing. He had continued taking dinner with the other "occupants," his dismissive term for the three old ladies he concluded were direct descendants of the witches in Macbeth. But he stopped eating breakfast with them after the first two weeks of their constant prodding and probing. Dinners would end soon as well.

I'll miss the cooking, he thought, *but not enough to abide those nasty sisters.*

He looked once more into the mirror as if looking directly into Elvis's room. *Those eyes that seem to take everything in and record it for all time. I'll miss those eyes.*

He had watched her perform, knew quite a lot about this special young lady, actually. *Perhaps too much to let her completely escape my presence.* He placed the little bottle he had received from his father in a bureau drawer beside a gleaming ten-inch needlelike implement encased in blue velvet. He picked it up turned its working end to the lamp, confirming its legitimacy and purpose, looked his mirrored-self straight in the face, then reluctantly returned it to the drawer.

He turned off the lamp, opened the door said goodbye to his possessions and muttered too low for anyone to hear, "Just another day at the office."

There was a light under the door directly across from him, the old ladies already cawing and jawing with one another.

Toil and trouble, Shakespeare's *Macbeth* entering his thoughts competing with his own *Book of Ruth: Quentin's truth.* He used the bathroom the tenants shared, but only to pee and that was done sitting down. He didn't need the add-on insult of splatter becoming a topic at the table, a complaint that had haunted him since childhood. He shivered as he thought of Mother Ruth.

　　　　　R. Wesley Clement

Shoes in hand, tote on his shoulder, he edged quietly toward the stairs. No light exited Elvis's room. The professor couldn't help himself; he touched the doorknob, turning it just enough to electrify his imagination. Suddenly in his mind he was a well-placed picture on her bureau observing the comings and goings, the dressings and undressings, watching her from within her own mirror.

He sighed, shifted his shoes to his other hand, unconsciously touching himself, and descended to the exit, ignoring the smell of coffee already signaling a new day, a fresh start.

Quentin didn't need coffee to signal new days or fresh starts, his past actions, like the wafting aroma reaching his nostrils, had dictated new beginnings periodically for the past twenty years. He closed the front door. Another sigh of resignation escaped his lips as he remembered his thirteenth year and all that followed.

A daily message mentally created during the worst of it entered his thoughts as if posted on the refrigerator door: *Avoid the avoidable, just watch and wait. Opportunity raises itself from despair. Not my problem, is it?*

* * *

Three ladies sat at the table observing the bottom of their first cup of the day. Mrs. Waslowski had bacon frying, scrambled eggs scrambling, toast toasting and a resupply of Seattle's number five brewing when a platter plummeted. The crash brought everyone's attention to Mrs. Waslowski, her arms still stretched up toward the top shelf of the cupboard.

"Oh dear—" exclaimed Kate.

"—are you injured?" cried Sarah.

Elvis was already across the kitchen taking a visibly shaken Mrs. Waslowski into her arms. "Let me serve you this morning. Sit down. I'll clean this up."

Thirty minutes later, breakfast was finished and the two sisters were offering up their latest complaint of the Propisser like a danish washed down with a bold brew.

"He's too quiet—"

"—to be a real person."

"He seeps through the walls—"

"—like that dreaded grinding sound."

Elvis cleared her throat. "I thought I heard him at my door this morning, I know he paused there. I swear my doorknob turned." The three ladies all shared the same shiver with widened eyes and hugged themselves.

"He's not a professor. He's a lecturer," she continued, sharing what she'd learned of his past, "It's a difference of stature from what I read. Apparently he really does know his subject matter. That's what allows him to move around so much, I guess."

The three ladies seemed content to let the usually quiet young lady keep the conversation moving. "I'm sure he's just an odd duck, and we're letting our imaginations run. I suggest we just forget about him. He's not even joining us in the morning anymore. Here's to that." Elvis raised her coffee mug as if she were toasting patrons at the bar.

The two sisters excused themselves, not thoroughly convinced, muttering all the way up the stairs about students they had taught who later turned out to be robbers or in one case a stone cold killer.

Mrs. Waslowski, an avid TV watcher, asked Elvis to join her in the living room. "There's something I want you to see." She turned on the TV, controlled the controller, found the recorded program and soon the two were watching a reality show. "You could do this, Elvis. This could be you."

Elvis swallowed her last bite of cookie, rose and hugged Mrs. Waslowski.

CHAPTER TWENTY-SEVEN

POLLY WANT A CRACKER

The cat in the hatch as Jacob dubbed him was still aboard, but never asking permission to board. Jacob was talking to the cat these days, even naming it Polly, not a talking parrot but still riding his shoulders when he exercised. This morning, he was asking Polly how she'd feel about sharing their morning time with a good friend.

"I know you'd like her Polly. She won't dominate our conversations. She's actually a really good listener."

Polly raised her tail as if testing the wind direction but offered no opinion. She moved silently around the deck as if staking her territory, not once glancing to the cabin below.

Jacob took that as a yes. Until he started getting sailing lessons, his time with Elvis would mostly be below deck. *At least, I hope so,* he thought.

"I'm going to ask her tonight, after we finish our show," he told Polly.

Weather was coming in, the sun slowly diminishing, the water quiet but turning one of those fifty shades of gray, like the book everyone was discussing at the bar. Jacob smiled.

"I haven't room for all those devices below deck anyway. I guess you'll have to help me win her over Polly. Just don't dominate the conversation."

⸻

The expansion was half-complete, and donors and collaborators were taking up most of Sean's time these days. Jacob, in running garb, climbed their hilly driveway and let himself in through the garage.

"Good morning, you two. Stella, are you going to run with me? I jogged here from the boat and, if you haven't run yet, maybe I could ask your opinion about a bold step I'm thinking of taking."

Sean answered first with a wry smile. "So it's Stella you're turning to these days, is it? I remember, back in the day, when you savored my take on things."

"Get over it, Sean," said Stella. "You're out of the running loop these days. You're more like chair-man of the bored," She finished, brokering no pity, humor being Sean's preferred prescription for his situation.

Both Sean and Jacob cackled. "Now that's an emergency room nurse right there, Jacob. All business and no sympathy for the afflicted." He puckered his lips sadly.

"Poor baby, it wasn't sympathy you were seeking an hour ago."

Both men roared, Jacob reddening slightly.

"That's kind of what I wanted to discuss with you—not you!" he stammered as Stella lifted an eyebrow. "Elvis. I want you to advise me in your best emergency room nurse bedside manner about Elvis."

Stella laughed this time. "Just let me get into my sneakers I think I know an old home remedy that just might do the trick."

* * *

Word had gotten out in the Old Port and the surrounding area about the direction *Troubled Waters* was moving. Several men and one woman, all in wheelchairs, sat nursing a beer at one of the tables. They didn't know one another when they arrived but now were animatedly swapping horror stories of injury, ignorance and isolation. Sean paddled over.

　　　R. Wesley Clement

"Thanks for coming in. My name is Sean," and with a big grin announced, "I'm a wheel-a-holic…. You hooked on that game show too? … Give me ten steps like A.A. gets and I'll rule the world."

The woman grabbing the circular metal wheel she used to propel herself, broke into song, parodying the summer hit, *It's All About The Bass,* inserting the word *Brass,* then laughing at her cleverness.

"I have had more fun in the last two hours, than since I don't know when," a guy introduced as Jimmy said, "and I'm still nursing my first beer. This place is awesome."

"Yeah well, maybe you might want to kiss a different nurse or get some take out when you leave," Sean kidded. "I gotta make a living you know." The table roared.

Freddy, watching from his stool, observed new people who would become regulars having a good time. He turned his head to study Jacob and Elvis huddled closely, discussing their music.

Gonna be a lot of new regulars. This is a whole new business model is what this is, he mused. He didn't notice the woman at the other end of the bar until she walked by him to the toilet. He noticed her then, though. He watched her return to her stool, mid-forties he judged, wounded, swaying slightly.

Without exchanging a single pleasantry, the lady whose body language indicated one seeking the privacy of a phone booth, huddled talking to her beer and her beer only. Freddy was smitten.

Now there's a building that is begging for renovation. I have reasonable rates. Freddy stayed with his Bud Light buddies for a longer time tonight leaving the Irishman Jameson to feign for himself. When it became clear that, for tonight at least, this was a private call the lady was making, Freddy decided he needed to have a conversation himself with good old Jameson. *But if she comes in again …*

Stella stopped in before leaving for work and Sean introduced her to his new circle of friends.

"Tonight is confirmation for me, thanks to you babe." He toasted his wife in their little booth. "Two months from now, Jacob and Elvis will have a stage to perform on. We'll have increased capacity six times over. I even found a guy, Jimmy, to begin an exercise program here in the mornings and maybe including the Back Bay when the weather's good."

"So how do I get rewarded for all this good stuff entering your life?" She took Sean's hand.

"How about we expand on that topic you brought up a while back. You remember, when I came home from that trip to Seattle?" He smiled, *"Energy into the effort* is what I remember you saying."

Stella's eyes teared up. "Sean, you just recited the lines I've been waiting to hear, and not just because I would like to have a baby. It means you've healed yourself. I knew you'd never want a kid until you believed in our future." She wiped her eyes with a bar napkin and hugged her man.

Meanwhile Jacob was also discussing the future with Elvis.

"I'm not real good at talking, Elvis. Maybe I should be singing this," he kidded, but his serious eyes betrayed him. He plunged into the ocean of uncertainty, no life vest in sight. "You've met Polly, well, we've been discussing how we'd like to learn to sail that house we live on. This is the perfect season too. Tourists are pretty much gone, and we'll have the harbor to ourselves. I haven't even gotten out to one of those islands yet."

He hesitated another moment then jumped in with both feet.

"So I guess I'm asking you to join me in uncharted waters Elvis. I'm asking you to come live on the boat." Not waiting for what might be a *no thanks Jacob,* he continued, "Freddy says he's leaving it in the water this winter anyway. And it has heat. You've used the shower in the parking garage. It's decent. I'm rambling on like a summer storm approaching." He took both her hands in his. "Bottom line, lifeline here, I love you Elvis. You make my heart sing."

Elvis the listener, the loner, the girl with no family, decided to speak to Jacob in the best way she knew how. She cleared her throat and broke into song; her own heartfelt lyrics and melody carrying the message.

 R. Wesley Clement

* * *

Two nights later, Elvis sat at the dinner table, unusually quiet. The two sisters had already gone to their room. The professor, a hit or miss dinner guest these days, was still out. Elvis rose to help Mrs. Waslowski with the dishes.

"What's wrong, Elvis? You barely touched your dinner."

Elvis, slowly running a dish rag under the faucet, struggled for the words.

"How can I be so happy and sad at the same time? You've done so much for me. I feel I might be letting you down. I won't be taking everything at first, not that I have much. You've met Jacob. Do you think I'm being hasty? I've only known him a short time, but it seems right."

"Let's sit back down dear." Mrs. Waslowski offered Elvis a molasses cookie and a cup of coffee. "When my husband was alive, we always had our talks with cookies and coffee." She smiled at Elvis. "You see, besides tasting good, they serve as a way to hesitate with an answer. Let's just enjoy a bite and it will allow us to think about what you need to say." She chuckled. "You're not supposed to talk with your mouth full anyway."

Elvis nodded her head. Mrs. W. had good common sense. She bit into a cookie and continued to listen.

"From my perspective, from my view of you, Elvis, I think you probably already know Jacob better than he knows himself." She took a sip of coffee, looking Elvis straight in the eye. "I watched you with Arthur, your caring ways and the insights you brought to that relationship. You kept Arthur laughing. He seemed to enjoy himself more with you than at any time he was with us. You were not just a caregiver; you were Arthur's friend."

She swallowed a bite of cookie. "You're Jacob's friend now, and he's a wise young man to recognize what he's found in you." One last sip ended the thinking required to ease Elvis' mind. "Our family will miss your energy and your kindness and your music. I won't tell the sisters. That's up to you to do."

Wednesday night was always pasta night, a garden salad and garlic bread riding shot gun. And Jell-O for dessert.

"I was just thinking of Arthur today and Jell-O popped into my mind," announced Mrs. Waslowski. The ladies all got a kick out of that, and Arthur stories accompanied dessert.

It was late September and two days of gorgeous fall weather had encouraged the opening of windows throughout the house. The kitchen curtains rustled as if they knew they might be breathing their last fresh air till spring, ebbing and flowing like the sea just a half mile away.

Professor Spence came down the stairs with a cross look on his face.

"Who entered my room and opened my window? I smelled it first. My own unique smells are thoroughly compromised. I have made it clear no one should darken my doorway. I say this in the kindest way possible, but my meaning is clear."

"I apologize Professor. Mrs. W. asked me to open the upstairs windows and I opened mine. Sarah and Kate thought it was a great idea as well. I knocked, I'm truly sorry. I didn't mean any harm," said Elvis sincerely.

"Harrumph." There was a long pause, and he gave one of those odd looks to Elvis. His cheeks flushed. "Well-well, no harm done I guess," he stammered. "I'm just a very private person." He gave that odd look again. "You're forgiven, Elvis."

The sisters traded glances. Mrs. Waslowski apologized as well and began serving dinner.

The professor gagged on his garlic bread, turning various shades of red, plum and ashen gray when Elvis told the table she would be leaving the family. The professor gargled with water, trying to free the obstruction. Finally gaining his feet, he left the table with the appearance of a weeble that warbles and might just fall down. They heard him stumble up the stairs and slam his door.

The ladies sat in subdued and stunned silence, finishing their meals, not taking dessert.

"Arthur wouldn't want to be part of this spectacle," uttered a bewildered Mrs. Waslowski. After genuine hugs and tears all around with the promise of visits and Elvis inviting the three ladies to the grand opening of the expansion of the bar, the two sisters went to their rooms remarking that they might need a rare evening toddy to get to sleep tonight.

Elvis and Mrs. Waslowski continued to sit in the oncoming darkness, the older woman finally taking the lead.

"If you've time before you need to leave, let me teach you the game of cribbage. My husband and I had long conversations over cribbage if you take my meaning."

Elvis nodded her head "My Grandmother's taught me cribbage, but I'd love to play."

I would love to gain a little insight into what had happened in kitchen earlier.

"I'll break out the board and brew us a pot of clear thinking."

* * *

The professor lay atop his bed, a sheet covering one foot, the shade and window that had been raised to allow airflow still a crime scene offering a dark portal for his thoughts to escape. The little circular pull on the shade moved back and forth in the evening breeze like a metronome.

The professor was a sequential thinker whose lectures were plodding footsteps of sameness, lectures that lulled his students into comatose attention. He could not find a single footstep of logic to explain what had happened at dinner. He was in a full sweat, his heart thumping loudly in his chest. There seemed to be nothing to grasp onto. What was this girl doing to him? He had planned to leave this house, but on his own terms. Elvis was suddenly in charge.

As he lay there, still overheated, the *way before* entered his head, the *way-way before*. He pleasured himself briefly, disjointed thoughts like counting sheep filling his mind and fell fast asleep. When he awoke, hearing voices outside his window, the professor pulled the closed shade slightly to the side and watched Elvis leave the building. He heard the sisters and Elvis saying goodbye.

Unfinished business. Elvis was unfinished business. *I'm not saying goodbye just yet.*

He looked into the mirror and scolded himself.

"You said you were done with all that after the mess in Savannah, nearly caught if not for your quick wits and a drug-induced lack of memory." Quentin moved to the bed and lay down, the memory of that incident and a dozen other *thrills of a life time,* as he termed them, bringing on an erection.

He thought back to his first encounter. That first time and the simplicity of it, the satisfaction it brought, even months after, was repeated twice more during his college years. He closed his eyes remembering, the images in his head moving to his physical self and he emptied himself into a washcloth as a bright acne-free young man entering Middlebury College for the first time, emerged on stage in his mind.

CHAPTER TWENTY-EIGHT

CAPTAIN JACK

September ended with a heat wave, shirts removed in backyards, smoke from barbecues signaling it ain't over till the north wind sings. Beachgoers from as far north as Bingham and Jackman made a weekend of it, making the three-hour trek. Knowing sun in the north didn't always hold up at the beach, their back-up plan included L.L. Bean in Freeport, or further south, the Maine Mall in Portland.

If the weather held, they could beach it, cruise the Old Port for dinner and frequent the many bars in the area. A last in-your-face hurrah before a string of holidays cleverly diverted your attention from the relentless cold to come.

Troubled Waters was humming on a busy Saturday night. Elvis would be moving onto the boat in the morning, she had spent several nights sharing a berth with Jacob, loving the closeness and the rocking motion that for some reason raised the memory of being in her crib looking up at her Elvis Presley mobile.

I guess Jacob has become the man who will watch over me. She smiled, looking at her redwood forest singing Billy Joel's *Captain Jack* to a room filled with buzzing bees.

One man was listening closely and wandered over to put money in the jar. Jacob thanked him and the man introduced himself.

"I thought I ought to offer a tithe to my church of choice since you just sang my confession. People call me Captain Jack."

Jacob smiled, not knowing what to say, shook his hand and turned his attention to Elvis roaming the room, filling beer glasses and selling shots.

"I really am, well once was, a captain. I joined the merchant marine in 1955 and got my captain's license a dozen years later. I captained boats through the Panama Canal—through the area that has had all the recent pirate attention all around the world." He sipped his beer quietly, watching for a reaction from Jacob.

"Freddy has taken me on down at Chandlers Wharf, taking over your mate's job in security." He motioned to Elvis who arrived with a pitcher and the little notebook she carried where she jotted down the patron's name and added it to their tab.

"I've seen you both down there on that 42-footer. Nice boat. Do you know how to sail her?"

"We actually haven't," Jacob said. "I'd love to learn, though. I've been reading some manuals, just haven't had the time really."

"Casco Bay offers some really pretty islands to explore, some gems really," he said. "Little Diamond and Great Diamond just offshore and further out Jewell Island. There are light houses, forts, a whole history lesson. I'd be interested in giving you two the tour. Freddy said he'd like to go to some of the places he hasn't been by in years, see if his purchase is seaworthy."

Jacob had signaled Elvis over and she heard the ending. They looked at one another.

"Before you decide, let me give you a quick tour of who I used to be, who I became and who I am today. I make no promises about tomorrow, but tonight's looking hopeful." He set down his beer glass, pointing to it. "That's mostly a prop these days, never really was a beer drinker." He picked it up and gazed into it as if the glass and its contents held the story.

"I had some money once, captained some very prominent people, made some insider information moves, married a great gal, had two kids, both gems themselves." He sighed looking inward.

"That was the used to be." He held up a finger, never letting go of the glass.

Like waves crashing over protruding rock, he told of his wrecked life. "Demon rum poured endlessly, drunk straight from the bottle toward the end. A nearly naked lifestyle offered up in ports around the world, girls passed around like shrimp on a platter." He looked at Elvis then lowered his eyes.

"Even through all that, I was still steady as she goes as a captain. One night we were attempting a tricky maneuver to enter a shallow cove. My assistant called me for advice but I was passed out below. He crashed a 150-foot yacht, though I was held responsible and lost everything I knew to be important. I wasn't at the controls but it was completely my fault." He looked straight at the two, reasserting his guilt.

"Couldn't find a ship after that, kept drinking though, bumming sea rides from captains I had known, and regaling the past. I fell further and further below sea level, would have drowned if not for falling deathly ill and diagnosed with pancreatic cancer, almost always a death knell." He held up two fingers. "That was who I became."

Then, suddenly, a smile, like the sun emerging after a damaging storm. "Who I am today can all be attributed to a nurse I met when I was at death's door." He stood suddenly. "Got to use the john, saving the new best-for-last anyway."

Jacob looked at Elvis with a questioning rise of his eyebrows.

"You're the one who seems able to divine a person's intentions. What do you make of this Captain Jack?"

"I like him. Add to that Freddy's inclination to check the background of anyone he's going to employ. I think he might become a good friend. I would love to see some of those islands. I used to live on one you know. Maybe Captain Jack can take me home."

Captain Jack didn't have to finish his story, when he returned, Elvis using Mrs. Waslowski's term regarding the professor simply announced, "You've been vetted Captain Jack. So when do we sail?" They all shook hands.

"I do want to finish my story sometime, turns out it's the best part, but I'll leave you two alone. Stop by my gate at the wharf, and we'll make plans. Best time of year to sail, at least for another month." He dropped a five-dollar bill in the jar and left his only beer of the night sitting there half full, or half empty—depending on your approach to life.

* * *

"Permission to board sir," asked a smiling Elvis who from somewhere had come up with a sailor's cap. She stood at attention saluting.

Polly saw her first but chose to ignore the request. Jacob looked down at his new shipmate framing the picture in his mind. *I'm going to have to get a camera or one of those fancy phones.*

"Permission granted. Did Stan give you one of his old sailor hats? He's a trip that guy!"

"Would you believe one of my grandmothers spent a short if not happy time in the navy in some place called Corpus Christie, in Texas?" Elvis went below for a cup of coffee.

"Bring that coffee up here, sounds like a great story to start our voyage."

Sitting on a bench seat that dominated twelve feet on the port side of the boat open to the elements, Elvis held her coffee in one hand and twirled the white sailor cap in her other, spinning up a piece of her past. Polly and Jacob both seemed ready for the story.

"When I struck out on my own shortly after grandmother one passed away, grandmother Elvira gave me her only memory of when she was about my age.

"'Everyone isn't your enemy,' she told me, I've had many opportunities to clean up my act over the years. What my sister and I had with you is the closest I can remember to being happy. Take this hat to remind you that you can sail the world but finding

R. Wesley Clement

happiness will come from in here. She touched her heart then she grabbed my hand.'"

Elvis stood up, downed the remaining coffee. "I'm going for a refill. Want one?" When she emerged, she handed Jacob his coffee and a beautifully crafted necklace, then returned to her seat.

Elvis pointed to the necklace in Jacob's hand. "Grandmother went into her room and returned with that necklace. She asked me to keep it but not wear it until I was settled in my head and happy in my heart." Elvis stood looked Jacob in the eye. "Would you do the honors, sir," she asked.

Polly, sensing this act was about to be a threesome, watched as Jacob set his coffee down, rose and placed the necklace where he hoped it would stay forever. They hugged and fell into one another, completing a dance step when the boat and the wave prompting it, as if reacting to the emotion of the moment, signaled its approval. Polly offered no opinion on the matter.

Stan who was doing his tour of the moorings watched from a short distance and smiled. *Love happy endings. That might make two,* he thought.

Polly, knowing when to say something, suddenly perched on Elvis's lap and began purring softly. Jacob took offense and kiddingly chided the cat.

"Hey Polly, how come you've never spoken to me?"

"We girls have to stick together, isn't that right Polly?"

Polly looked at Jacob, cocking her head as if telling him to just get over it.

CHAPTER TWENTY-NINE

CASCO BAY
AND BEYOND

The early autumn of 2014 had been particularly warm and calm. Jacob and Elvis were spending a Wednesday morning drinking coffee, watching the sun paint the water as wisps of vapor were sucked skyward. They were trying to debate the predisposition of a prowling Polly.

"She does what she does because she's a woman, simple as that. I have never been able to figure them out," said Jacob.

Elvis, shrouded in a blanket on this first day of October, offered no witty repartee. "I grew up with women. Only women. And as much as I'd love to, I can't fault your thinking."

At that moment Captain Jack appeared and his experience with felines was questioned. He sipped the offered brew and stated simply, "I have no use for cats. Loved dogs as a kid, though. I haven't really spent a lot of thought on the subject, I'll admit."

Polly moved as far away from Captain Jack as close quarters allowed. Elvis watched and laughed. "She understands every word, I swear."

Captain Jack checked his watch. "It's nine thirty now. I checked the forecast before I left the apartment. Going to get up to 74 degrees today, wind is coming out of the east-southeast at 3.5 knots. Perfect day for an easy sail.

R. Wesley Clement

"Freddy should be here anytime, I'm just going to check fuel and test the instruments. We'll sail if there's enough wind, motor if not. This will be hands-on learning for both of you. I'll ask for your help, and when we get underway let you learn how everything works in tandem."

Freddy arrived in outlandish seafaring garb. He looked like he belonged on *Love Boat.*

No one laughed louder than Freddy himself as the comments were cast. "Get me to sea quickly, Captain. I may need to drown myself," he laughed.

Then, simple instructions were given.

"Before we go anywhere, I'll explain terms like port and starboard since we're a team with only one captain." He smiled. "I'll show you two basic knots to do and two basic nots-to-do, and, no, I didn't stutter." Everyone laughed. "Please pay attention for the next hour, and we'll get underway."

When Captain Jack started the engine, Jacob was in the bow ready to bring the mooring line aboard. Elvis was awaiting orders to do the same in the stern. The small triangular sail called a burgee was blowing in the direction of the wind. The mainsail had been raised, though not completely, and a working jib was attached and ready to be pulled aloft on the captain's orders. Chandlers Wharf was just a short distance from Little Diamond. That would be the first leg of their sail.

Captain Jack was a full-time teacher for the day, explaining the buoy system and the meaning of red and green lights on the markers. "It's like a road system in a way. Instead of staying between the white lines, you use the buoys. By the way, you'll find a boat doesn't turn in an arc like a car. It pivots on a point."

Sailing 101 day one was a huge success. They sailed past Little Diamond, skirted Great Diamond, hung a right, keeping Long Island on their port side. They stopped on Peaks Island and had a late afternoon lunch at *The Cockeyed Gull.*

———

The fall colors were beginning to claim ownership of every piece of rock that offered life.

"In my experience," said Captain Jack, looking out at the beauty, "viewing the islands from the water gives you a perspective you just can't get landside."

The return trip was a shorter leg with the sun racing them to see who would give up on first.

"We have to be at the bar by seven thirty," said Jacob. "Sean and Shellee are holding down the fort. Sorry to have to run, but Elvis and I need to clean up." They grabbed their garb and headed for the shower.

"I'll batten down the hatches. You'll see me later anyway. I haven't completed my trip around my life yet. Freddy, will you assist me?"

* * *

Sean was telling a funny story at the bar while a group of wheelies at a table hollered that they wanted to hear the joke as well. He interrupted his story long enough to shout out, "Wait your turn. You get cut no slack in here. You know that."

The table cheered. They loved Sean. He had given them their nights back and the respect that allowed being chided and scolded in good fun.

Jacob went behind the bar to check on quantities.

The bar erupted with laughter and after getting a series of high fives, Sean turned and welcomed his tree in the forest.

"Well Mr. Redwood, it seems you gained a little autumn color out there on the water."

"What a beautiful day, Sean. You and Stella will have to go next time. It was awesome, man." Jacob watched Elvis begin her round of tables, all the while chatting away with Shellee as they worked the room. "Captain Jack is the real deal. I could tie you up in knots right now that I couldn't even name this morning."

"I'll leave that to Stella thank you very much."

The tone of the evening was set: a warm autumn evening, successful sail or beach day, delightful dinner, hump day reached. It seemed there was a smile on every face.

By nine thirty, the bar was loosened up, lubricated and laughing. It was the perfect time to break into song. Elvis had not merely been a watcher on the water, she had composed a song she intended to sing to Jacob tonight with the regulars understanding the closeness of the two. The audience had hushed when Elvis took the mike.

"You haven't heard this before," she announced to the audience and Jacob. "The music will come later. Tonight, just listen to the words. It goes like this."

> *It's not often that you find one*
> *As rare as diamonds in the sand*
> *But when you gaze on open water*
> *You realize such day might be at hand*
> *Today totally filled my senses*
> *Autumn colors filled my eyes*
> *Seabirds offered up suggestions*
> *Sails flapped with breathless sighs*
>
> *Looking starboard I see my Jacob*
> *He fills my sense of taste and smell*
> *Can't wait to touch and hold him*
> *I'm complete and all is well*

After lowering the mike she finished with "I love you Jacob."

The audience put their hands together. There was no hooting or hollering; they knew they had witnessed a special moment—bar napkins all around.

At the end of the bar, one patron was even more touched. He sat there feeling he had been right all along. A man whose own senses seemed to be on alert twenty-four-seven had sensed that there was a reason he was attracted to the girl in the rooming house. *My god, we're soul mates.*

He stumbled from the bar, not ready to reintroduce himself. He had lines to rehearse, a methodology different from the one he had previously used to prepare. He was in love without knowing what love even means.

When Elvis moved out, so did the professor. He now inhabited a room in a motel on route one in Scarborough. He drove slowly, bombarded with data and stimuli, his mind racing but resolve cementing itself, stiffening his entire body. He was a mannequin of mobility.

He entered his room lit the lamp and removed his disguise. Moving immediately to the cheap set of drawers, complete with a Gideon's bible, he lifted the velvet covered case and opened it, the stainless syringe holding the disposable needle gleaming in the lamplight. Quentin had never used it. He'd studied the effects the little bottle of liquid might provide but timing was everything.

Perhaps it's time. I'll need to practice once though. For Elvis, everything has to be perfect.

 R. Wesley Clement

CHAPTER THIRTY

A MONTH OF TYING KNOTS

Nights were cooling down; sweaters and light jackets, dusted off and donned. Tourists were dwindling, becoming sparse as November would be rearing its head at the end of the week. Halloween would be crazy this year, landing on a Saturday.

Sailing had continued. Freddy so impressed he decided the captain might be more valuable showing prospective buyers some of his properties from the water. Jacob and Elvis quickly agreed when Freddy-the-businessman offered to reduce their rent a certain dollar amount with each voyage offered to his clients.

Sean and Stella, the captain and his fiancée, Freddy, Stan, and Jacob and Elvis taking turns at the tiller for their first voyage. Captain Jack had spent the month as teacher in the floating classroom, quizzing, challenging and offering a vocabulary of nautical terms, and at least fifty ways to knot your lover.

Captain Jack finally finished his own back story, introducing the nurse who had nursed his soul and healed his heart. The weird part was that Stella knew the fifty-five-year-old nurse. She'd worked with her on occasion. Stan knew her too; she was his sister. Ebony was just that, dark and strong, a rare wood indeed. When the captain and his new first mate boarded, there were hugs and greetings of surprise all around.

Elvis looked on in wonder. *What a small world it is. Maybe my mother might find me yet.* Jacob took her hand and looked at her quizzically.

"Just wishing and hoping," she said.

The remaining foliage in the landscape of the shore was dressed in muted browns and offered something closer to a black and white snapshot than the Kodachrome of just a short month ago.

They were all dressed in colorful sweaters and jackets; their bright smiles matching the cloud color. Watch caps kept the wind at bay, the sun offering light but a lot less heat. Captain Jack took over the controls and fired up the engine as they moored on Peaks Island.

Lunch was delicious with everyone ordering something from the sea. Today was special. New found friends, fresh sea food followed by fresh blueberry cobbler and vanilla ice cream, bringing groans from everyone. Laughing like fools all, Jacob showed his back, and Sean boarded for the trip back.

The foliage might have passed its peak, but the new colors of fall were definitely still in vogue in the Old Port. During the last week of October, for four days, a harvest celebration took place on the waterfront.

Stella pushed Sean's wheelchair past a flotilla of colorful tents that featured cuisine from around the world. The smell of fresh bread and pastries rose into the crisp-as-an-apple air. Demonstrations of various cooking techniques, along with delicious proof they work, were available.

Braden was carrying his son in front of him in a baby bag.

"Hey Sean. Maybe Jacob could use one of these with you." When Sean's reply took flight, Braden put his hands over his son's ears. "Son, your daddy's cousin doesn't really expect me to do that, he's just having fun."

While Braden's wife chatted with Stella, the men talked about the expansion, which was coming along nicely.

"We're going to open the room even though it's not finished," said Sean. "The work is done during the daytime anyway, and

R. Wesley Clement

it's all finish work. We're going to open for Halloween with a big costume party."

"Sounds like fun. My wife and I have played about all the cribbage I care to. You might not recognize us, Sean, but we'll be there." A further thought then. "Actually, you will probably recognize us if you've been paying attention.

* * *

Halloween, Halloween, oh what crazy things are seen.
Witches' hats, coal black cats, Halloween.
Troubled Waters is hosting a Halloween costume ball.
Come dressed as your favorite character, stay in character and win a door prize.

* * *

Stella dressed as Cruella De Ville, the wicked lady in Disney's classic. She even had a stuffed Dalmatian hanging from her belt. Stella wouldn't be drinking, though; she was with child.

Sean, dressed as the Black Knight from *Monty Python And The Holy Grail* had placed a hobby horse head on the end of a skateboard and was even lower to the ground than his usual means of travel. A goodly number of costumed creatures lurking close to the ground tested the new roomy expansion. Sean and Jacob escaped to the new office for just a moment and high fived their effort.

"Stella deserves the credit. She knows me better than I know myself."

"We'll have to plan a way to thank her," said Jacob with a nod. He was dressed as a giant redwood with painted cardboard surrounding his girth and a crown of evergreen boughs completing his effort. His arms protruded from holes in the cardboard, giving him freedom to raise his mug.

"Don't drip tree pollen over everyone tonight, Jacob and get them sneezing. They'll blow their cover."

Both men laughed, shook hands and returned to the party.

Elvis was dressed as Elvis Presley in a fitted one-piece bodysuit offering the only clue to her gender.

Freddy came dressed as a loan shark with a gangsta fedora and glued-on mustache.

Captain and Ebony were dressed as salt and pepper shakers.

Braden and his date, let's assume it was his wife, were unrecognizable as zombies, costumes that reflected the lifestyle they'd been living since their baby boy arrived, denying them sleep. When Sean approached them, Braden uttered in a zombie voice, "Told you you'd recognize us.".

The night was star-filled. Boys and girls rang doorbells and filled candy bags on every street, their breath beginning to appear by nine o'clock. Portland's finest, on alert for pranks, prowlers and things that go bump in the night walked the Old Port laughing at all the crazy getups.

Professor Quentin T. Spence in his slime green costume with a matching mask hiding his face appeared as if from the book itself. Gollum had come to life, no longer lurking in an underground cavern fed by a river. Tonight he entered a different body of water—*Troubled Waters.*

When he'd read the details posted on the bar door a week ago he realized opportunity was knocking once again. Tonight a trial run and, if successful, his rendezvous with Elvis before the snow flies.

He had been in the bar a total of three times previously, wearing a wig, fake beard and padded oversize suit. He had avoided being recognized by Elvis. During those visits he noticed a good looking woman of around forty, always on the same stool, always seemingly lost in her own thoughts, swaying just a bit when going to the single toilet. The three times he'd seen her, she was fending off a man who seemed to be a regular, a regular pest at any rate.

She was here again tonight and not in costume. Seemed like she was here for a long time, not a good time. Gollum who pursued Bilbo Baggins in the quest of the ring would attempt a practice run tonight. So much for the promise he'd made when moving to Maine. He recalled a line from a biblical passage in King James.

'Touch not; taste not, handle not.' Where's the fun in that?

With the vote by raised hands taking place at midnight, Sean was the easy winner. He had pestered people all night long, hitting them lightly on the legs and thighs with the rubber sword he wielded, all the while challenging them to "Stay and fight like a man."

Interestingly, Gollum was a close second as he seemed always in character, slinking and sliding in the shadows. When his name was called, he slunk completely out of view and left the bar. He went to his car and got out of his costume. The woman was still at the bar when he left. He lurked once more just across from the bar, waiting for the lady to exit. She finally navigated the exit. The man who always seemed intent on offering her a ride was left standing in the doorway, a lone shark rather than a loan shark.

Quentin watched and listened, the only sound a distant siren and the clacking of her high heels on cobblestone, in the distance, light laughter but too far away to cause harm. He followed at a distance and when she suddenly took several steps into a darkened doorway perhaps to void her vodka, he was on her immediately, offering a kind word and a grip.

Squeezing her arm as he raised her slumping form, he took attention away from the pin prick of pain even now entering her bloodstream. She would remain lucid enough to be guided without complaint to his vehicle.

"Come my precious," he said aloud.

CHAPTER THIRTY-ONE

IF IT WALKS LIKE A DUCK

Parking is never easy in the Old Port. Free parking is an endangered species and no parked car goes unnoticed for very long. The blue Toyota Corolla was observed by an employee on the morning of November 1, but given the level of revelry from the night before, allowed some slack. Besides, it was Sunday.

Bright and early Monday morning, Officer Gary Malbon was called with the complaint. The car was registered in the state of Ohio; the tag not due to run out until June 2015. The officer continued his foot patrol after a walk around the car and called it in, breathing into his hands to keep them warm. An hour later, he was on base at the *Home Plate* sliding a piece of toast through the remains of a hearty breakfast.

His phone vibrated, and he had a name and an out-of-state address. No wants, no warrants. "Check the location again. If it's still there, we'll have it towed." With those orders in mind, Officer Malbon had a third cup of coffee, razzed the regulars, popped in to pee and continued his rounds.

He got back to the area around nine thirty, the day warming nicely, the Old Port stretching and yawning, sun beginning to peek into windows. The car was parked in an overflow lot owned by the Portland Regency Hotel on Silver Street. Without a reason,

R. Wesley Clement

but curious, Officer Malbon entered the lobby of the hotel and approached the front desk.

"Who called in about the car in the lot?"

"Good morning officer, that would have been me; though I didn't find it, our security guy did. Just a minute I'll call him in. Say, if you'd like a cup of coffee, help yourself from that silver urn over there."

Officer Malbon took a seat near the window in a very comfortable chair and waited. That was what more than half of every work day entailed—waiting. This morning, it was a short wait as a small fat man approached in a dark blue mid-weight jacket, his name pinned on the right side. It seemed Darryl Winslow would be the source that ended this morning's wait.

"Good morning, Darryl."

"How did you know my name?"

Officer Malbon gave him a look that shouted, *Ahhh, Yuh Think?* Darryl looked down at his name tag and reddened.

"Anyway, I found the car. Yesterday, actually. I asked the night shift guy who comes on at eleven. He said he's seen the car there every night for a while now, but nobody had complained and it was always gone every morning by the time his shift was over."

"Till now," Officer Malbon said.

"What?"

Officer Malbon took a deep sigh. "No one complained TILL NOW, Darryl. Anyone ever see the driver coming or going on one of those every nights?"

"Not alive, no."

"So a dead person saw the driver?" deadpanned Officer Malbon.

Still not catching the ebb and flow of this conversation, Darryl played what the officer said on mental rewind, until a wave submerged him, and he finally got the drift.

Redder still, he said, "No, it's on tape from three nights ago."

"Wow, that's good police work, Darryl. Whose idea?"

"What idea?"

Officer Malbon was dying inside, about to throw a who's-on- first into the mix, but the day was lengthening—this had to end.

"Say, you think I could watch a first run?" A blank look covered Darryl's face. "The tape, Darryl. The tape."

"Sure, the officer who suggested we look at the tapes said to have it available for you." Officer Malbon nodded, rose and followed Darryl into an office behind the main desk.

The tape showed the car being parked at seven thirty, the lights at the end of the lot giving a shadowy image to the scene. It was clearly a woman, tall and thin, hair to her collar, dressed in what looked like jeans and a dark sweater, high heels. She stood, posing as she lit a cigarette, the flame lighting her image with a brief flare. The video showed her walking to the end of the lot and exiting on Silver in the direction of Fore Street. Officer Malbon watched the tape once more.

"So this car has been parking here regularly but not during the day, I surmise, or it would have been checked before, correct?"

"Never reported during the day, no."

"The night guy has seen it every night for a while though and it's never been here in the morning, till yesterday morning, correct? Pop that tape, will you? My boss is going to want to see this."

He left the hotel, his mind turning it over.

"Why would someone leave their car in a lot that draws scrutiny, knowing it would get towed sooner than later?" he asked aloud. "Really bad Halloween hangover? Maybe. Really good hook-up? Possibly. Bad clam experience? Probably not."

By the time he reached police headquarters on Middle Street, after one more walk around, he had covered three-and-a-half miles and the sun was heading in a different direction.

The sergeant wasn't in, so he knocked and entered his lieutenant's office and put the tape on the desk. The lieutenant looked up. She tilted her head quizzically.

"What do you think?"

Obviously an invitation to sit and chat. Officer Malbon, a seasoned veteran of seven years on the force with no grandiose ideas about becoming detective, was actually a pretty good one.

"You know, Lieutenant, a long walk can clear the mind, scintillate the senses. My long walk today has me smelling more than the usual odorous odors I pass in my walk-around."

"I've been chained to my desk all morning, Officer Malbon. So what's the smell on the street today?"

"Wrongdoing. I smell wrongdoing, the degree of which I have not determined, but definite wrongdoing. By the way, Lieutenant, I can see you in chains and black leather. Maybe a doggie collar."

"No wonder you're limited to foot patrol. You're on drugs, obviously. You're hallucinating, Officer."

The good-natured ribbing ended, and Officer Malbon laid out what he'd seen on the footage, what he surmised from the number of times the automobile had been parked there previously and good old economics.

"The owner had to know it would be reported, towed, impounded and a significant cost to get it back. Not good economics. So for my money, the owner has not been able to get back to her car."

The lieutenant had been listening carefully.

"I came to the same conclusion," he said. "The photo and identification of the owner offer a starting place. If the surveillance tape is a match, then some well-placed calls to hospitals would be step two. I'll get the photo lab to blow up her license photo. We can start showing it around see if anyone saw her Halloween night or before, or after, for that matter."

"What's the lady's name, Lieutenant?"

"Rae Anne Howes from Chillicothe, Ohio."

CHAPTER THIRTY-TWO

"'TIS AN ILL COOK THAT CANNOT LICK HIS OWN FINGERS' – ROMEO AND JULIET

Quentin managed to get the fading female to his car with no one noticing; others were in a similar state, happy all. By the time he'd reached the outskirts of the city, his passenger had melted to just below window level. A line from Shakespeare entered his head.

Oh true apothecary! Thy drugs are quick.

"Hopefully not as lethal," he chuckled.

The little motel was completely dark, two other cars signaling inhabitants in rooms 212 and 215. Quentin had picked a room with a view of the woods, the last room in a motel with one floor, yet the rooms all beginning with the number two. Ambitious or hopeful, determined Quentin when he'd signed on for the winter.

Room 230 lit up briefly as Quentin parked and extinguished his lights immediately. He left the woman in the car while he opened the car door, the room's door, then the bathroom door and turned on the bathroom light. He relieved himself, offering an extra congratulatory shake to old Gollum.

"Well done, old chap."

R. Wesley Clement

He went back to the car, opened the passenger door and, looking around once more, lifted the woman's dead weight off the seat, mostly dragging her the 15-foot distance and dumping her on his bed.

Door closed. Drapes closed. Lamp lit. Quentin began by smelling her essence. Liquored obviously and a lingering smell of tobacco, but beneath that a sweet smell of something earthy. He studied the still form, guessed her age as early forties. Thin, attractive, but a worn look to her quiet countenance. Her breathing was shallow, though regular.

He tasted the earthy smell of her neck and the light, salty taste of being human. He touched her first, from tip to toe without removing her high heels sweater or jeans. He lay down beside her, hugged her to himself, and another line from Romeo and Juliet entered his head.

He uttered the line aloud, "Tempt not a desperate man."

While hugging her, he imagined how this encounter might have occurred in a natural way. But he had nothing to compare it to, no normal experience.

"A wasted thought," he said aloud and got up. The sounds of the squeaking bed seemed magnified by the woman's stillness. He loomed over her still form, reaching slowly taking off each heel.

Talking to himself, as if they were holding a normal conversation, he told her what strong calf muscles she had as he peeled her jeans. Halting to knead them, he noticed a varicose vein that had found its way to the surface just to the inside of her right knee.

"Nobody's perfect, isn't that so my precious? Adds character, don't you think?" He folded the jeans and placed them on the chair. Snow white lace-edged panties topped well-shaped legs. Her sweater, well-worn but soft and comfortable to his touch, slid from beneath her with scant resistance, almost as if she were helping Quentin disrobe her.

He watched her shallow breathing, his eyes following her breasts to the flat stomach leading to the mound at the top of her legs. He brushed it lightly, wondering if awake she would be as easily stimulated by touch as Gollum.

Quentin reached behind her and removed her bra. He studied the well-formed breasts and lightly licked each one, tasting once again the saltiness of life. He felt Gollum responding. He slid her panties slowly down the length of her body as if removing the peel from a favorite fruit. He smelled her overall essence and moved to the bureau. He covered an alert throbbing Gollum, posed her perfection using pillows, then slowly entered the cave beneath the river, in search of the prized ring.

"Come, my precious."

* * *

No missing person's reports and no crime reported as yet. Tuesday found hospitals being alerted with pictures sent by email. No hits.

Officer Malbon had a hunch and asked to start his shift later in the day so he could follow up with some of the Old Port bars within a reasonable walking distance to the hotel parking lot.

He mapped out his route, deciding to go as far west as Center Street, not much happening west of that. He walked these streets day-after-day and had met a significant number of people who trusted him. North as far as Spring Street he'd go. He left the police station on Middle Street at four o'clock, walked to the parking lot at the Regency, stood facing Silver and took a right, just as the woman in the video had done.

A homeless man approached him asking which shelters would be open tonight. Officer Malbon told him Whole Foods Market would be setting up tents, cots and portable heaters in their parking lot every night until Christmas. "It's a walk, but it's worth it. They are offering soups and sandwiches. It's up on Somerset and Franklin. By the way, you haven't seen this woman in your travels have you?"

The homeless man studied the poster and shook his head.

R. Wesley Clement

"But if I do, I'll ask for you. Thanks Officer Malbon, you're one of the few who don't hassle me."

Officer Malbon watched the poor guy head in the direction of Whole Foods, pushing his worldly possessions toward another uncertain night.

Probably should have given him a buck or two, then on a clearer thought, *Nope, it's not on me gotta' find your own answers.*

By seven o'clock, Officer Malbon had reached the bar, *Troubled Waters.* He'd stopped in on several occasions for an after-shift beer. Sean was behind the bar. Jacob was sitting at a table with Freddy. The bar was quiet at this hour, several patrons nursing their day; the good and the bad on their thrones.

"She looks vaguely familiar but I'm not sure," answered Sean when shown the photo. "Let's ask Jacob."

Officer Malbon showed the photo to Jacob who studied it. "I think she might be the lady who adopted that stool on the right. Freddy is this the gal you keep striking out with?"

Freddy who was clear-eyed at this hour took only a moment before recognizing the lady.

"That's for sure the woman, Officer, haven't seen her for a few days, though."

"When did you last see her?" Officer Malbon asked casually, trying to hide his excitement.

"Halloween night. She wasn't in costume, but she was here watching the action, listening to the music."

"Did you talk with her? Did she seem upset?"

"She was exactly like she's been nearly every night for the last month or so. Preoccupied with her own thoughts. She stayed a little later than usual, watching the crazies, I guess. She was weaving pretty good when she left. I offered to drop her off. She waved me away at the door. She alright?"

"That's what we're trying to determine. We found her car. We haven't found her. Did anyone leave here around the same time?"

———

Freddy reached back into the reptilian brain that had been in charge of him at that time of night on that particular night.

"I remember seeing someone across the street standing in the shadows. A guy. I watched her get up the street, and then I came back in."

"Any chance you'd recognize the guy if you saw him again?"

"Nah, it was too dark."

"One more question. Did anyone in here that night seem to be paying special attention to this woman?"

Freddy had paid special attention to the woman that night, all night, asking her to dance twice but being politely refused. Suddenly he remembered the shadow-dwelling creature who seemed to focus on two women throughout the evening, one being the woman in the photo, the other being Elvis.

"You know there was one guy," he began.

When Officer Malbon left the bar, he'd heard of the stranger, certainly not a regular, from Jacob, Sean and Elvis. She came into the conversation late but perhaps offered the most insight.

"It was Gollum, from Lord of the Rings. He was a nasty little creature. I heard him use the line from the book, *my precious,* several times that night. Once when I was going to use the bathroom and the lady in the picture was headed there at the same time. He bowed and said *after you, my precious.* The second time it seemed he was about to strike up a conversation with me but couldn't bring himself to speak. He finally just walked off muttering something about *my precious* under his breath."

Officer Malbon had solved at least part of the mystery; the rest was still in the wind. He got back to the station, sat down, clarified his notes and wrote the report that would be on the lieutenant's desk in the morning.

CHAPTER THIRTY-THREE

ONE DOOR CLOSES AS ANOTHER OPENS

No more sailing for the year. The sails were all removed and stored away in one of Freddy's warehouses. Captain Jack had been put in charge of winterizing the boat, which would remain in the water through the winter, securely tied up in its mooring.

Jacob, Elvis and Captain Jack sat aboard on Wednesday, November 5, discussing the weather as the sea fog rose like the steam off their second cup of coffee.

Captain Jack looked out over the water and remarked, "Think about the different lives that are being touched by this very body of water this morning. People perhaps heading out to fish for the day aboard a trawler or in a wooden skiff trying to secure the day's meal."

"Maybe they're sitting just as we are, or maybe rich fat cats looking out from a balcony are having their third cup because they got up earlier than we did," laughed Jacob. "Speaking of fat cats, Polly must be sleeping in again. She hasn't been aboard the last two mornings. She's missed her first and second cups."

The missing Polly triggered a thought in Elvis.

"It's been four mornings since that woman was last seen. Something has obviously happened to her, and I can't shake the feeling that I should know about this. Kind of creepy, really."

Jacob jumped as Polly landed right in front of them at that moment.

"*That* was really kind of creepy. Did I just summon that cat or what?" They all laughed. "Maybe I could summon up that woman too. Give me your hands."

"Not funny Jacob, not funny."

"Sorry, just trying to make light of a mystery we're not really tied to except by happenstance."

* * *

Quentin showered, shaved and dressed in casual khaki's and a collar shirt and sweater, was humming as he prepared for an eleven o'clock meeting with the grant team at the college. Monday and Tuesday, he'd called out ill. He couldn't miss another meeting. Students would be taking the first course, using the new curriculum in a scant two months. It had to be approved by the English faculty within two weeks.

He finished his coffee from the little two-cup pot he had on the nightstand, the last nutty slightly bitter taste fueling his thoughts. He brushed his teeth, smelling and tasting the peppermint flavor of the toothpaste.

As he combed his hair, the little lamp on the nightstand allowed reflected in the mirror. The bed sat rumpled, sheets and blankets twisted, pillows stacked, the man in the glass a shallow shadow person seeing none of what had occurred in the room. Rather Quentin looked into the mirror to first check that there were no blemishes present but really to reflect on a very pleasant learning experience.

He'd learned a lot about himself over the past three days and nights. He now considered himself a master mixer of mischief. The drug had kept the woman just below the level of consciousness yet pliable, with just a small additional dosage twice a day.

 R. Wesley Clement

He'd learned he had the ability to think on his feet. He thumped his chest. He'd also found great patience. His plan was to get rid of her by Sunday night, but things didn't work out exactly as planned. Plan B had emerged, and Gollum seemed pleased with the postponement.

What on earth possessed the motel owner to rent out room 229 for two nights was beyond his understanding. I mean really, what are the odds? Through the paper-thin walls, he'd heard what had to be a traveling salesman settling in, singing to himself, right up until there was a knock on his door and he heard the girl's voice. Quentin then understood what all the singing was about.

Thank god the man must have had a schedule to follow and checked out yesterday afternoon. The only good that came out of the tryst, which Quentin heard on full alert, was how Gollum reacted to the level of moans seeping through the walls. Quentin's acute sense of hearing was a stimulant he might just want to add in the future. Gollum seemed pleased even now.

Later, my precious. Hold that thought, though.

Quentin had traversed into uncharted waters in trying to find a place to leave the woman. He waited until well after dark, the November night heightening his senses, the stars gleaming an extra brightness, every sound magnified, the smell of wood smoke filling his nose as he drove slowly through a little town west of Route One.

Not wanting any connection to the area he was living in, he drove through rural areas offering the remoteness he was seeking but not the hope of discovery he sought. There seemed no good place. He wanted her to be found alive not a frozen corpse he'd have to acknowledge.

So far, no harm no foul. He gazed just beyond his headlights to the shadows right and left.

By twelve thirty in the morning, he was in the city of Portland.

In plain sight. I'll just leave her in plain sight. He looked at his passenger, slumped and still. *She'll have no memory of this.*

He drove by the parking lot of Whole Foods and saw tents and a sign that offered a place to stay for the night for the poor and trodden down. He parked on the roadway, walked slowly toward a tent and peered in. No one in this one yet and on a cold night, everyone should be tucked in by now.

He returned to his car and backed into the parking lot as near to the tent as possible. He helped his poor—what would be viewed as inebriated, if spotted—passenger into the tent and onto a cot. He administered one last dose and added a healthy pinch more. *She should sleep right through breakfast, perhaps even lunch.* The lights surrounding two sides of the parking lot shone, bearing witness.

* * *

On Wednesday morning, when Jacob, Elvis and Captain Jack were toasting the day, Quentin T. Spence was admiring himself in the mirror and the lieutenant was drinking Starbucks from a travel mug. She was reading the report Officer Malbon had left on her desk. The sergeant was back at his desk, but Lieutenant O'Connor was interested enough to stay with it.

Lieutenant Colleen O'Connor read between the lines. The very reason she'd entered police work was staring her in the face. This woman was missing for a reason, and in Colleen's mind, a man's misplaced lust was probably at work.

Ten years ago, she'd been violated at Middlebury College by a fellow student. She could have reported it, probably should have. Instead, she used her anger to spark what she really wanted to do with her life and left the college without finishing the semester. She moved back in with her family and began taking courses in law enforcement at the University of Southern Maine. Most of her credits from Middlebury were accepted and three semesters later she had a bachelor's degree in law enforcement. She entered the State Police Academy in Vassalboro, Maine, and graduated top of her class.

R. Wesley Clement

She worked the roads of Southern Maine first as a trooper, then later promoted to detective. Colleen visited every crime scene and honed her investigative skills. She married, had a child and later still became a single mom when all the old clichés about policemen not making good mates became her own reality show.

Her failed marriage prompted her to apply for a detective's position with the Portland Police department, which allowed her to see her parents a little more often, and they became the support system for her son when she worked the crazy hours that fighting crime involved.

She stared at the picture of her four-year-old son Addison, straddled atop the shoulders of her brothers in an apple orchard, an apple hiding all but his eyes, and smiled to herself. Single but fulfilled. She re-read the report, set her shoulders, and resolved to find this woman and the man behind the mask. Somehow, she just knew this was more than a Halloween masquerade.

CHAPTER THIRTY-FOUR

THE WAGONS BEGIN TO CIRCLE

Rules are rules, and it was in this spirit that the tents were being dismantled for the day in the parking lot of Whole Foods at eight in the morning on Wednesday, November 5. An array of grocery carts were being filled, not with produce and tasty food choices from the store looming in the near distance, but rather the meager possessions that would be carted throughout the city as the homeless disappeared from sight.

Alfred, the daytime security guard, had been given the fun job of moving the migrants. He had a sense of humor though and tried to use it to prod life and movement from the tents. He was down to a last tent where there'd been no reaction to his efforts.

On his first trip by, he'd seen it was occupied. This second trip had him entering the tent, whistling, using the get-up-you-sleepyhead voice and tone he used to get his own kids down to breakfast on a school day. The woman lying there didn't stir. He hated to do it, but he shook her gently—no movement. *Passed out still from too much firewater, probably.* He'd give her another half hour then let management deal with it. Alfred was not Arnold Schwarzenegger; he would not be back.

Management came, observed and responded. They were not in the mood to comfort creatures of the night during business hours. A call was placed to the police department and an hour

R. Wesley Clement

later Officer Gary Malbon sauntered up drinking his second cup of coffee of the morning to have a look.

He spoke gently but with authority to a lifeless form whose head was turned away from his voice. He placed his still half-full cup on the fabric floor and shook her gently When she failed to respond to his voice, he took his flashlight from his tool belt turned it on to look at her profile. Something stirred in his mind and his pulse quickened. He grabbed her shoulder and turned her face up. He had located his missing woman.

Her breathing was shallow; the sleep too deep. He smelled her. No alcohol in her breathing. He called his boss and then called for an ambulance.

The lieutenant arrived the same time as the ambulance. She instructed Officer Malbon to interview any of the homeless still in the area to see if anyone had witnessed the woman arrive. Lieutenant O'Connor followed the ambulance to the hospital.

"I'm not letting this gal out of my sight till we've talked," she vowed.

Officer Malbon interviewed three of the night's inhabitants; he missed the crucial fourth, an early riser heading for the Back Bay to pick up any returnables.

* * *

Troubled Waters had the usual crowd for a hump day. Braden and three lawyer friends sat in the original bar space, nursing the latest craft ale being offered from Gritty's Brewing Company. Jacob, being the tapper of all barrels that drew their first breath on the premises, had recommended it.

"Imagine Taylor Swift all hoppy, duetting an original breakup song with the guy she was named after, James Taylor." Jacob smiled. "So an in-your-face first sip with Taylor, then a smooth-afternoon-at-the-lake finish with James."

The ale, poured and emptied lived up to the hype and the three lawyers raised their glasses to Jacob.

"The man knows his ales. His singers too," saluted Braden.

Elvis was doing a soundcheck on the little stage erected in the new part of the bar. The addition was ninety-five percent finished, with only Sean and Jacob envisioning what else was needed to have it the way they'd dreamed.

Sean was sitting at a table with the wheelies planning a late November *Rally of Recognition,* as they were calling it, to be held on the Back Bay just a month from now on Saturday, December 6.

This group of shut-ins, following Sean's lead, were fighting to reclaim their dignity. They had approached the same businesses that helped create the expansion, and now funds to buy a full sized handicapped accessible bus complete with two shifts for full-time drivers topped the list. Crowd funding was being considered, but only after their own efforts. Spirits were high.

Elvis began her performance with a number of her standards—her covers of Elvis and, more often of late, Elton John, who Jacob seemed to favor from his piano background.

"Billy Joel must be on tour," complained one patron who favored his music.

"One last song before I turn the mike over to Jacob," she smiled. "I'll make sure Billy stops in tonight," she promised, nodding to the complainer.

"Jacob hasn't heard this one. I just wrote it today, sitting on the boat tied up for the winter like it was a prisoner serving time. For some reason, I began thinking about the mother I lost when I was just two." She looked to Jacob then. "By the time I repeat the chorus, Jacob, you can join me. Knowing you, you'll have the music written by then." She cleared her throat. "I call it, *Oh Mother.*"

I can feel you, you haven't gone to dust
You're still out there, that much I have to trust
You're still moving, I can sense it in a breeze
I can hear you in the rustle of the trees

Chorus:

Oh Mother, dare I believe you can hear me
Oh Mother, throw me a saving rope
Oh Mother, I feel you're somewhere near me
Oh Mother, my heart is filled with hope

You're not a ghost crab hiding in plain sight
Have you reached out
Are you somewhere in the night
I have my own story now with so much more to say
Why can't I find you
Please let me find you
why can't I find you
Please don't stay away
Chorus:

Oh Mother, dare I believe you can hear this
Oh Mother, throw me a saving rope
Oh Mother, I feel you somewhere near me
Oh Mother, my heart is filled with hope
My heart is filled with hope

The regulars knew Elvis and most of her story, and nodded silently. The other bar patrons simply appreciated a beautiful voice and applauded.

Stella, sipping a club soda, went to Elvis and they hugged, Elvis crying into her shoulder. Jacob was helping mop Elvis dry when Officer Malbon approached Freddy at a table in the new room.

"We found the woman in a homeless shelter. I haven't heard back from the lieutenant, but it appears she was drugged and dropped off. We have a match from a picture license, some lady from Ohio."

"Any leads on what happened and by who?" asked Freddy.

"Nothing yet, but I'd like to follow up with you and Jacob and Elvis. Sean too, if you can spare me a minute."

"I'll rustle them up. We can meet in the little office just through that door."

They met but little else surfaced. Elvis still too emotional to help. She vaguely heard the officer say "her name is Rae Anne Howes" but little else. Stella joined them and said she'd keep her nose to the ground at the hospital.

For the regulars, the rest of the evening was subdued. Jacob played haunting piano solos with no words, and Elvis didn't sing another song. Freddy ditched his friend, Jameson, didn't invite Bud to join him either, for that matter. The mood seemed to infect the room, and by midnight, the bar crew was cleaning up and closing early.

Sean had not said much, mostly listening.

"When Stella gets home in the morning, I'd like for you guys to come over. She might have more information on this woman."

"My mother's name is Rae Anne you know," Elvis told him. "These feelings I've had lately, getting all emotional, thinking about her. That song I sang tonight was about her." She teared up again.

Jacob took her hand. "Let's get out of here and go home, get some rest and do as Sean suggests. We'll meet over coffee in the morning."

Freddy who had been eerily quiet said, "This is my town guys. This is not supposed to happen in my town." He shook his head, leaving *Troubled Waters* with a clear head for the first time. He got to his car and drove straight to the hospital. He wasn't waiting till morning for a report.

     R. Wesley Clement

CHAPTER THIRTY-FIVE

MORE MYSTERY AND MEDICINE

When Freddy arrived at the hospital, he asked to speak with Stella. He told her what Elvis had said about the woman's first name being the same as her lost mother's.

"She also said she's been getting these vibes and her emotions are surfacing, as you witnessed after that song."

"Interesting. The woman is just beginning to stir, though it may be premature, a lady officer is sitting just outside her door. You might want to talk to her."

Freddy approached the officer and introduced himself as a friend of the people who owned the bar. He told her of his observations and very limited interaction with the lady over the past month. He then told her what Elvis had shared an hour earlier.

"Stranger things have happened. We have contacted her last known address in Ohio, the one on her license, and we're waiting to hear."

Freddy studied Colleen O'Connor as she spoke. He smiled suddenly. "You wouldn't happen to be Irish would you?" When Lieutenant O'Connor nodded, he added, "Well, I am a rare Irish Jew who would be honored to buy you a cup of coffee from the cafeteria," he paused. "Furthermore, I will hand-deliver it to your door."

———

Lieutenant O'Connor gave him a tired smile. "I need to get up and walk anyway, think about what you've told me. I'll join you in the cafeteria. You can still buy, though."

By two o'clock, it was clear the lady wouldn't be ready for an interview just yet. Lieutenant O'Connor called dispatch, and they sent an officer to sit outside her room.

"Nobody gets in except the nurses and doctors. No one. You understand?"

The officer saw the wisdom in responding with a determined nod of the head and a strong, "Yes, Lieutenant, understood!"

* * *

Officer Gary Malbon began his walk from the station house at seven in the morning. He was determined to interview any of the homeless he'd missed the morning before. First things first, though. No stationhouse coffee for Officer Malbon; he walked east for several blocks then took a left onto India Street. *Two Fat Cats Bakery* was a treat he offered himself once a week. Coffee always, but their danish was to die for. He headed north on India, crossed to Franklin and turned right. It was a straight shot then to Whole Foods.

The tents were just beginning to be taken down, the overnight residents, a disheveled-looking lot, packing up what looked like a shopping-cart parade. Gary was about to make a general announcement when the same guy he'd directed to the shelter several days ago approached.

"Officer, I heard about that woman, when I got back here last night. What tent was she in anyway?"

Officer Malbon walked to the location where a tent was just now coming down.

"Right here."

The homeless man began wringing his hands, looking down.

"Did you see the woman when she arrived?" the officer asked.

R. Wesley Clement

"Not really. But I heard a car back up near that tent, and I heard a door close." There was more nervous twitching of torso.

"But you never saw the woman?"

"Nope."

"Did you see anything?"

"Yes sir, I did." All the while, the homeless man was contorting his body like a snake trying to unsnarl itself from a bramble bush.

"What's your name?"

"Edwin Workman, sir."

"Okay Edwin, you and I are going to stop dancing now. Tell me everything you saw, heard and even imagined about that time and that tent."

"Yes sir." He rubbed his five-week-old beard and pushed his hand through his greasy hair. He tried to compose himself, looking as if he were about to take the witness stand. "I heard the car door close. Some time passed—not too much—and I heard the door close again." He reached way inside his thoughts, trying to separate truth from liquor lingering.

"I got up and looked out and I saw the car leave." A look as if asking, *can I be excused now your honor,* crossed his face. Edwin was not offering any more than the question begged.

"Could you describe the car? Did you see the plate, by any chance?"

He sighed. "It was pretty dark. It was a small car, maybe a Honda Civic or a Corolla. I'm pretty good with cars."

"The plate. Did you see the plate?"

"I was getting to that. It was a green plate, I remember three letters and some numbers. I remember the letters, not the numbers. Only because they are my initials. EDW. Edwin Davis Workman. That's me. I don't remember the numbers, but I know my name for sure."

Officer Gary Malbon could have kissed the guy but settled on giving him a ten-spot.

———

"Lunch is on me, Edwin. I'm going to call into headquarters. You stay right here. Someone will be here to write down everything you told me. Edwin, you might just turn out to be a hero."

Edwin raised his hand like a schoolboy.

"Is it all right if I clean up first? I don't smell like I ought to be indoors."

"Tell you what. I'm going to see that you are taken to headquarters and allowed to clean up. Then you can write out what you saw and heard. But don't wash any of that memory away." Officer Malbon smiled. Edwin caught on and shyly smiled back.

The officer called the station and asked for the lieutenant.

"Stay right there. I'm hooking a ride with the officer who's been dispatched to Whole Foods. We have a witness and a partial plate. While you're waiting for me, check out a green plate with the letters E as in Edwin, D as in Davis, W as in Workman. They're on a small Civic or Corolla. That's all we have. Let's hope it's enough. By the way, make sure there's plenty of soap in the men's shower. I'll explain when I get there."

A nosy newshound heard about the unconscious woman found in a homeless shelter while nursing a double espresso at a *Coffee By Design Coffee House*. A paramedic was comparing horror stories of his work when he mentioned police involvement and an unconscious woman, possibly drugged. The newshound listened more closely.

Might just check out the hospital, see if there's a story there. Maybe a line or two, anyway.

* * *

By local news at six, the woman's picture from her license was four stories into the nasty mix of muggings, drugging and highway mayhem.

Tonight a woman lies in a comatose state in a local hospital. Police believe foul play put her there. Have you seen this woman before? If so, call Portland Police Headquarters at 207 999-3333.

* * *

Elvis was sitting in Mrs. Waslowski's living room, watching the news, a napkin holding a molasses cookie in one hand and a cup of coffee in the other. She had called Mrs. W. earlier in the day and asked if she could visit.

The late afternoon began with hugs all around, the twin sisters telling of their newfound independence, no longer sharing a room but rather living across the hall from one another. They didn't elaborate, but Mrs. Waslowski shared the truth with Elvis after the two ladies retired to one room or the other for their afternoon toddy.

"Their independence was from necessity, really. Blame it on an argument at TJ Maxx," she laughed. "They don't close their doors, though. I hear them finishing one another's sentences from one room to the other. It's like a ping pong match." She sighed. "It has worked out for the best though. After that horrid man left, I decided I didn't want any more boarders. I'm too old for the drama." She patted Elvis's hand. "Except you, dear. You can come back and live here anytime."

Elvis shared all the exciting things going on at the bar and her recent sailing trip.

"I think I'm going to make this ship ride a voyage," she kidded. Then the serious expression she'd had when she entered returned.

Mrs. Waslowski who had spent a lifetime *reading people's faces,* as the line from the Kenny Rogers gambling song and her late husband's favorite went, read right through to the real reason for the visit.

"What's troubling you, dear?"

"There's this woman. She's been at the bar most nights for a month or more. She drinks too much and doesn't talk to anyone. She listens to Jacob and me sing, then she leaves. Anyway, she was missing for a few days, and now she's in the hospital. Mrs. W., her first name is the same as my mother's, and I have been having strange feelings and my emotions have me crying. I'm not a crier." She paused. "Is it possible?"

They watched the news together, and Mrs. Waslowski lent support to the idea in Elvis's head.

"Let me just warm up the car, dear. The wind is whipping up white caps, I'm sure. That weatherman won't be bearing good news till spring. What is it you young people say? Road trip. Let's take a little road trip."

CHAPTER THIRTY-SIX

ALL NEWS IS LOCAL

Quentin sat in his motel room, watching the same local news that was being absorbed throughout the listening area.

"Well, she's been found and she's alive. All good news at the end of the day." He spoke into the mirror, congratulating himself aloud for his creative approach to disposal. He smiled then as he began to silently, reflectively, retrace his steps looking for any missteps he might have taken.

I'm sure the owners of the bar and Elvis recognized the picture. There's nothing there to connect me. I didn't see anyone at that shelter. I believe some good actually came out of all that. I certainly added to my knowledge base. Let's move on, shall we?

A plan began to take shape in his mind. *I think Gollum would enjoy a week away. The grant is in the hands of the powers that be. It's getting cold here. A return to the sunny south for a week or ten days might just be in order.*

"What do you say, Gollum, my old friend, road trip? After your latest extended stay in that cave, I don't suppose you want to be left in my hands?" He chuckled. "Almost time to claim our precious, don't you think?'

* * *

Mrs. Waslowski carefully parked the car. Elvis took her arm and entered the hospital. Stopping at reception, they were told the woman could have no visitors. When Elvis insisted she might have knowledge of the woman, she was ushered to the officer sitting outside room 210.

Lieutenant O'Connor was back in the chair after ending her shift, racing home, hugging Addison, and devouring a turkey wrap.

Elvis and Mrs. Waslowski approached the lieutenant and introduced themselves. The lieutenant called hospital security and asked for someone to relieve her for a short time. The women took the elevator to the ground floor, not saying anything as yet.

"Let me get you ladies something to drink. Have a seat."

"I'm fine, thank you. Mrs. W., do want anything?"

Lieutenant O'Connor returned with a single cup of coffee, and Elvis told her story from the beginning. When she finished, the lieutenant drained her now cold cup and spoke.

"I would say you have a vested interest in this lady. You know, in my line of work, I'm always saying you couldn't write these stories. This may be another one of those."

She took Elvis's cell phone number and Mrs. Waslowski's home number. "I'll call as soon as she wakes up. I promise."

* * *

Three nights later Rae Anne was fully awake. That added pinch Quentin administered was a doozy.

At two twenty in the morning, Stella who had taken a special interest because of Elvis was alerted. She was in the room trying to orient Rae Anne when the lieutenant arrived. Between sips of ice chips that slowly moistened her parched throat, Rae Anne provided very little to the mystery.

"I remember leaving the bar, getting sick and that's it. How long have I been like this?" she rasped.

"A full week now. Halloween night a week ago is when you disappeared. Do you remember where you were staying? We have your name, your car and your license, which indicates you're from Ohio. Is that right?"

Rae Anne nodded her head, it still hurt to talk.

"Were you staying in Portland?"

"I'm living in a little camp trailer in Old Orchard," she rasped. "I got here in September, right after Labor Day." The effort of the response had her seeing stars.

By three thirty, the lieutenant had what she needed from Rae Anne, and a weeping Rae Anne had the news she needed.

An address in Old Orchard would be checked in the morning. She had a call to place to an anxious young woman. Her heart was full of sorrow for this woman who had endured the theft of her child but never stopped looking.

* * *

Elvis got the call on the boat at five in the morning. The lieutenant had gone to headquarters and written her report and placed the order for a call to the Old Orchard police department. The crime had happened in her city but coordinating with the Old Orchard's police chief was protocol.

"She's really spent, Elvis. I wouldn't expect her to be alert before noon. I'll meet you there. I'm very happy for you. You've found your mother."

More news that's fit to print was on her desk as well. She opened the folder. The partial plate was a rental plate from Vermont. The green color was a clue. In Montpelier had rented the car to one, Quentin T. Spence.

When she read the name, Lieutenant O'Connor suddenly went white and her arms turned goose flesh. *It's a small world, after all. It's up to me to settle accounts.* A look of steely resolve entered her eyes. *Have you been being a bad boy since we last met, Quentin ? As my father used to quote his father …Is it time for a trip to the woodshed?*

* * *

The lieutenant requested Officer Malbon come to her office at ten. He was standing looking at the diplomas she had received, all indicating extra merit.

"I have just a short time, then I have to meet a young woman at the hospital, but I wanted to bring you up to speed. We have a tag number and the car wearing it is indeed a Honda Civic registered in Vermont to a car rental company. We have a name, Quentin T. Spence. Though we have not found out who he is, I know who he is." The look on her face was almost a grimace.

"We don't know where he's living. I'll fill you in later on how I know this man. Officer Malbon I have been impressed by your efforts. Good police work. I want you to stay on this case. I will notify your sergeant. Tonight, we'll let the media do a little reach-out for us. The name is not common. Someone else must know who this man is, and what he's doing in Maine."

* * *

Elvis was in the corridor, nervously waiting for Lieutenant O'Connor, a bearded, long-haired giant was rubbing her shoulders and trying to settle her emotions. Elvis introduced Jacob as her fiancé.

"It might be better for Elvis to come in alone with me. Just until we get through what I'm sure will be traumatic. I'll come out and bring you up to speed, Jacob. Maybe what I tell you will trigger something."

They entered the room. All monitoring equipment was gone, and Rae Anne seemed to be resting comfortably.

The Lieutenant cleared her throat. Elvis stood just to the side and slightly behind.

"Rae Anne, are you awake? There is someone who wants to meet you."

R. Wesley Clement

Rae Anne opened her eyes and blinked several times, shaking the cobwebs away. Elvis came forward and touched Rae Anne's hand. All the strange feelings Elvis had been experiencing disappeared in that touch. Rae Anne squeezed her hand and managed, "At last, oh my god, at last," her eyes filling with tears.

There was no need for a hug yet; the connection had been made. Elvis not a crier by nature—all cried out really—did not cry now. She stood holding her mother's hand, remembering the promise all that time ago when she said goodbye to the little ghost crab on Flagler Beach.

Rae Anne cried though, for a hundred reasons, some of her own doing and some for the doing of others. The end result of those doings was holding her hand now, and in an instant she let the anger seep out of her. Elvis felt the negative energy leaving her mother's body. Suddenly her mother smiled, looking ten years younger. Suddenly Elvis could see some of her own features emerge.

The lieutenant left the room and spoke with Jacob.

"I don't think Elvis's mother knew her attacker, so there's plenty of time to fill her in. Does the name Quentin T. Spence mean anything to you?"

Jacob thought, spun it up, down, and round and round memory lane and came up with nada.

"Elvis ever mention the name? Freddy maybe or Sean?"

Jacob shook his head. No, he'd never heard the name.

"You see I don't think this was random. I think this guy had been in your bar before. I'm not at liberty to divulge all that I know. But I will tell you this. It was a planned attack."

*　*　*

Mrs. Waslowski was watching the six o'clock news on Sunday November 8th when she heard the name of her former boarder mentioned as a person of interest in a kidnapping and possible drugging. She immediately tried to contact Elvis. Just an hour before, however, Elvis had finished informing Jacob and Sean she was going to be out of the loop for a while. She had a mother who needed mending. She then turned off her phone.

CHAPTER THIRTY-SEVEN

HEADING DOWN THE EASTERN SEABOARD

Quentin was singing to himself on Sunday evening. He'd spent the day on his computer, mapping out various places he might go. West and north first. He figured a quick stop in Montpelier for some funding, then he would head south in as straight a line as possible. The news was just coming on and he paid it scant attention—nearly missed it—until he heard his name, which put focus to what had merely been white noise.

The commentator moved on, but Quentin quickly changed channels, hoping his name would surface again. NBC channel returned from a commercial break and suddenly a picture of Quentin, obviously from his college yearbook, was staring him dead in the eye. He didn't need to hear the rest. He snapped off the set and sat down on the bed.

How did this happen? Could the woman have been conscious?

With that last dose, no way. Even if she had somehow regained consciousness, she didn't know him. And his name. Who came up with his name and his college picture from Middlebury?

He took a deep breath and rose; his thoughts leapt into action.

"Change of plans here. No mountains in my future. The straight south piece is still viable. No Elvis. Not now at any rate. There's no time. Perhaps we can scrape up another diversion for

Gollum in one of the little towns I'll be traveling through. Damn you, Gollum, you've gone and done it haven't you?"

Gollum remained lifeless, listening, all the while knowing that at the moment he might be sorrows' obsession, but a stronger obsession would surface in the coming days and he would respond.

First a disguise would be in order and while he didn't listen to the details, he was sure they must have his plate and vehicle identity as well. He went to his computer and googled a highway map of the eastern half of the country from Maine to Florida.

By nine that evening, he was on the road. Ditching this car would be a lot easier out of state he figured, and an early start while there was still at least some traffic on Interstate 95 should make him obscure if not invisible. He had not donned a disguise, as yet; if they saw his car, he would be revealed anyway.

He got within a mile of the bridge that separates Maine from New Hampshire when traffic suddenly slowed. Without knowing, he knew. He reacted immediately and took the last exit in Maine. He pulled into an all-night convenience store parking lot and parked as far away from the light as possible. Quentin began to play the blame game—a learned man sitting there reciting old parables he'd heard as a child.

Suddenly he hated the woman he'd spent three nights with. It was her fault. A parable, *The Fox and the Lion,* came to mind along with the line *familiarity breeds contempt.*

Quentin's mind was racing and for a man who prided himself on having a logical step-by-step scientific orientation, this was not pleasant. Suddenly his senses, those reliable barometers of his own sense of well-being were under attack. He heard sirens that weren't in the vicinity, people talking in their homes hundreds of feet away. He heard a cash register open though he was still in his car.

The hundred smells of Kittery, Maine, wafted through his closed windows and the light, the light was blinding though parked in the shadows.

　　　R. Wesley Clement

Quentin was under attack from his own worst enemy, his own best friend—himself. In his mind his mother regained control and placed a Wheaties box in front of him, looking at him with contempt. "After all I've done for you, ungrateful little shit," she was saying, then buried her head in a black bottomless cup of coffee.

Quentin began to hyperventilate, his heart racing. A cold clammy moisture seeped from his pores, his involuntary system taking charge, shutting him down. He couldn't stop the blinking of his eyes; like a traffic light gone rogue. He collapsed in the seat and forced his eyes to stay closed. Even with his eyes closed it seemed a locomotive was heading straight at him.

He must have slept. The black of night was blacker still and there was frost beginning to appear on his windshield when he opened his eyes warily. His breathlessness had subsided—he was calm now but shivering uncontrollably. He turned on the engine and turned up the heater.

He had dreamt his way through every line of prose and poetry that ever reinforced his belief that he was special. *My dreams are intact at least,* he thought, and one of the lines he'd dreamed had given him the start of a plan.

He entered the convenience store and went to the men's room. Standing at the urinal the exact wording escaped him, yet it seemed important that he be able to quote it line for line, a new mantra he would now live by. In a stream of his own making, holding Gollum in a detached way, the words came to him.

Adopt the character of a twisting octopus, which takes on the appearance of the nearby rock. Now follow in this direction, now turn a different hue.

Quentin's features relaxed. He remained at the urinal lost in thought as another man with an urge entered the room. Quentin smiled as he turned his head. He was a different man now; he was a man with a plan. Coffee to go was in order and he mixed several blends together in a 24-ounce cup deciding on a French vanilla creamer to sweeten the deal. The old Quentin wouldn't have dreamed of lightening his joe.

He headed back toward Portland. He practiced between sips, looking in the mirror. *This is me being obscure,* another look, *me being simple,* the sweetness of the brew prompting the final line, *me being less.* He drove into Sanford and slept once more in a remote area.

It was Monday morning. He took out his cell phone while driving and when bars appeared, he pushed call. His father answered as he always did.

"Just do your best son. That's all you can do." The wording might change but the message was always clear. Quentin found himself suddenly that small boy who always academically pleased his father. Not going into detail he asked his father to wire him money through Western Union as soon as possible.

There was no long dragged-out conversation; there never had been. No enquiry about the need for money—no words wasted—no emotions unraveled. As simple a transaction as a two-dollar bet in the window at the racetrack. No goodbye, good luck, just gone.

Quentin took what made sense to travel lightly with and ditched the car. He took off the license plates and flung them into the woods. An hour later, a disheveled man with a slight limp walked into a Smartstop seeking the customer service desk. He left with the wired money and several purchases that would help this octopus become a rock.

CHAPTER THIRTY-EIGHT

AN UNEASINESS AS THE GARMENT UNRAVELS

Elvis opened the blinds in her mother's room. She had not left her bedside since arriving. Looking out into the gray of a November morning, she studied the landscape. Without leaf now, the hills in the distance seemed the drab color the ocean sometimes reflected. There was no sun as yet, the car windows in the parking lot below clearly marking those who had yet to end their overnight shift. A thick film of frost on the grass was a stark reminder of what would be months of Crayola's new favorite color—bleak.

Her mother stirred. Elvis turned, their eyes met and her mother smiled.

Ah, there's the sun rising now. Elvis smiled in return.

Stella entered the room with a small tray. "Medicine for you Elvis," she grinned, offering a paper cup of coffee to her best friend. "And for you, Mrs. Howes, good news. We'll be moving you to a regular room this morning."

Two hours later, following a breakfast of egg and toast, and a fruit cup, Rae Anne was in a room on the top floor. Elvis was again at a window, and her take on the day brightened. The sun, not relinquishing control just yet, had risen with authority, melting last night's frost, adding a sparkle and glisten to the grass. Looking within the darkness of the woods from a higher perch revealed a few spattering's of color within the gray ring at the picture's edge.

Some of the trees are refusing to give up, thought Elvis, *just as mother hadn't, and I didn't.*

Rae Anne, her hair combed and fresh from a nurse-assisted shower signaled Elvis to sit on the bed beside her.

"I have a lot to tell you, some good some not so good. It's a story that has a happy beginning and now a happy ending but in the middle, well, I could write a book—at least an Elvis song."

She told of her love of a little toddler who sang constantly, and cried only when she was being abandoned.

"You remember that jailhouse, Elvis?" Rae Anne broke into a smile. "You made quite a hit singing that Christmas song." Then she turned serious, "There's no nice way to say this Elvis. Your grandmother stole you and ran away with you." She shook her head as she remembered the empty parking lot when she got out of jail. "And then you were gone. I looked everywhere, but I couldn't find you." She took Elvis's hand.

"I eventually married a nice man who had two children of his own. I tried to forget you, hid my feelings. I never told my husband about you because I thought he wouldn't understand. In the end he didn't." She wiped her eyes. She blew her nose.

"Here's some worse parts. A few years back your father surfaced, and I offered him money if he could find you. All without telling my husband anything. Six months later, Billy, your father showed up claiming he'd found you in Florida and demanded money. He had lost his front teeth in a fight of some sort and he was liquored up. You never met him did you?"

Elvis shook her head no, not speaking, not willing to interrupt.

Rae Anne continued, "I got a thousand dollars from our checking account, figuring I could replace it before Vern, that's my ex-husband, found out. Anyway, that didn't work out. Billy came back, and Vern heard it all. Not very understanding for a supposedly Christian man. Billy left, and I was sent. Didn't even

R. Wesley Clement

get to say goodbye to the two kids I had come to love. I worked and drank my way to Florida." She shifted uneasily on the bed.

"I found your great aunt. I'd seen her in the courtroom years earlier but never met her. She looked like she was at death's door, working at her little booth in the flea market. I think she actually felt sorry for me. She told me you were headed north the last time she saw you, that you had summered in a little town near the coast."

"I have a drinking problem, Elvis. I never expected to find you in a bar, but I hit every one of them with the lame idea that maybe you'd be singing somewhere. Your great aunt said you were getting famous down there, and that's why they left. So here I am, and here you are." Tears were streaming down her face but she held Elvis's gaze.

"Why didn't you tell me who you were when you were coming in every night?"

Sniffling, she said, "I saw you with that handsome young man, and you seemed so happy. I didn't feel I had anything but a bad past and present to offer. I don't think I was ever going to return after that Halloween party. I guess I have fate to thank for supplying me the opportunity, no matter the circumstance."

"Well you're here now, and I am not letting you lose me again. Jacob will be here this afternoon. We'll make plans for when you get out of here. We have a friend, Freddy, actually he's the guy who kept trying to get you to give him the time of day. He's wonderful. I'm sure he can get you a job and a place to stay." In Elvis's optimistic mind the matter was settled.

Jacob arrived with flowers and a box of chocolates. He hugged Rae Anne, and his strength of character and concern brought forth a sigh from her.

Elvis offered, "That's what he does to me too, mom."

Jacob reddened but beamed.

Small talk led to news of the day. It was just in passing that Jacob mentioned the name Lieutenant O'Connor had quizzed him about.

"What did you just say, Jacob?" Elvis gasped, suddenly pale.

"Say that name again."

"Quentin T. Spence."

"That's the Propisser—I mean the Professor—I mean he lived where I lived," she bumbled, her eyes wide. "Oh my god, I have to call Mrs. Waslowski. She might be in danger, and the sisters. He hated them."

Jacob watched his normally even-keeled shipmate unravel for a second time, this time fear replacing concern. "You call Mrs. W. I'll call the Lieutenant."

Lieutenant O'Connor, who had been planning on coming to the hospital, was just wrapping up an update with her squad. She arrived at the hospital within fifteen minutes.

Elvis gave the briefest of details about the professor, insisting they go at once to Mrs. W's home and calm her down. "I'll be back as soon as possible, mom."

"I'm not going anywhere. I'll be right here."

Mrs. Waslowski met them at the door. She ushered them into a kitchen that smelled of freshly brewed coffee and molasses cookies. Needing to gain control over her fears, she insisted on coffee and cookies all around.

"Mrs. Waslowski, I think you're safe. We believe Mr. Spence has left the area. It's only a matter of time before he's caught." Lieutenant O'Connor bit into a cookie and washed it down with some coffee. "My God, these cookies are delicious."

The lieutenant shared all she could about the suspect and learned of where he'd been working. It was another lead, maybe, though probably that ship has sailed.

Phone numbers were swapped, and assurances made. The lieutenant ate one more cookie and washed it down one more time.

"I think we've seen the last of your professor until he's caught."

Mrs. Waslowski, who had lived a lot of years and seen and heard and discussed similar stories over coffee in this kitchen with her late husband, wasn't convinced, but she kept that thought to herself.

R. Wesley Clement

CHAPTER THIRTY-NINE

IN AN OCTOPUS'S GARDEN IN THE SHADE

He got the idea when he entered customer services. No one made eye contact; they simply performed their duties with limited voice direction. After finding the items he needed, standing at the end of a line of seven people, he simply took stock of this environment.

Well lit, organized by department worker ants doing what worker ants do. He heard no greetings, saw no interaction beyond someone seeking assistance to find something. The light came on once more. Quentins octopus could blend in nicely in Smartstop Blue and White.

He went to the bathroom and donned the baggy jeans and tee shirt. A bulky brown sweater added girth and anonymity. He pulled the baseball cap low, shading his eyes, though he favored the Red Sox he didn't need to be offered high fives every time one of the rabid fans recognized a kindred spirit. A college logo, a gator of some sort with the letters UF seeming to ride the gators jaws, would be his mascot.

In just the briefest moment of whimsy, he asked the clerk if he'd ever seen an octopus as a hat logo.

"Just kidding," he said, ending the conversation. He located a Wi-Fi hot spot for his computer and turned it on. There was a bus stop and a Smartstop in this town.

Let's keep it simple. Let's keep it lowly, he thought as he sat at the bus station ready for the ride back to Scarborough. He had stayed in Scarborough before and had at least an understanding of the area. He rubbed his already grizzling persona and transformed into that simple, lowly self. The old Quentin had returned, though in a different form.

Arriving in Scarborough, he realized he'd need transportation. He bought a local paper and took a cab to the Starbucks on Route One. Sipping the boldest blend offered, ignoring the sweetener for the moment, he sat and perused the local paper. Everyone, it seemed, was selling vehicles before the first snow hid them from view.

He found a private sale offering a 2001 Toyota Camry for eighteen hundred dollars cash. One owner. Gold color. Excellent running condition. Owner has passed.

As anonymous as you can get, thought Quentin.

* * *

"My husband passed away a month ago," the lady announced as soon as they had seated themselves at the kitchen table. "I don't drive myself. Plenty of my lady friends do, so it's time to clean the closets," she confided. "You didn't know him of course, but truth is, he was a son of a bitch." She paused for effect. "He loved that damn car more than me."

Quentin sat silently. This new Quentin listened; he didn't speak. He remained simple and lowly. He turned the cap in his hands, affecting a man beaten down by life.

The woman went on and on, emptying and refilling her coffee cup, each cup revealing more and more of her distaste for her late husband, her facial expressions suggesting her home-perked brew had gone sour, then bitter, then dumped down the drain.

Finally Quentin had heard enough; he'd stopped accepting a refill a gallon ago.

 R. Wesley Clement

"I'm down on my luck," he began humbly. "I got laid off two months ago." He nervously twisted of his hat. "I've found a job, but now I'm going to need transportation to get there." He mumbled as if squeezing his last dime; even his mouth seemed unwilling to open with the offer. "I can offer a thousand dollars." Then, in a eureka moment, he added even though his last dime would most certainly be disappearing, "Twelve hundred if you'll allow me to drive on your husband's plate just for a day or two until I get it registered."

"What a nice man you are!" she exclaimed, not having a clue about registrations and restrictions. "You're giving me two hundred extra dollars for just a day or two of driving? That seems more than fair. You know, my friend Mildred said I should haggle and not let it go for less than eight hundred. She's going to think I'm a smart old broad getting twelve." Smiling, she offered her hand, sealing the deal.

Quentin rose reluctantly, sighing continually. He counted out twelve new hundred dollar bills, signing nothing, but suggesting she let him use her late husband's license as well for the two days. "That way it's all legal," he confided.

"John just paid two hundred dollars a coupla months ago to keep his plates. I told him then, John you're not well enough to drive, so why waste the money, huh? He shoulda listened. He never listened."

Quentin exited the driveway with a car that was clean inside and out. He looked at the license and then in the mirror. No blemishes. He looked different somehow.

While in the coffee shop, he had looked for a room to rent. Not a motel, he was sure the police were all over his last residence by now. No, he would find a kindly woman who would take him in. Perhaps a widow he might find at his next stop, the Scarborough Smartstop. In the meantime, if necessary, he would stay in a homeless shelter.

———

Holiday music was playing loudly and every department shouted, with slashed prices, their wares would make Christmas complete.

John A. Thomas was hired on the spot. He filled out the necessary paperwork, using a made up social security number. It could take years for that bureaucracy to catch on. And when it did, if it did, it would just be a matter of transposing numbers to start the process all over again. He shook his head. Charles Dickens, his favorite author, entered his mind as he completed the job application. *A smattering of everything and a knowledge of nothing.*

He did a tour of the store, familiarizing himself with sound, sights and smells. The old Quentin might be gone, but this John A. Thomas was just as savvy.

He started work the next day in the electronics department. He knew cell phones and computers well enough to offer assistance but wouldn't think of giving advice. *We have lots of choices* would be his line of the day every day.

Two weeks passed. He'd spent only two nights in a shelter before befriending an elderly lady from housewares. She had a friend who had a friend who had a friend, and before you could extend this sentence further, he had a place to stay on Spring Street in Scarborough, the same street name as his former boarding house in Portland. He thought of Elvis and had to remind Gollum to keep it simple and lowly.

Thanksgiving found Quentin sharing a simple meal of turkey with stuffing and gravy, potatoes, peas, squash, boiled onions, pumpkin biscuits and cranberry sauce, with a widowed lady of seventy-five. Quentin sat, absorbing his fullness, smells lingering.

The old lady, happy to have company, was humming as she cut the apple pie and brought it to the table. Sipping a cup of dessert coffee, Quentin realized at that moment how alone we all are. He could most likely travel from town to town, state to state, and share meals with a hundred old ladies in the same situation. Not the worst idea he decided.

     R. Wesley Clement

                              *   *   *

I'll have a blue Christmas without you. Quentin froze. The King's voice wailed over the store's speakers. Suddenly, his obsession with self, his wants and needs and desires replaced the cautious, careful, simple and lowly John A. Thomas. He would be Quentin again one last night.

I know where you work. I know where you live. I know what I want, each phrase echoing in his mind as the sounds of Elvis Presley left the building.

CHAPTER FORTY

STOCKINGS ARE HUNG

The holidays were a blur. From Veteran's Day to Christmas, holiday music was the one constant. The economy was improving, everyone said so; people were hiring though only seasonal was promised. Like the snow covering the ground that would be gone by the afternoon, nothing is permanent.

Captain Jack had installed a large gas heater on the boat, venting it through one of the sliding windows in the cabin. When people asked about wintering on the boat, "cozy as a clam" was Elvis's response; "amazing what body heat can do" was Jacob's comeback.

Jacob brushed off the snow that had fallen overnight and called for Elvis to join him on deck. Polly had been there. Her tracks circling the perimeter were reassuring in a way. Ten minutes into their cup and conversation, Polly was suddenly in Elvis's lap.

"Why good morning, Polly. Where did you sleep last night?

Or are you like Sean, a clock-watcher overnight."

Jacob chuckled, "I see you were here earlier. Sorry we missed you."

Polly rubbed against Elvis, then, smelling Jacob on her, moved to neutral territory.

"I don't think she likes men, Jacob, and you in particular."

"I hate to think it, but I'm sure you're right. Still haven't figured out why she chose this boat." Jacob pointed his coffee cup toward the newly snow-covered islands. "Now there's a Christmas card right there."

It was December 19, just five shopping days till Christmas.

* * *

Elvis was now singing Christmas tunes as her part of the nightly show. She felt like she had already received the best present ever (next to Jacob of course).

The bar was packed, old room and new. Sean declared the new addition complete and a large decorated tree stood at attention just to the right of the stage. Elvis used the tree as a prop for a lot of her Christmas songs and a chorus from the bar patrons accompanied nearly every song.

There were a few stool-sitters who couldn't muster the energy or the interest to wander into the new room. One customer with a sandy beard, owlish glasses and a baseball hat sat at the end of the bar, observing nothing and everything. When asked, he was John. Then the conversation ended. He came to the Friday night show, then showed up again on Monday, December 22. He was sitting on the same stool when a man approached Elvis and Jacob and spoke to them together for a moment. Then they took their place on stage.

Troubled Waters was rocking for a Monday night. Sean's wheelie group were all in attendance, discussing their recent fundraiser on the Back Bay. The official funds raised amounted to twenty-four hundred dollars and that didn't figure in sponsors who would provide prizes for a silent auction in the spring. With a drink or two under their belt, some were doing wheelies and just having fun in general.

Sean sat among them, nursing a coke. He had stopped drinking in support of Stella who was with child.

"We women have to do it all, Sean," she lamented, "the fetching, obviously the carrying, then the birthing and the nursing." This conversation had taken place right after Elvis's mother had been found and the perils of motherhood took on new meaning for Stella.

On the stool, Quentin reflected on a busy last few days. Saturday night and then a test run Sunday evening. It was a simple plan really. *A simple plan for a simple man,* he sang in his head. *Maybe Elvis can sing it to me,* he merrily mused. He went back over the past few days in his mind.

Saturday afternoon, his early morning shift over and done with, he changed his clothes and donned his invisible sweater and a ball cap with no logo. He drove down near the water just up from DiMillo's Floating Restaurant and finally found parking on a side street. He wandered along Commercial Street, the sidewalks still wet from the dusting they'd received.

When he got to the condominiums that claimed Chandlers Wharf as their own, he spotted a security person so he walked past a ways and crossed the street. Ten minutes later, he was back and had made a decision—in plain sight would work here too.

Quentin entered the parking lot where no one seemed on duty at the moment. He walked to the little building that allowed entrance to the wharf. A black man in his mid-fifties was on duty. John introduced himself as a person new to the area who might be interested in renting a slip in the spring.

"Would it be alright if I walked on the wharf to check it out?" he asked.

"I don't see any harm in that. Just let me know when you leave. Sign here if you would. Sign it again when you return, if I'm not right here."

John A. Thomas walked through the little gate and down a ramp to the boat slips. He knew which boat he was looking for; he'd paid attention at the bar. Their boat, *The Last Tango,* was

R. Wesley Clement

directly on his right with a large white, one-eyed cat sitting on deck, staring at him, just daring him to board.

John merely saluted and continued his walk. He went to the far end of the wharf and walked up a ramp that looked like another possible exit. He couldn't be sure but he'd find out. He returned Saturday evening and checked out the comings and goings of security, how busy it all seemed. During the week, he decided. At night, he decided. That would make the most sense. It was pitch dark by five o'clock now.

Wednesday night, hump day, will have the pre-Christmas revelers in fine spirits. Yes, Wednesday will do nicely.

Sunday afternoon he repeated his excursion looking for places that might afford the best opportunity. The two love birds always seemed to be together. But he had a plan if it came to that. The parking lot at night seemed the best place; he could visualize the action.

I can approach her, looking for my car. She's such an innocent, she'll help a man laden with gifts find his vehicle, perhaps put them in the trunk as well.

He returned to the little room on Spring Street in Scarborough for a dine-in dinner date with the little old lady who couldn't seem to get enough of his attention.

Pity that, he thought as the old lady wobbled into the living room with two after dinner toddies in tow. *If Gollum could just see clear to be a little less discriminating, we could explore dark places all across this great country of ours, at all hours of the day and in plain sight.* He smiled sweetly and thanked the lady.

"Here's to you," he toasted. The old lady practically melted.

———

CHAPTER FORTY-ONE

SNOW COVERS ALL TRACKS

Wednesday morning, the day before Christmas Eve, festive colors were absent from view for the two hardy sailors who intended to be on the water all winter. The color of the day was a grizzled grim gray from waterline to horizon. The pallor predicted precipitation.

By nine o'clock, Jacob and Elvis, both becoming weathermen in their own minds, were placing bets on the amount of accumulation.

"Okay, so you're saying half a foot," she said. "Is that right, Jacob? Now is that by your own exaggerated measure or are we talking a ruler here?"

Jacob nearly spilled his coffee, "I see you woke with a sharp tongue," he laughed and scolded. "Did you hear that, Polly? Questioning what a man holds so dear."

Polly as usual seemed to be taking a feminine view and cozied up to Elvis.

"I haven't heard any reports since late yesterday, but they were talking storm of the century," Elvis said, petting the cat.

"Speaking of exaggeration, those weather people concoct scenarios that would keep us all under our beds for a week at a time." He looked at his beautiful first mate, wrapped in a colorful afghan. "Now if they suggested we stay in our beds for a week, that's a scenario I'd buy into," he continued rather shyly, "see if I could meet your ruler requirements."

Elvis blushed, stroking Polly's white coat. "You're embarrassing Polly, Jacob. Anyway I'm going to agree with the weatherman for once. Look at that sky. It mirrors the water, a foot at least."

The bet was set. As usual, Jacob, being a man, claimed Elvis's body as his prize if the storm sputtered.

Elvis giggled. "You're more predictable than that weatherman, Jacob. I for one would like a pedicure. Shellee took off her shoes at work last night and eight little elves appeared with Santa riding one big toe and Rudolph the other. That's what I want. And know this Jacob, it's expensive."

* * *

One o'clock that afternoon found the first flake falling, landing directly on Polly's nose. She sniffed the air with derision, looked out over the bow of the boat, then leaped lightly to the dock, abandoning ship for higher ground.

* * *

One o'clock that afternoon found Smartstop a flurry of activity with people talking to one another. The subject? The impending storm just a day before Christmas Eve. Grocery carts competed with stocking stuffers and big screen TVs. The lines were unusually long. Gathering abandoned carts in the spacious parking lot became a priority. Quentin, nearing the end of his shift, nervous with anticipation, had spent the morning in the stock room mindlessly resupplying shelves as associates on the floor witnessed a wide-eyed mission-driven mob.

He donned his coat and baseball cap, and walked to the parking lot, summoned to help retrieve carts that could now be tracked in the accumulation that was turning tar to off-white slush.

———

He was pushing a stack of six carts, slipping his way back to the storage area when he heard his name called. His new landlord Mrs. Ellison was slowly making her way to join the congregation.

"I'm so glad I saw you Mr. Thomas. I'm going to pick up extra groceries and wanted to know if you'd like something special for Christmas Eve. I think we're in for it."

Quentin had not heard a forecast. Just the typical paranoia seeping into the stockroom. He had no idea what the lady meant. Mrs. Ellison was quick to spread the gospel. "They are predicting anywhere from a foot to fifteen inches, and thirty mile an hour winds into Christmas Day. Would you like some special treats Mr. Thomas? I think the town will close down by dark this evening."

Quentin finally understood that his afternoon and evening plans were probably ruined, certainly in jeopardy at any rate. He could cancel the reservations at the motel in Biddeford, though that was the least of his concerns. He couldn't think clearly with this old lady yapping at him. He simply threw up his hands, ignored her and walked away, the carts slewing their way to a hard landing against parked cars.

He punched out, refusing offered overtime and drove immediately to the rooming house. He gathered what he needed and headed into Portland. He'd be damned if he'd spend Christmas in a house with an old lady.

The whiteness of the road was attacking his sight; the reality of his disappointment was making him think rashly. Gollum stirred as if dictating the terms of this delay.

One more test run then. He touched himself. *It would be a shame to waste that reservation.* With a look of resignation he turned back south and followed route one into Biddeford. He checked into the room he had rented for the next three nights. He went to the phone book , looking for social clubs in the area. He found the listing for an area Eagles Club and dialed. Yes, they would be open to the public tonight. They had a pre-Christmas wedding reception planned with a dance to follow.

  R. Wesley Clement

Quentin revisited plans that, at least for now, would not include Elvis.

* * *

By seven o' clock, it was clear that this would be no normal night. The six inches of blowing snow that Jacob had predicted were already on the ground, keeping everyone but the regulars at home. *Troubled Waters* had no water on the floor from entering patrons, no wheelchair tracks at the entrance. Sean, Jacob, Elvis, Freddy and his new friend, Lieutenant O'Connor, sat at a table, eating up a beef stew that would go to waste if not consumed.

Elvis asked Colleen if there were new leads in the case.

"He's left the area we think. If not, he's changed his appearance by now and is trying to blend in. It's just a matter of time before he hurts someone else. We have warnings out in fifty states and at least that many false sightings have occurred."

Jacob and Sean discussed closing the bar at nine. "Why don't you all come to my place for a drink? I'm sure Stella would like to wish you a Merry Christmas. It doesn't sound promising for opening on Christmas Eve, anyway."

Elvis walked to the entrance. It looked like a deserted desert of white sand that refused to stay in one place. She smiled, already planning what color frocks her elves would wear during the holidays. Jacob, watching, saw her smile when she turned, snapped his fingers in disappointment but couldn't help chuckling.

So the evening of December 23, 2014, would pass quietly into the forgotten history in the Old Port. Now in Biddeford, Maine, just a short ride south, French Canadian history was about to be celebrated in public.

CHAPTER FORTY-TWO

LANGUAGE BARRIER

Biddeford has a fair number of citizens with French heritage. Maine itself has a fair number of communities populated by former French Canadians, many arriving from Quebec in Eastern Canada.

Different cultures bring their own unique traditions to whatever town or city they live in. One of the very special events that French Canadians celebrate is marriage. A strong Catholic upbringing accents these special moments.

The wedding of Paul Lemieux and Marie Poulin was held at the Catholic Church on a late Wednesday afternoon on December 23, 2014. An early evening reception was to follow at the Eagles Club.

Many of the invited guests grumbled when they received their invitations. "A Wednesday wedding? What were they thinking?"

To the soon-to-be-married couple, it made perfect sense. There was no competition for the use of the church or the reception hall. The couple would celebrate Christmas and their honeymoon in Cancun. Negotiating their vacation during the holidays added three days to their honeymoon stay. If their friends couldn't make it, they understood; gifts would be sent in their absence—hopefully money.

Once the elderly priest arrived, the vows went off without a hitch, though he was heard swearing about the lack of road maintenance by the city. Red-faced from wind, embarrassed at getting caught using blasphemy and the two port wines he'd consumed earlier had him cutting to the chase and a much shorter version of a Catholic wedding was consecrated.

* * *

Quentin arrived at the Eagles Club at six thirty and found a large gathering of people milling about. One wall of a long hall was lined with white cloth-covered tables. A centerpiece of colorful flowers signaled the place of honor set for the newlyweds. Another white-clothed table held a wedding cake topped with a smiling bride and groom. A large, open wooden floor separated the long tables from the round top tables similarly garbed and intended for the guests. The bar area was in a separate room and it was there where Quentin placed himself to watch, to find and to act.

The happy couple arrived as if the wind had blown them in; the bride hustled into the bathroom to reassemble herself. The noise level increased as cameras and phones recorded the first dance, the reception line, father and daughter dance, mother and son, and on and on. A professional photographer herded people like cattle as he followed his script.

Quentin watched.

About an hour into the proceedings, the waiting ended.

Quentin had found.

At nine twenty-three, he acted.

The maid of honor was in tonight's limelight simply by an act of biology; she was the older sister of the bride. She went through the motions with a pasted-on smile.

Charmaine Poulin shunned the spotlight in her normal environment. She was a librarian in an elementary school in Falmouth, Maine, a town just north of Portland, an avid reader who dreamed of inhabiting a world that existed a hundred years ago.

Her literary heroes lived in the latter part of the 1800s; they all spoke and wrote in French. Her college degree in the romance languages satisfied her thirst for knowledge but, practically speaking, wasn't a game changer when seeking employment. In her fifth year as a librarian, she helped kids rhyme their way through Dr. Seuss and laugh at Robert Munsch, and in their last year of elementary school, directed fifth-grade girls to Judy Blume, all the while feeling stymied as a person.

When the required smiles and formal photographs were satisfied, she moved to a corner of the room and nursed a wine cooler. Suddenly a man was standing in front of her table, gazing down at her with a warm smile.

"You look as alone as I feel. Would you mind if I joined you?"

"Be my guest. We can be alone together," she quipped without looking up.

"I like that line. Perhaps I'll use it in the future. My name is John," offered Quentin, sliding into a folding chair. She looked up then. After introductions and small talk, their love of literature emerged, and their conversation warmed. By ten o'clock, it was clear they were socially compatible. John dropped his simple and lowly persona, for here sat a woman who could appreciate academic excellence. John explained away his current situation, and Charmaine understood completely since she too was living and working in a world that celebrated mediocrity.

There would be no need of a room at the Biddeford Motel. Charmaine was ready to leave and invited John to drive her back to her apartment in Falmouth. She said her goodbyes to her parents and her sister, claiming to have a headache.

Quentin couldn't believe his good fortune, this girl seemed intent on allowing him to explore all parts of her French heritage; Gollum throbbed with anticipation as they drove into what was becoming a very serious snow storm.

Charmaine settled into the seat beside him like a favorite shirt. She fiddled with the radio and squeezed herself in her excitement, sneaking quick glances at the driver whose focus was out the windshield.

All the while, snow pelted the windshield, testing the wipers' resolve. The rubber on glass screeched and squawked, matching the rhythm of Charmaine's pulsing heart. She acted. Suddenly her hands were all over him, caressing the hair just above his shirt collar, brushing the length of his arm with her hands. She traced his profile with her finger, stopping long enough to lightly pass it beyond his lips. She leaned into her effort brushing Gollum in passing as if melting a stray snowflake.

Quentin experienced a sensation new to him. Suddenly he was on the receiving end of a scientific search. Her touch created a heightened awareness in all five of his senses that was overwhelming. Her perfume was so heady he could taste it. He could hardly wait to ask what senses he had filled in her, when this evening ended.

Outside this cozy cabin, the windshield was being pummeled with blowing snow matching the intensity of the storm inside. Overwhelming the defrost feature, heat from all sources fogged the window glass. When Charmaine gripped Gollum, Quentin lost control. He shifted in his seat, preparing to release his belt; Charmaine shifted herself as well.

Quentin took his attention away from the road for just a moment. As she took him in her mouth, they plummeted off Route 295 North. The last visual captured in the headlights was a road sign showing Falmouth, 2 miles.

So close, yet so very far away.

———

CHAPTER FORTY-THREE

PINS AND NEEDLES

"People just don't get it, do they?" muttered the paramedic as he strapped an unconscious Quentin onto the stretcher. His vital signs were stable but by all indications this guy was going to require some serious stitching up. "Looks like some inner trauma too. Stay off the road people. Mother Nature is having her way with us. Don't mess with Mother Nature."

The second ambulance carried Charmaine Poulin. She was more fortunate. Her position at impact with her head just below dashboard level for some reason, found Quentin's mid-section, cradling the blow.

The first officer on the scene was even now telling of finding the poor victim with his belt unbuckled—not his seatbelt—fly down and his oldest, best friend exposed to the snow that was entering the shattered windshield.

"Looks like he was shifting gears and lost control," he deadpanned.

Charmaine was transported for observation. She was shaken up, but it appeared she'd sustained only bumps and bruises.

The emergency room was pretty quiet with more people heeding the weatherman's advice than not. Bars had closed early. Stores with extended hours had grudgingly turned out their lights at normal closing times.

The lights were on in the emergency room, though, and it was Stella who received the bloody, unconscious-yet-groaning accident

R. Wesley Clement

victim. After getting him to an operating room and into the hands of the trauma surgeon on duty, Stella returned to speak with the officer who had information that might reveal who should be notified.

The officer showed Stella the license and wallet he had taken from Quentin's pocket. "Says here he's one John A. Thomas from Scarborough. Tough old bird, I'd say, to even survive the crash. He's not a kid. Born in 1942. What's that make him 73, 74? His head was covered in blood. Like I said, tough old bird."

"I'll try to locate someone. Just leave his wallet. We'll put it in a secure place," said Stella.

"Yeah we're done here. No crime I can see. Just bad timing, I'd say."

"What do you mean?"

"Well the billboard he hit just got completed before the storm hit. Wasn't there yesterday."

"Seriously?"

"Yeah it was an empty field. Funny story, though, when you think about it. Can't write this story," he said. "The sign was supposed to be up a while ago, put up for the holiday season. Got delayed but I guess the message got through tonight."

Stella waited. The officer continued. "I searched the immediate area for debris before it could be covered by the raging storm. Can you guess what the billboard had suggested to Quentin just before he hit it? DON'T DRIVE DISTRACTED, DELIVER YOUR PACKAGE SAFELY THIS HOLIDAY SEASON." He laughed all the way out the door.

The receptionist on duty in the emergency room thumbed through the phone book and found a John A. Thomas listed at the address on the license. She buzzed Stella so she could make the call.

It was after one in the morning. The lady answering the phone had obviously been asleep.

"Is this the residence of John A. Thomas?"

<hr>

"That's how it's listed in the phone book."

"Are you Mrs. Thomas?"

"Yes, I suppose I still am."

"This is Portland General Hospital. I'm sorry to be calling at this hour."

"Well, better late than never."

"You've heard the news then?"

"Not really news now is it?"

"I'm not sure I understand what you mean."

"I mean it was over a month ago that John passed away in your hospital, and this is the first call I've received from you people. Bills, you've sent bills, but not one word of condolence. And then out of the blue you call me at this ungodly hour? I'm not impressed!" Mrs. Thomas shouted into a receiver and hit the end call button.

Stella stood shocked, the phone still at her ear. She checked the license again. The victim was still in surgery but she slipped in and did a once-over of his visible part. This was not the body of a 74-year-old man, half that, maybe. She dialed the Portland Police Department and suggested that some kind of law had been broken and tossed the accident back into their lap.

"Do we need to deal with this tonight? You say he's unconscious and still in surgery. We're short-staffed here. This storm is a nightmare of fender benders. If morning is early enough, I'll leave a note on the sergeant's desk."

"Fine by me, I'll let our morning people handle things. This guy isn't going anywhere tonight.

* * *

Officer Malbon was not very happy. Christmas Eve morning and on duty. He was not some rookie who needed to earn his stripes. He was up for promotion for god's sakes. He had promised his wife and kids they would do some last minute shopping today.

R. Wesley Clement

He'd been called at seven fifteen in the morning when two newbies suddenly caught the flu overnight. "I bet I could trace that flu down to its source in half an hour," he grumbled to his wife as they shared a cup of coffee in the kitchen. The day was just dawning. The good news was the storm had suddenly veered out to sea, and the sun should be shining by noon.

"Maybe you won't have to work a full shift. We could meet you at the mall," said a hopeful Mrs. Malbon.

"Should actually be an easy day." He sighed. "Christmas Eve and all, most people actually being polite. So yeah, let's hope for that at least."

Officer Malbon donned his hat and jacket, and silently thanked the guy for plowing his drive early. He backed out of his garage and eased his way down his driveway, which was clearly defined by a three-foot bank on either side. The road was plowed but slick with a light windblown snow cover.

Could have been a lot worse, he thought as he took in a wintery postcard that for a few hours would hide the dinginess of a city in December. Railings and signs all wore new finery this morning while tree limbs shivered in the lingering wind, trying to shake off a coat of white. Smoke rose from white rooftops and many of the cars on the road were painted by the same artist.

The scene brightened Officer Malbon's demeanor, and by the time he reached headquarters, he was humming Christmas carols. First stop this morning, after visiting his desk, would be a second cup of coffee.

He looked at the brief note that would be sending him to the hospital to follow-up an accident with someone apparently driving on a dead man's license. He greeted the sergeant with a *Merry Christmas* and a plea to be the guy to get off shift early if it was possible.

"My wife has plans and the two yahoos who called out are screwing them up, so a little help here if you can, Sarge."

———

Officer Malbon stopped at a Starbucks, bought a pastry and washed it down slowly with a new bold blend, just because it was Christmas. He was in a good mood.

"I love the holidays," he sang aloud as he pulled into a parking space at Portland General.

He walked into the emergency room, gathered the license and wallet and sat down to figure it out in his own mind before calling the nurse. The accident victim was out of surgery but still in ICU.

"Can I get an update on his injuries?" asked Officer Malbon.

"The doctor who operated has gone home, but I'll get Dr. Wolf in to speak with you. He's on duty this morning."

Dr. Wolf was swift and succinct.

"I'm very sorry to report the victim is still in a coma. When he does come to, if he comes to, he's going to be in tremendous pain and will require strong medication that will keep him from being coherent for some time."

"What injuries were sustained, doctor?"

"He has a fractured skull, which has been addressed. Whether his brain is injured remains to be determined. There was a slight brain bleed and swelling. Time will tell. He suffered a collapsed lung. He has facial fractures that will require reconstructive surgery if he survives his other injuries. And his penis was nearly severed."

"Ouch!"

Officer Malbon tightened his gut in sympathetic pain and felt himself shrink.

"Can I look in on him? Is the woman who was with him still here?"

"Yes, I believe she was held for observation but will be dismissed shortly. You might want to see her first."

Officer Malbon entered the room of Charmaine Poulin. Her mother and father were readying her exit.

"Miss Poulin, I'm sorry to bother you, but I'm following up on last night's accident. It seems the man driving the vehicle is not the man on the license he was using. Can you help me out with that? Are you alright, by the way?"

"Just sore. Thank you for asking."

Mr. and Mrs. Poulin were clearly not happy with their daughter and stood back muttering to one another. Charmaine glared at her parents who had not completed their tirade or asked her how she was.

"I met the man at my sister's wedding reception last night, and we started talking. We shared the same interest in literature. He wasn't drinking heavily, he offered me a ride home and suddenly, wham, bam, here I am," which evoked a little smile. "Is John alright? He seemed to be in great pain. He was unconscious and groaning when he left in the ambulance."

Officer Malbon could feel the friction.

"Mr. and Mrs. Poulin, do you mind if I speak to your daughter alone for a moment?"

Mr. Poulin started to protest but Charmaine insisted.

"Dad, it's okay. I'm not a kid now and I wasn't a kid when I accepted the ride last evening. So please leave us."

When the door closed Officer Malbon probed lightly into last night's happening.

"No, he wasn't an invited guest. He was just there. French weddings are festive occasions that we like to share with others and we often hold the receptions in public halls." She paused and took a deep breath. "Anyway we hit it off. He was nice and he crashed because of the storm, I guess. I have no idea why he would be using a fake license. He clearly was an educated professional, well-spoken and charming, really."

"Well, I guess that's all I need for now. I'll get your contact information from the desk. I'm sorry you were hurt. Have a Merry Christmas, Miss Poulin. I'll be in touch," he tipped his hat.

Officer Malbon's next stop was the ICU wing. He found the room in semi-darkness with monitors blinking instructions and information. The man was swathed in bandages clearly still in a coma.

"I guess I need to call Mrs. John A. Thomas and see what she knows. *Whose sleeping in my bed?* said Poppa bear."

Over the phone, Mrs. Thomas was about as helpful as she had been to Stella.

"I need to see you within the next hour, Mrs. Thomas. I can come to your home, share a cup of coffee and straighten this all out or I can arrange for you to be brought to headquarters. Your choice."

With a cup of coffee that needed refilling, Officer Malbon had managed to drag the story of the sale of her late husband's Camry out of the reluctant witness.

"How is it then, I'm asking one last time before I lose my patience, Mrs. Thomas, the man left with your husband's license and registration?"

"I didn't see the harm. He said he needed them for only a day or two until he could do whatever you do when you buy someone's car. My husband paid good money to register his car just like you're supposed to do, then he died. What a waste of money, I told him."

"Mrs. Thomas, bear with me here. So this man answers an ad to buy a car. You never saw him before or after, and he was apparently driving on your late husband's license for weeks. That's your story?"

"One hundred percent gospel, Officer. I had no idea what I did was wrong. John was a bastard. He never shared anything with me. I was just being kind to a stranger. Where's the harm?"

Officer Malbon returned to police headquarters and wrote his report. He bugged his sergeant for the next hour and by three o'clock, he was at the Portland mall with a wife and kids who wanted to show him some stocking stuffers they would like.

"We'll leave the big stuff to Santa," they said.

R. Wesley Clement

CHAPTER FORTY-FOUR

HAPPY HOLIDAYS

Ignorance is bliss, or so they say. The laughter and good-natured noises exiting *Troubled Waters* were all about celebrating Christmas Eve among friends. Eggnog was the preferred drink. Sean had mixed up a batch and it was being offered free of charge—in moderation of course.

The white lights that framed the bathroom door had been replaced the week before with twinkling blue, green and red LED lights that Jacob had somehow managed to synchronize with his piano keyboard. Jingle bells had the lights dancing, while a solemn carol slowed them.

Freddy was entertaining a table that included Elvis, Sean, Stella, Rae Anne, Braden and his wife Marcia, Mrs. Waslowski and Freddy's new best friend, Lieutenant O'Connor.

At another table, the wheelies were in attendance. Five of them tonight, delivered in the new van that advertised Braden's law firm, a local bank and various corporations. Captain Jack and his savior, Ebony, shared a table with her brother, Stan and his wife.

Nobody in the room had a clue that lying in a coma just a short distance away was a man with a possible brain injury, facial fractures and a nearly severed body part that had been doing his thinking for a very long time.

The bar was due to close at ten o'clock. Then the real celebration would take place with one special announcement that had only been finalized in a video chat a day before. When the bar had cleared of all but these close friends, presents were exchanged.

Jacob gave Sean a handcrafted bracelet with an engraving of the Black Knight swinging his sword on the front and the words *Troubled Waters* beneath it. The meaning was clear to Sean as he hugged his bearlike friend. With no legs, the Black Knight of Monty Python fame still demanded his pursuers come back and fight like a man. Sean certainly exemplified his spirit.

Sean gave Jacob a set of bronzed keys to the bar. His eyes misted.

"You're going to be running this place, Jacob. My interest has changed and now all I want to do is improve the lives of the handicapped. I'm starting a non-profit. It's already been promised substantial funding from various veteran organizations. I haven't even tapped the private sector as yet.

"Stella is going to manage all the health-related issues and paperwork while I do the public relations and fundraising." Heads nodded and hands clapped. "Braden is handling all the legalese stuff. Thank you, Braden." Sean held up his hand. "And, by the way, the Black Knight will still be patrolling these waters with sword in hand, just battling for a different cause."

Jacob spoke up as well.

"I have a gift for you, Elvis, back on the boat, but I also have something here that should bring a smile to your lips this evening." He grabbed his iPad and held it out for all to see. The screen suddenly lit up, and Carson Daley was staring at them. He spoke.

"Elvis, I had the opportunity to watch you perform a few weeks ago. You are a very talented young lady. It's my pleasure to announce that you have been selected to appear on next seasons *The Voice.* Congratulations, and we'll see you in the spring. Merry Christmas by the way."

The room was silent for a moment as all absorbed what they'd just heard. Then they broke into cheers, hugging Elvis and each other. Rae Anne held onto her baby and cried.

It seemed it would be a Merry Christmas to all and to all a good night.

*   *   *

The holidays were merry indeed for Jacob and Elvis. Jacob asked Elvis to be his wife.

"Not immediately," he kidded. "Let's see how I handle rejection. I'm not giving up just yet on Polly warming to me, but if given more time and she doesn't, I just don't know how I'm going to absorb it. Besides, I think a wedding on the boat this summer would be awesome. Captain Jack can sail us to some of the islands up the coast. We'll go visit where you lived, maybe climb that mountain you climbed that's so famous. Named after a car. What's it called?"

"Cadillac Mountain. That would be awesome, Jacob. As for Polly, I think she must have had a mean male owner somewhere along the way, so don't take it personal," she said solemnly.

*   *   *

Lieutenant O'Connor put the case of Quentin T. Spence on the back burner. It seemed clear he'd left the state. Officer Malbon was promoted to sergeant in the first days of 2015. His one assignment from his beat as an officer was to follow up on the man who crashed his car while driving on a dead man's license.

"He's conscious, but he's not out of the woods according to his doctor. I'm hoping to get to talk with him by week's end."

"That sounds like a plan. I'd also like you to assist me in running down any leads that might surface regarding Spence. He has to be somewhere."

*   *   *

Out of intensive care but still critical, Quentin lay with most of his face covered with bandages. The doctors were trying to wean him off the most potent medicine, and Quentins mind was becoming clearer even as his body registered increasing pain.

Pain in his face, his entire body ached and his privates were on fire. January 7, a Wednesday in the new year two full weeks after his car plummeted down an embankment gathering speed and hitting a billboard support pole head on, Quentin was slowly coming out of the fog. His memory of the accident was just beginning to have clear edges.

It was snowing heavily, I had been at a club, I met someone, we seemed to get on well. Quentin closed his eyes exhausted. *Perhaps chapter two tomorrow.*

The doctor entered, checked his eyes, his pulse and several of his injuries.

"If you can hear me and I think you can now, there are some questions about your insurance. This might sound uncaring, but you're going to require a good deal of reconstructive surgery to your face and your penis." The doctor cleared his throat. "This hospital will care for your immediate needs, but I'm afraid, if we're going to be doing reconstructive surgery, we'll need to use a specialist and they'll require proof of insurance.

"I will stop in again in the morning, and you'll need to tell us where we stand. We do not know who you are, but we do know your condition, and that is going to require your consent and a source of payment."

The door closed and Quentin, with this wrinkle thrown out there and no idea in the world how to deal with it, summoned the nurse to give him a source of oblivion. His mind cleared for a moment, and he remembered who he was and what a strong mind he possessed.

Perhaps I can dream up a way out of this, he thought before blessed relief was upon him.

  R. Wesley Clement

During the next few doctor visits deny-deny-deny became Quentin's only defense. He had totally frustrated the doctor as he mumbled a lack of memory of who he was, what had occurred, "I'm afraid I'm a blank slate at the moment."

"There are people who want to question you and I see no reason not to let them in," the doctor said. "Perhaps they can clear up your confusion. At any rate, your initial injuries have healed enough for you to be released by the end of the week, Monday the 13 at the latest. If you can provide proof of insurance before then, I would be glad to see the reconstruction of your face and private area scheduled."

The doctor opened the door and signaled Sergeant Malbon into the room.

Sergeant Malbon looked at him. His swelling was still apparent; blues, purples and mustard yellow offering a mask that Quentin could not have mixed more cleverly from a painter's palate. It was a short interview and Sergeant Malbon left with no new information on who he was.

Quentin, for his part, knew time was of the essence. They had his picture. They had his name. It was only a matter of time before his employer would be contacting authorities.

I have to think this through in a scientific manner, let's do an inventory here. He looked around the room. The monitors had all been removed.

It appears I'm going to live. He looked at himself in a hand mirror he'd requested. *Even my father wouldn't recognize this face.*

He touched each part of his anatomy that still pained him. His face ached but it was bearable, and the heavy drugs had been discontinued. He had yet to rouse Gollum, but the pain down there was still persistent like a toothache. He got out of bed and made his way to the bathroom on rubbery legs. He nearly fainted from the effort and sat on the toilet with his head down. He looked at Gollum for the first time since the accident.

"Oh Gollum, what have they done to you, my precious?" There was no response. At least it was healed enough to allow liquid to wind its way through. The bed pan added as the bag disappeared but the ache remained constant, rising with each discharge. Quentin raised his head, looked in the bathroom mirror and blamed the woman. Charmaine.

"She got me into all this, perhaps I can arrange for her to get me out."

 R. Wesley Clement

CHAPTER FORTY-FIVE

WINTER OF DISCONTENT

At police headquarters, things were beginning to come together. An inventory of what had been found in the wrecked auto from several weeks ago was finally on Lieutenant O'Connor's desk.

Sergeant Malbon joined her in her office and filled the lieutenant in on the interview that morning.

"The guy is saying he can't remember anything, including who he is. Some may be true. Some bogus, in my opinion."

"Let's check out what it says in the report."

One shirt and one pair of pants. Pretty basic. Pants, 34-inch waist. Shirt large.

One pair of black work type shoes, size eleven.

One Smartstop vest, size large.

The lieutenant looked at Sergeant Malbon, "What do you garner from any of this?"

Sergeant Malbon stroked his chin.

"Who carries an extra set of clothes around with them unless they plan to change on the fly? And Smartstop workers distinguish themselves with those vests, right?" He was getting excited. The lieutenant looked on not saying a word.

"So, let me fly with this a minute," he said. "He's a Smartstop worker who works away from the town he visited that night, but it wouldn't be over an hour away," he cleared his throat. "The weather wasn't exactly travel-friendly that day as I recall. Anything else in the report?"

"Nothing that I can see. Description of the damage, where it's housed, that's it."

"So what do you think of my analysis, boss?"

"I think you need to dig out the phone book and call every Smartstop within an hour of here and see if they have an employee who hasn't shown up for work in the past two weeks. And when you locate it, give me a heads up. I'm going to call around to some of the other police departments, see if they have any missing persons from the same time frame. This guy had to be living somewhere. Hopefully someone has reported him as missing. By the way, excellent police work, Sergeant."

* * *

The knock on the door was tentative, followed by a head appearing as if unattached. The room was dark, the blinds closed, the voice a whisper. "John is that you?"

Lying there faced away from the door feeling sorry for himself, plans still fuzzy, Quentin at first ignored what might be white noise. The second time he heard his assumed name, he turned and viewed a silhouette of a head bathed in harsh corridor light. Still not sure who it was, his own reply was tentative.

"Yes, it's me, John."

Full in the room now, but not attempting to add light yet, a woman moved to the bed. "It's me, Charmaine. How are you feeling?"

Quentin's eyes widened, trying to capture enough light to add focus to sound, a sudden flash that focused his plan at least. A prayer had been answered, if not a prayer, at least one of the options he had considered. He took her hand.

"I'm actually a mess, and I need your assistance."

     R. Wesley Clement

"No one knows I'm here. I snuck by the nurses' station. My parents have been giving me a rash of crap since that night. I feel as responsible for all this as if I were driving myself. Dammit. It was an accident. Get over it, I told them."

Quentin, wily and with a knack for self-preservation, said, "I have some things to tell you about myself, nothing earth shattering, but I need to get out of here first. Can you help?"

"Tell me what to do. It's not like we're criminals. You can stay with me if you need to."

"I'm going to need some clothing, and they have my wallet, so if you could buy a few things and get back in here without being seen, I have a plan taking shape in my head."

"I have taken a leave of absence from my work. At least a month I told them. So I'm free as a bird, John, or whatever your name is. The police asked me all kinds of questions, but I really didn't have anything to tell them. All I know is you were nice to me, and we seemed to have a lot in common. I'm going to hang my hat on that for now."

John squeezed her hand a little tighter.

"If you could get back here this evening, this plan will work best in the shadows of the night. My face is a mess, Charmaine, but it can be fixed if I can get to my resources."

"I'll be here by eight tonight, and don't worry that I care about your scars. It's the person that matters, don't you think?"

Quentin couldn't agree more.

*　*　*

Sergeant Malbon dialed the Scarborough Smartstop. It was his third call. He was connected to the manager after being put through the usual hoops. While on hold, he tried to recreate what had taken place to give him the sergeant stripes he was now wearing. Doing real police work. Patience, he decided and a love for his career choice had kept his nose to the grindstone during the past seven years.

Don't forget the love of a good woman, the sudden thought of his wife at home, raising the kids had him smiling to himself.

"This is the manager. How can I help you?"

"We have a man with a Smartstop vest lying in the hospital. He's going by the name of John A. Thomas. I'm calling the area Smartstops to see if any are missing an employee using that name?"

"You called the right Smartstop. What's your name? We don't give out information about our employees on a regular basis."

Sergeant Malbon gave just enough information to get what he needed from the manager.

"Does he have a locker there?"

"Just a shift locker. Nothing is allowed to be kept overnight. I can double check for you. He's been missing for over two weeks. Many of our employees are a bit transient, so we weren't alarmed since he's only been with us a short time. He joined us just before the holidays."

"You must have a photo of him. He didn't have a picture badge on his vest. Just his name."

"We'd have one on file. If you are coming down here, I'll have his folder ready for you. If I'm not right here, it will be in customer relations with your name on it."

"That would be great. I will try to get down there today. Thanks so much for your help."

"He was a good employee. Did all that was asked of him and kept to his own business. Frankly, we were considering bringing him on as a regular hire. I hope he's going to be okay. Tell him Manager Bob asked about him."

As it turned out Sergeant Malbon didn't get right down there because Lieutenant O'Connor had made a discovery.

* * *

It was Stella who made the startling discovery an hour into her shift. The emergency room was quiet and so, Stella being Stella and having the inside scoop on the man she had directed to emergency surgery was curious to see this man who was defying detection.

"Who is this masked man?" was the question that moved throughout the corridors like the constant smell of Lysol that reminded everyone of where they were, full time, all the time.

Stella saw the rumpled form in the near darkness. The blinds were closed, light seeping in, but just barely, from arc lighting circling the building. She walked to his bed and studied the still form. Too still she decided after a minute. She turned on the light in the bathroom. The patient was gone, plumped up pillows provided the form.

* * *

Quentin was discovering Charmaine's apartment at about the same time Stella was discovering his escape. The plan went without a hitch, and Charmaine stopped for fast food and a cup of coffee on their way to Falmouth. A more normal skin color was slowly overtaking the garish Halloween mask that was Quentin's face. Charmaine was sympathetic and that was just the prescription the doctor ordered to his way of thinking.

"I'll pick up any stronger pain medicine you need in the morning. I have extra strength Tylenol if that will do for tonight."

"Charmaine, you are a life saver. Tylenol will do nicely. I am feeling better already." He stretched out on the couch and closed his eyes, thinking how fortunate he was not to be discovered and recuperating in a jail cell. He motioned her to his side and squeezed her hand.

Charmaine, a prisoner of her own loneliness, was like a lap dog savoring any human touch. She began to rub his shoulders lightly, his arms, his chest. Quentin not used to a different pair of hands offering him affection, warmed all over.

It was odd. The two of them cuddled, then slept together, Gollum remaining neutral and silent and sore. This was all new ground for Quentin. Here was a woman, nearly a stranger, offering a port in the storm, not asking anything for herself, putting herself at risk of trouble with the law. Quentin muddled all this even as he remembered cuddling several weeks ago with what had been his latest experiment before unleashing Gollum.

So this is what a normal cuddle feels like, innocent, warm, like comfort food. It was hours before he allowed his scientific mind to rest.

When Lieutenant O'Connor arrived at seven in the morning, the news of the accident victim's escape from the hospital raised a red flag. Sergeant Malbon was holding two cups of Starbucks when he entered his office and handed her one.

"We'll be drinking this on the fly. Something isn't sitting right with me and it's not the cup of coffee I had earlier. On the ride to the hospital, let's figure out what we have and, more importantly, what we don't have."

Sergeant Malbon shared his Smartstop story and waiting photo.

"The rooming house didn't give us much except this man wore expensive clothing, though it was bought with the idea of fitting in, not drawing attention. The lady of the house simply loved him and she's sure there has been some mistake." He rolled his eyes. "What's up with these old ladies?"

"Did he escape on his own or did he get help?" asked the lieutenant. "I'm leaning toward help. Someone must have driven him somewhere. You are not going to wander a Portland night in the winter in the condition he's in." The lieutenant was all business this morning. "When we finish with the staff at the hospital, we'll make that trip to Scarborough and see exactly who we're looking for."

* * *

The file was waiting exactly where the manager had said it would be. When Lieutenant O'Connor opened it, her jaw dropped and she swore.

R. Wesley Clement

"Holy shit!" Sergeant Malbon waited for a more informative follow-up. It arrived with a flourish. "It's the professor! He's been in our backyard from the beginning." Her pulse raced and her body began to shake. She shook her head as if dislodging a summer pest. Before she could stop herself, she dropped onto a chair in the customer services department of the Scarborough Smartstop and began to weep.

"We were so close."

Officer Malbon touched her shoulder and offered a tissue.

When the lieutenant was back in control, she took a deep breath.

"Let's go through both cases again. We must have missed something. I want to examine that wreck again. I can't believe he didn't mean harm to that woman he was with. We'll need to speak with her as well."

CHAPTER FORTY-SIX

NO KNOWN CURE

Lieutenant O'Connor and Sergeant Malbon were once again in the office discussing their latest discovery— a syringe.

"I just knew there had to be something there," suggested Lieutenant O'Connor, "he clearly injected Elvis's mother and now we have the proof."

"I can see how it was missed, stuck up under the front seat like it was. Nobody had any reason to be actively looking beyond the obvious, a liquor bottle or beer cans and such," offered Sergeant Malbon.

"Yeah, he wasn't drinking and driving, he was planning on drugging. Just, not himself."

"So what's your plan, boss?"

"We have eliminated everyone from the old lady he was living with to the lady he bought the car from. Though those ladies are naïve enough to have helped if asked I swear. One still finds nothing wrong in letting him drive on her late husband's license and registration, and the other insists she'll provide counsel to clear his name." The lieutenant shook her head, "When we interviewed her and told her what was taking place, she actually smiled. Said that was the kind of action her late husband had dreamed of when he moved here. *Pizzazz, this John showed Pizzazz,* whatever she meant by that, it didn't sound good to me."

"So we need to talk to that lady, Charmaine is it?"

R. Wesley Clement

"I can't see her being involved, but you just never know, do yuh?" Sergeant Malbon shook his head, having seen lots of those you-just-never-know-do-yuhs bear fruit.

*   *   *

Another Wednesday night at *Troubled Waters* found the usual cast of characters sitting around one of the tables, adding chairs so they could all hear and offer an opinion. Lieutenant O'Connor had shared what she could responsibly share, knowing all their lives had been touched somehow by Quentin.

"He's holed up somewhere nearby, I can sense it. We found his drug kit so there's no question, Elvis, he drugged your mother. How is she doing by the way?"

"She's moved in with Mrs. W. and the two sisters. She's taken over the cleaning and household duties in exchange for rent. Mrs. W. is going to do the cooking, though. No one can cook like Mrs. W." Her lips drew into a nostalgic smile, then suddenly flattened into a look of concern. "Are they safe, do you think, with him still out there?"

"I think so yes, if we can catch him quickly. He's still healing. He's not an immediate threat, but we do need to get him soon." She took Freddy's hand; she had put a sparkle back in Freddy's eyes. He had parted ways with his old drinking buddy, Jameson, settling for just two meetings a night with his friend Bud.

"Have you people considered that maybe Elvis was the intended target for this guy?" asked Sean, offering an insight that hadn't been explored before. Perhaps he was far enough removed from all the drama so he could see the big picture.

"Think about it. He moves in where Elvis is living, coincidence yes, yet Elvis herself said she was uncomfortable with his actions but chose to ignore them. Then he just happens to show up at our bar. Coincidence? I think not. Correct me if I'm wrong, Lieutenant, but I've seen enough cop shows to buy into their theory that there's no such thing as coincidence, especially twice."

The lieutenant looked at Elvis sitting there, a beautiful innocent concerned for others, not thinking she could be the target of any evil intent.

"I didn't know this back story. I do know Quentin T. Spence has never shown any interest in older women except as a place to hide. In fact, I think he hates older women. He's threatened by them. Mrs. Waslowski herself said he seemed undone by the gentle chiding the sisters embarked on, testing his mettle, they told her, when he went to his room all flustered."

Jacob had been listening to all this, opening and closing his hands as if wringing the neck of a chicken intended for Sunday dinner.

"I don't like this one little bit. I'm going to show Stan that picture. Make sure he keeps an eye out for this guy. He's all scarred up you say? That ought to make things easier if he does come around."

"This is all nonsense," chided Elvis. "I worry about Mrs. W. and the sisters, and now my mother staying there. That's my concern."

* * *

Meanwhile a ways up the road, Charmaine was cooking a late dinner for Quentin. He told her the truth from the book of his mother Ruth, with a twist of Quentin thrown in which would never make it to the nonfiction list.

He had a wife, he said, a child which he was sure wasn't his, he said, a career in real estate that went the way of the economy five years ago and, though it was coming back, he didn't intend to be part of it. They had separated, she wouldn't leave him alone. She demanded child payments; he had no money, so finally he just left his old identity in a trash barrel and took on the identity of the dead guy John A. Thomas.

Charmaine was sympathetic and needy herself, to a fault.

"I'll take care of you, John. Keep that name, I like it. It's an honest name. That's what we'll build together. Honesty." She was beaming.

    R. Wesley Clement

"I have a little money, and two more weeks of sick time. Let's get out of here, head to where it's at least a little warmer. Virginia maybe. I have a cousin in Virginia we could stay with or we could just get a room on the beach."

Quentin knew in his heart the police would find the needle case eventually and that would lead them to Charmaine's residence.

This woman is reading my mind I swear, he thought.

"Let's leave at first light," he said aloud. "Don't tell anyone anything. Don't even call your cousin. Either we show up or we don't. No obligations."

They ate the smothered pork chops with a mushroom sauce, frozen green beans and rice pilaf and went to bed sated and satisfied.

Charmaine began to rub Quentin's shoulders and massaged his soreness as if on a mission. She took a deep breath and brushed Gollum for the first time since that fateful night. Quentin stirred but didn't protest. A feathered touch followed, Gollum stirred but didn't protest. Charmaine parted the opening of the pajama fly and warmed to the task. Gollum regained consciousness.

Quentin, almost comfortable with the level of pain he was living with, decided to give it the old college try. When Gollum responded, unsheathed from obscurity at last, Quentin smiled to himself, feeling safer than he had in quite some time. A subtle shift of positions allowed Gollum to disappear into the dark cave. Quentin's last thought was *I think this might all work out just fine in the end my precious.*

* * *

The knock on Charmaine's door was early, just an hour after sunrise on a beautiful January morning. Cold overnight, the temperature when Lieutenant O'Connor started her car was minus ten degrees.

She picked Sergeant Malbon up at his home and handed him his favorite coffee, Starbucks, a Yukon blend that commanded attention.

They parked just down the street from Charmaine's apartment and sat there for a moment, savoring their coffee and the solitude of the moment.

"With the snow piled up like that, I'd say there's only one way a person could go. Would you agree?"

"Unless he's got a dog sled and a team of Huskies," kidded Officer Malbon as he sipped his own taste of the wilderness.

"Okay, we walk to the door together. I knock and step back. If you are threatened when and if he comes running out, shoot him right in the lower mass if you get my meaning. It would serve him right. Not that I'm still angry." She winked.

An hour later they had the landlord opening the door, voicing their concern for the tenant's well-being.

Sergeant Malbon found plenty of food in the refrigerator, the remnants of what looked like a dinner for two in the garbage, "unless that girl eats three chops at a sitting," said Sergeant Malbon as he used a pencil to probe the leavings. They found an address book and called her mother who had no idea where she could be.

Several names thought to be friends were called, all with the same result. Her cousin Rachel who lived in Virginia according to the address book, and the number listed was called. She was just getting ready to leave for her work as a restaurant hostess but swore she'd not heard from her cousin Charmaine in the last three months.

"My gut tells me they are together, and she has no idea who she is traveling with. Let's find out her make, model and plate number. Get it out to every state north and south, east and west. I want a high alert issued. This girl is traveling with a very dangerous wounded animal."

* * *

It was a sunny morning in Maine. Charmaine was driving her sensible gray five-year-old Subaru wagon, Quentin was holed up in the back seat. They made good time on roads that were cold but clear of ice and snow.

R. Wesley Clement

No Interstate 95 for Quentin, he had Charmaine's smart phone talking back to him. Siri told him everything he needed to know. Frankly after several days with the woman, he was already getting tired of Charmaine's voice. It came across as sharp and wheedling.

He studied the little bit of hair showing above the headrest, moving in cadence to her voice and imagined her out of the picture.

Just need to think this through. He shut Siri up, then looked once more at that little bit of hair. *Were it just that easy.*

One of the few women Quentin had not been able to control lately was Mother Nature. The clouds piled up as they entered Connecticut heading for the New York border. Quentin was driving now and Charmaine dozed with her head on the sofa pillow she sat on when she drove.

Quentin turned on the radio, it didn't take long for a weather report to surface. Six to eight inches all the way to Maine. The storm was coming up the eastern seaboard. High winds and poor visibility would add to accumulation and what looked to be a "miserable mess of moisture," the weather man quipped, laughing like a fool. Quentin snapped off the radio and touched Charmaine's shoulder. "Let's find a little town with a drive-through and get a room. This storm is coming in fast."

Charmaine opened her mouth to answer; Quentin closed it for her with, "That was a declarative sentence, dear. It does not beg a response, just letting you know, about the weather I mean" but meaning so much more than that.

Charmaine, no slouch in the language department, knew exactly what was meant and her heart tore just a little as the real Quentin began to emerge. She placed a little check mark along all the others that had hurt her over the years.

Early yet, maybe that was just a slip, we'll see. She closed her eyes. *Let him find his own damn fast food feast.*

The storm turned every car to white once more, covered their plate and allowed them to get a room in the town of Fishkill, New York.

———

CHAPTER FORTY-SEVEN

A DIFFERENT KIND
OF STORM

I *thought I was a little strange at times, but this girl is off the charts in her demands.* Two weeks in one room in Fishkill, New York, had Quentin focusing on the Kill part of the town's name. Gollum seemed to be the only happy camper in this relationship.

Her breath smells in the morning, she leaves her towel lying about, everything's just thrown down—and her voice is to die for.

He smiled at his own wit and a bothersome ever-growing inventory of insults he'd just love to throw out entered in his head.

Alas, he still needed her, but not for much longer. He was healing nicely, the sinister rainbow of colors more like yesterday's rain, barely noticeable. Gollum, bent but unbowed, was fully operational and Quentin still had it in his mind to finish this business with Elvis. She entered his mind now every time he allowed Gollum his own way with Charmaine.

Charmaine had about had it too. She kept her opinions to herself but it was now clear she had made a terrible misjudgment; John was not someone she could spend the rest of her life with. He was petty, demanding, self-serving and the past two weeks had her thinking she was the parent of an unruly child.

That damn wedding had had her imagining she could be a bride herself the accident brought out her nurturing instincts along

R. Wesley Clement

with guilt all thrown together. A terrible caution thrown to the wind had her fleeing the police for god's sake. She too was looking for a way out and, unlike John—or whatever the hell his name was—she didn't need any more of this. She was not on the run!

Opportunity and decision crossed paths as she sat in a coffee shop, not yet willing to return with the groceries the man of the house—as he now called himself—had demanded, not requested, demanded, the jerk. She had walked the short distance to the grocery market and now to the coffee shop. It was a beautiful sunny morning with blue skies and white non-threatening clouds chasing one another like kids on a playground.

I should be in class right now. Hell, those kids were less demanding than John. She had watched the sky, all the while thinking, *we are being chased too, and I'm sick of this cloak and dagger drama.* When a policeman entered and moved to the counter to order a coffee, Charmaine made a decision. When he approached the table to add a soft landing for his brew, she moved toward him.

"I think I'm in trouble and I want to go home, that's all I can tell you right now. If you will take me to whoever I need to talk to, I'll explain."

The officer replaced his lid and offered, "Tell me about it on the way."

Quentin saw this morning as an opportunity himself, and his own decision found him leaving the motel within five minutes of Charmaine's shopping trip. He took her car. For the last week he had insisted they needed to go south; he was sure they could disappear in Georgia. He had worked there once after all and knew the terrain. This was a seed he had planted as he planned his real destination, hide in plain sight still his mantra, the octopus his mascot.

Once more a knock from officer friendly brought no response and the six armored and armed officers accompanying him were left with their powder dry.

Jacob had shown Stan the picture of a younger Quentin T. Spence, the security man at Chandlers Wharf recognized him immediately.

"He said he was interested in buying a berth for his boat. He walked right by your boat for sure."

Jacob shared that information with Sean. Sean shared that information with Freddy. Freddy texted Lieutenant O'Connor, and once again they all shared a table that evening before show time.

"We still haven't caught him, but he's on the move. The woman who has been with him is cooperating fully, hoping to get a wrist slap and really, maybe that's all she deserves. She now knows who he is and she's still shaking."

The lieutenant scraped her chair a little closer and confided, "We're told he's probably heading toward Georgia, that's what he told Charmaine Poulin. I personally think it's bogus. He's probably either ditched the plate or the car by this time." She scraped her chair even closer. "I've studied these guys. He's a classic narcissist, short-term fixes for all areas of his life. I for one think Sean nailed it," she paused and looked Elvis straight in the eye. "I think you are unfinished business Elvis. I think he plans you harm."

Elvis made sure she had eye contact with everyone at the table.

"You know, when I lived in Florida, there was this little ghost crab on the beach. He could emerge from his little hidey hole and, unless you were paying close attention, you wouldn't notice him. He was clever, he could sense when you spotted him and disappear as if by magic.

"Listening to you all talk about this man all he's done and how he disappears as if by magic, I think the only way to catch him is to get him out of his hole and fill that hole with sand while something or someone makes him believe he hasn't been spotted." Then, trying to make light of the situation, she added a line from one of her favorite movies, *Forrest Gump,* deadpanning, "and that's all I've got to say about that!"

Everyone laughed lightly, but already in Lieutenant O'Connor's mind a plan was taking shape, if only Elvis would agree, of course.

* * *

 R. Wesley Clement

Quentin re-entered Maine on February 3, driving a car he had traded for on a private used car lot at a guy's house. This guy clearly lived on the margins and Quentin had no problem trading a five-year-old Subaru in excellent shape for a ten-year-old Toyota Corolla with 167,000 miles on the odometer. The one suggestion Quentin made with a wink was that the Subaru probably could use a paint job and a month or two inside under cover. Best time to sell is the spring anyway—enough said.

In ways that could not begin to be explained, Quentin ended up in Hollis Center a town of 4,000 plus residents, a mix of urban workers and reserved retirees and a good number of elderly women living alone. This town west of Portland allowed Quentin to once more hide in plain sight.

He perused obituaries online in the local library and identified a prospective widow who might take him in. The widow had lived here for four years, the couple having come to Maine to retire in the country, but near everything her husband had insisted.

The obituary sung the man's accomplishments and his courage. The only piece of near everything, besides bingo, Steven Palmer encountered was an urban hospital that did all they could for his prostate cancer. Sheila was left in a state she knew nothing about and no relatives within visiting distance. Quentin called on her exactly six months after her husband's death.

Within the hour he had explained away his terrible accident and unfortunate circumstances. Two cups of coffee later, he was moving his meager wardrobe into the spare room.

"I'll pay you what I can when I find something."

"Have you considered substitute teaching? The pay isn't terrible, and you can keep looking for something better. By the way, have you eaten yet you poor man? And I thought I was the only one with problems."

Quentin did in fact substitute in the elementary school after using his uncle's name and a made up on the spot social security number. *I won't be here long enough to raise an eyebrow.*

———

The youngsters were curious about his scars, but kind. Quentin substituted for a total of two weeks. He liked kindergarten best, remembering how impressed his teacher had been when he could read on the first day.

On a Friday afternoon, after teaching a full day, Quentin ventured into Portland for the first time in a long time. The days were beginning to lengthen in a meaningful way, and the parking lot at Chandlers Wharf was clear of snow. Captain Jack was back doing security until sailing weather returned. A man entered and struck up a casual conversation. He might be renting soon in that condo building yonder and wondered about friends visiting, would they be able to park here? Captain Jack answered his questions and the man melted away when the captain had to direct someone to a space and collect a fee.

The next morning, Stan was on duty and reviewing a dented fender that "had to have taken place in the parking lot," the owner insisted. "It was fine when I parked last night but this morning there's a dent. Had to have happened here."

"Let's just take a look. You say you parked at four thirty in the afternoon." Stan fast forwarded the tape to that time. He waited for the camera sweep that panned the entire lot in fifteen second intervals back and forth. He found the owner's car and when he paused the tape, it did indeed show a dent-less fender.

"See I told you so, no dent right," said the man who had been wronged.

"Let's see if we can see who parked beside you and for how long. Might not have been the first car. We get people parking for a half hour, an hour or the night."

Stan was looking at the captain standing in the lot talking with someone. Then the captain walked away to assist a customer. Then the man was gone. There was still no one parked next to the dented vehicle. Now the captain was back. Now the man who had been talking to the captain was by the security shack. Then he was

R. Wesley Clement

gone. Stan suddenly had a funny feeling. He left the man with the dent still talking to himself and dialed a number.

* * *

The lieutenant reviewed the tape, still unsure what she was seeing. She called Elvis who had lived in the same house with the man and Elvis in turn called Mrs. Waslowski. By ten in the morning, four ladies sat at Mrs. Waslowski's kitchen table having coffee and molasses cookies. The lieutenant put the tape into the portable machine and turned on the screen. The three ladies knew the seriousness of it all and quietly watched the man and his movements. It was Mrs. Waslowski who rose, went to her kitchen window staring at a late winter scene unfolding, she nodded to herself. She knew, one more nod, she knew she knew. She brought a second round of cookies and waited to be called on.

Elvis couldn't be sure.

Elvis's mother Rae Anne had never been coherent so she had nothing to offer.

The lieutenant had only seen him years ago.

When they turned at last to Mrs. Waslowski, she sighed and told her story.

"My late husband always said I saw way too much for my own good. Kids left in shopping carts while their mother was two aisles away. The man striking his wife in the car in front of us. People stealing in a department store. I could go on and on. Guess I do see things others don't."

She cleared her throat. "That man on the screen is Quentin T. Spence." All eyes focused on her. "My husband would never play poker with me either because I always knew when he had a winning hand or losing one for that matter. It's called a tell. You probably know what I'm talking about, Lieutenant. It's a little physical quirk that reveals something you don't even realize you

———

Troubled Waters   277

are revealing. Quentin T. Spence has a tell. And that man on the screen, he has the same tell."

The three women waited. Mrs. Waslowski seemed almost embarrassed. She reddened slightly then just said it out, "He touches himself." She asked the lieutenant to replay the tape and when the tell told, she said "Stop the tape." It was subtle but it happened at least three times. "He just lightly brushes himself like he's removing lint. He did that when he lived here, a nervous habit I guess, but noticeable."

The women with eyes wide looked to Mrs. Waslowski, too stunned to speak.

"You should come to work for me Mrs. W. You are quite the observer of human behavior."

R. Wesley Clement

CHAPTER FORTY-EIGHT

ONE IF BY LAND. TWO IF BY SEA

Funny thing about those ghost crabs, they seem to mirror some of the same penchants as Quentin T. Spence. They are scavengers, predators and being nocturnal, they favor the shadows and dark places. They blend in well with their surroundings, able to hide in plain sight—a mantra for Quentin.

He felt good about his latest excursion to the ocean's edge. Obviously Elvis was still living on the boat. He had wondered if she'd winter there. He sat at a table in *Two Fat Cats Bakery* on India Street in the Old Port, sipping a cup of coffee, slowly opening and closing his eyes, pondering his past, present and future, employing his scientific method of planning. He sighed. Smell was dominating. He was having difficulty getting past the wonderful aroma of handcrafted pastries that filled the room. He shook his head like the Magic Eight Ball he had played with as a kid, waiting for an answer to appear.

Sergeant Malbon entered and secured a coffee and a pastry to go, never even glancing his way.

Quentin noticed that, appreciated that. He felt his present was secure, in his mind, he read the answer he was seeking from the black globe: *it is decidedly so.* He revisited his recent trip to the boat where one word summed up the location: secluded.

Still too early in the year to be attracting visitors, it seemed Elvis and her man-friend were the only inhabitants at this marina wintering aboard. Quentin had watched from a distance and viewed the large bearded boyfriend leaving in the late afternoon on most days. Sometimes Elvis accompanied him; sometimes she didn't. On days she left on her own she was very punctual. Leaving the boat at exactly seven o'clock. Quentin knew which days those were.

As to the future, he decided a nice slow trip to Mexico and, after securing travel documents, perhaps to a Central American country where he could teach English, perhaps at the college level.

This would be Quentin's first conquest without using a calming influence on his victim. *Can't count Charmaine,* he thought. *She was more than willing. Besides, if anyone was a victim it was me.* Fingering the scars hidden beneath his beard and frowning at the painful memories, he took a sip. Gollum had reacted with a newfound pleasure at not being cloaked. He would be diving into this commando, so to speak. He just loved that word *commando.* He chuckled to himself, toasted himself.

"Let's get all the senses involved here," he said quietly to himself. "Watch the giant leave, wait and watch, listen, set off the little diversion in the parking lot. Sneak past the security shack down the wooden pier, take a right and, bingo, there's *The Last Tango.* Like a house in the country with no neighbors for miles around."

He had googled a similar boat on the internet and with a closed hatch the living quarters below the surface would greatly muffle sounds of a skirmish. He had a plan to hopefully avoid the skirmish part, for that matter. The little multi-tooled jackknife in his pocket could be used to convince Elvis, if it came to that. *I'm sure that won't be necessary.* It was clear from his time at the rooming house that Elvis was fond of Mrs. Waslowski. He would merely inform Elvis any confrontation would be harmful to that wonderful lady he had hidden away. She would be let go when he had finished his business.

"I walk away, she walks away. What's that term they use in sports? No harm, no foul."

Upon leaving the coffee house buoyed by what he saw as a foolproof plan, he suddenly viewed what just might be an extra ace in the hole.

"Sometimes I even surprise myself," he said as he crossed India Street with a purpose.

* * *

Lieutenant O'Connor had secured an around-the-clock observation team. She was sitting at her desk when Sergeant Malbon called in that Quentin T. Spence was sitting quietly at a table in a coffee shop when he left. Nothing happening as yet.

"We have someone near his car. I think this is going to happen sooner rather than later. He's been scouting out the area for the past several days. I think he'll strike when Jacob leaves by himself."

The lieutenant had explained to her superior they needed to catch this guy in the act. With all the information they had, it was all still circumstantial, or it had been unreported or unproven at the time of the offense.

"If we can catch him doing, what in his own mind he does best, all the circumstantial becomes supporting evidence, and we can put him away as a serial rapist for the rest of his days."

* * *

The sound of a six o'clock bell penetrated the semi-darkness. A fog horn also sounded, echoing the end of daylight on this first Friday in February. Those watching observed a bearded man wearing a captain's hat enter the parking lot at Chandlers Wharf and skirt security. Lieutenant O'Connor indicated she could be on the scene in minutes.

"Keep the suspect under observation, but let him get to where he's going. Intervene only if he tries to leave the boat or Elvis signals distress."

The man walked down the wharf, paused and looked carefully at the name *The Last Tango*, then climbed aboard, three officers descended the ramp as quietly as possible.

Several moments passed then Elvis screamed, the microphone planted aboard signaling the time to end this. The officers rushed aboard just as the man was trying to climb back out the hatch. He made a move that one officer felt was threatening and the officer shot him point blank. Lieutenant O'Connor arrived just as the ambulance was loading the man, an oxygen mask signaling he was still alive.

After making sure Elvis was okay, the lieutenant and Sergeant Malbon rushed to the hospital to make sure Quentin T. Spence did not get to enter a hidey hole.

The scene returned to normal and Elvis called Jacob to tell him it was over. She was shaking but assured him she was okay and would be at the bar by eight. She needed a shower to remove the smell of that terrible man.

She had heard him enter the hatch, had seen the boots descending the stairs. She smelled the sour unwashed odor invading her little cabin and didn't wait for him to turn around before she screamed.

* * *

Quentin was being rushed to surgery and Lieutenant O'Connor was brushed aside as she tried to reach his stretcher.

"I only need a second. Just let me view him so I can write my report," she asked plaintively.

"If you can give me ten minutes to fully evaluate the next steps and diagnose the trauma," the doctor suggested, "I'll let you make your identification before he goes into surgery"

While Lieutenant O'Connor and Sergeant Malbon waited at the hospital, Quentin was walking casually to the now deserted security shack and descending the ramp.

He had watched the homeless man go through his script without a flaw. Elvis even screamed on cue. Everyone dispersed when the poor man departed with lights and sound. Quentin, unlike the ghost crab who shuns the public eye, simply walked to the parking lot that was quickly emptying, silence replacing the excitement of minutes ago.

Elvis wrapped in a towel and winter boots was just boarding the boat when Quentin spied her. He waited two beats then followed, gazing once more at the back of the boat, *The Last Tango.* The name suddenly took on a whole new meaning. He quietly stepped onto the little wooden platform designed to aid entry to the boat itself.

At that moment, Elvis poked her head from the cabin below. Their eyes met. Elvis's widened with shock to see the man she thought had been shot running toward her. She slipped and fell the last three steps into the cabin. She struck her head and nearly blacked out; Quentin was at her side, comforting her, assuring her.

Elvis opened her mouth to scream but Quentin covered it with a gloved hand. Then in an instant it seemed, Elvis was tasting leather from another glove being forced into her mouth. Words accompanied the hushes.

"My precious, all is well."

Quentin waited until she stopped struggling, trying to regain her breath, then told her he had Mrs. Waslowski in a hidden place and would release her if she did just as she was told.

"My car is just up the street, if you get dressed, I'll take you to her. You can see she's safe and all will end well."

Elvis stood stock still with fear.

"I won't hurt you Elvis. Just do as I ask, and you'll be home by morning. I promise."

———

* * *

"It's Edwin David Workman!"

When they were finally allowed to see the patient, Sergeant Malbon identified him the homeless man with the initials EDW. He had given them the first lead in the case months ago.

"That son of a bitch played us like a saxophone," fumed Lieutenant O'Connor as they ran back to the squad car. "Let's hope to hell we get people there before he strikes." Siren's squawked, lights flashed, tires squealed, all descending back into the Old Port toward the Atlantic Ocean.

Quentin waited as Elvis donned jeans and a sweat shirt. The girl moved as if in a daze. They emerged from the hatch.

"PUT YOUR HANDS UP!" demanded a voice on the bullhorn. Quentin leapt backwards and pulled Elvis with him down the hatch. He pushed her into the little toilet and closed the door.

Got to think this through scientifically, then he remembered his deny-deny-deny approach.

He hollered up the hatch, "I have a weapon with me and will use it unless you back away!" Suddenly taking charge he demanded, "Give me someone in charge to speak with!" *Bluff with intensity, bluff with vigor, bluff like your life depends on it, Quentin.*

When Lieutenant O'Connor reached the boat, the standoff had been in place for ten minutes.

"We have him trapped in the boat. He has the girl down there with him, says he's armed. No way of knowing if that's true or not. He's demanding to speak with someone in authority."

"Give me the bullhorn, Sergeant. I'll speak with him but there's no way in hell he's getting off this boat, not with the girl and not on my watch."

Lieutenant O'Connor spoke from the wharf directly facing the boat.

"Quentin, you are hearing the voice of an old classmate from Middlebury, Colleen O'Connor. Do you recall when we last met?"

R. Wesley Clement

She waited. "Think about it for a moment, it was a long time ago, but I remember like it was yesterday. With your scientific mind, I'm sure you can leaf through your past conquests in record time." Once more she waited.

"So we meet again, only now I am wearing a badge and a gun, and this time, you have to pay for your deeds, Quentin. Let the girl go and come out with your hands up. You'll have a good long time to compose that letter of apology you owe me and a lot of others. You have exactly two minutes and then we are coming down those stairs."

Quentin felt like he'd been punched in the gut. He was shocked to hear that name, so that was why she left school. He moved to just below the opening.

"Ah, Colleen. I'm afraid restitution will have to come another day. I am indeed coming out in the allotted time, but Elvis will be in front of me and she will have a knife to her neck and, though I will regret it, I will use it. So back every goddam person off the wharf or this will end badly for more than just myself!" He added calmly, "Now you have a minute and a half."

Lieutenant O'Connor took a deep breath. She decided to stall for time, think this through.

"Okay Quentin. We're backing off," she announced through the bull horn. "EVERYONE OFF THE DOCK NOW!"

Quentin popped his head out of the hatch and saw the deserted, barely lit dock, the shadows as deep as the darkness. The bluff with intensity had moved him along this chessboard, eliminated the pawns at least, there was still a queen to contend with. He summoned Elvis and pushed her up the steps ahead of him, holding her sweatshirt in a sturdy grip. They reached the deck, and he played his next bluff.

"We'll be walking out of here now, and any attempt to interfere will cost this girl her life. I have nothing to lose, Colleen." He began mixing quotes from different sources in a montage of desperation.

———

Everlasting dark surrounds me below, stand thee out of my sun; no moth me, I seek no light, only a pale trail of stars as guide."

"He's lost his mind," whispered the lieutenant. She stood on the ramp leading down to the wharf, then made a decision and began walking slowly down toward the boat.

Pushing Elvis ahead of him, Quentin reached the edge of the boat, one foot still aboard and the other on the little raised step leading down to the dock. He opened his mouth to offer more of his twisted passages when a screech pierced the night white fur flying flew at him with ferocity.

Polly, as if summoned, was a mound of fur and claw, scratching and biting, ripping at his scarred skin. The suddenness and savageness of the attack sent him toppling backward. His arms flailed in the air, trying to grab onto a railing that didn't exist.

He landed on the scant five feet of wharf and tried to stand but the furious cat was all teeth and claws in his face he stumbled backward. Dressed as he was, shocked as he was, his eyes torn and still covered by Polly's claws, Quentin T. Spence really didn't put up much of a struggle. Briefly an unrecognizable passage escaped his muffled lips, then, arms reaching, he fell into a very cold, very unforgiving Atlantic Ocean.

Polly ran up his body and just as his boots submerged, deftly leaped back onto the dock and into Elvis's arms. One eye trained on the space where Quentin had left the building so to speak.

Six cruisers sealed Congress Street. Blue lights shocked the darkness like a never-ending lightning storm. Sergeant Malbon ran interference for the lieutenant, pushing back an ever-growing crowd with a harsher voice than his normal temperament allowed. He waited until she'd disappeared down the wharf before barking one more command and following.

Officers were using flashlights to probe the blackness. On the boat Elvis was wrapped in a warm blanket, Polly on her lap. Lieutenant O'Connor stood at the water's edge with her gun drawn almost lamenting that she had not been the one to end this.

There was an officer trying to get a statement, but Elvis simply looked into the blackness of the February night as if expecting Quentin to rise at any moment. Polly remained on alert as well, her fur on end and a look with that one eye that would have discouraged the hardiest drunken sailor from trying to board.

* * *

Three nights later on the second Monday of February, all the players in this drama had to push two tables together. Sean and Stella sat holding hands, wondering what kind of a world their unborn child would be coming into.

Mrs. Waslowski, Rae Anne, and the twin sisters, Sarah and Kate, discussed the weather and the very newly discovered factoid that molasses cookies did seem to actually taste good with a Maine crafted malty ale.

Lieutenant O'Connor and Freddy chatted about the kinds of things that newly formed couples chat about. Interestingly, the name Quentin T. Spence never made it to the table.

And Polly was there. In a place of honor with a meal to boot. A puss'n boots smorgasbord. She never offered an opinion of Quentin either.

Jacob and Elvis sat listening to the chatter, gazing into one another's eyes, knowing they had weathered the storm of the century and were still afloat. Elvis spoke slowly and in a hushed voice only Jacob could hear, "What happened will never reach the pages of my little book, Jacob." Ever the optimist, Elvis closed this chapter with a repeated line, *"And that's all I've got to say about that."*

EPILOGUE

March 18, 2015, a Wednesday night in the Old Port. Once again all the gang was in attendance and the overflow crowd at *Troubled Waters* moved between rowdy excitement and utter silence. It was nine fifty-five and the commercial was just ending. The crowd quieted as the lights turned to a shade of blue that could only be manufactured. The big screen showed the judges kidding one another, then it quieted as they tried to sense what was to follow. The padding of footsteps entering the stage.

The music rose and a voice filled the room. This was not a voice fighting to be heard but rather a voice telling a story of love and loss, of hope and betrayal, a story of resilience and in the end hope once again. The words wove a tapestry that spoke to everyone in the room, human beings all, with their own unique story being spun in a way that included them in the chorus.

When the song ended it was Blake Shelton, one of the four chair turns, with the chairs emptied and all four judges on their feet, who said all that needed saying.

Holding his Starbucks cup, looking like Giant Jacob directing traffic, he asked, "Honey what's your name?"

"Elvis."

He chuckled to himself, looked at each judge and shook his head in amazement. Then he offered, "Why are we even going to hold a season? I'm ready to vote right now. How about you America?"